OBFUSCATE

WORLD OF BLOOD: BOOK TWO

KILLION SLADE

SPIRIT

A Division of Draconian Publishing

Cover art: Ravven Kitsune http://www.ravven.com/

Published by Spirit, an imprint of Draconian Publishing.
P.O. Box 1000
Conrad, MT 59425

First Edition:

6x9 paperback ISBN 13: 978-0985938178

Obfuscate is a standalone reading experience, containing interactive content. Obfuscate contains links to youtube videos, please visit WorldofBlood.com to explore cut scenes, character dossiers, and extended versions. We encourage you to access and discover our complimentary "second screen" addition.

If you are familiar with how QR codes work, you can scan the above code to access the page. We hope you join us in this interactive adventure.

If you purchase the print edition you will find QR codes embedded in the text. On the Worldofblood web site you can discover how these QR codes work. We hope you join us in this interactive adventure.

Acknowledgements

I would sincerely like to thank my editors. You simply—rock my bobby socks! I'm a huge advocate of surrounding myself with people who are smarter than myself and I never consider my editors a necessary evil. They are necessary angels!

In taking what they have provided and applying that knowledge, it has grown my craft and taken decades of time off the books. You have made me a stronger writer through blood, sweat, tears, and gallons of whiskey. Thank you Lisa Lane, Jami Gold, Mary Ann Peden-Coviello, and Virginia Smith.

AND ... where would any book be without its beta readers? I have a trusted crew to totally tell me how the cow ate the cabbage and I wouldn't expect any less from them. I sincerely thank you for being bloody honest and helping me work out the kinks. This novel reflects your feedback and love. :-) Thank you Ahnah, Alicia, Billie, Tara, Cindy, Ginny, Vix, RomaLee, and Becca!

Dedication

For My Family.
To both my virtual family and friends and real world family.
For without you, my dreams could not have come true.
For with you, I have found true inspiration,
love, compassion, and kindness.
Namaste.

Contents

Author's Note

Thank you for being awesome! If you have come this far, then I sincerely thank you for purchasing and reading Obfuscate. I hope you have already read Exsanguinate [Book One] and are as anxious to reunite with the characters as I was to get them back here in your hot little hands.

A couple of changes since you've last read. I've expanded on the foreign language dialects since there are so many International characters. This book includes a glossary of words and references featured in other languages to help you understand their context. There are no made up words in this book. All words have references to how they are spoken in cultures all over the world. I hope you'll join me in celebrating the beauty of so many languages.

Lastly, I share this book with you from real, heartbreaking experiences I've had in my own life. Several chapters were gut-wrenchingly difficult to write, but were intensely therapeutic in my own grief recovery. My heart goes out to everyone [especially parents] who have challenges with grief and depression in their lives. This book is dedicated to you. <3

I hope you will enjoy this book series, the quirky characters, and share them with your family and friends. Thank you for joining me on my journey. Let's continue the ride!

~Killion

Prologue

I failed. I should be dead.

The schism of words replayed again and again as though they were a needle stuck between a track and a scratch on an old vinyl record.

I tried to open my eyes and sit up but found my head was wrapped and I'd been tied down.

What the hell? Where am I? Have I been captured?

I leaned my head closer to my hands and pulled on the strips of cloth covering my face. Rewarded with searing pain, I jerked my head away, sucking in a breath. Immediate and intense, the sensation behind my eyes was the same torment from a jammed toe against the bed frame in the middle of the night. Agonizingly slow to dissipate.

My eyes! Did they take my eyes?

I wrestled against my bonds and kicked my feet hoping to find some sort of escape. Something fell, clanging to the floor. It sounded as though a hundred steel marbles scattered, bouncing in every direction. My runaway imagination insisted the calamity had to be a bloodied tray full of shiny, sharp implements.

I can't see ... how can I get out of here? Breathe, Cheyenne, think.

I leaned over again and bit the thick, padded belts holding my wrists. Blood pooled in my mouth as my lower lip snagged on a buckle. I spat out the blood and felt along the length of my mouth with my fingertips. Hard, plastic stitches lined my lip as if I were a forgotten rag doll in a creepy carnie show. Were they trying to sew my mouth shut?

Unholy hell, what are they doing to me?

I knew it—it was a trap. I should've listened to my guts. Cannibal vampires. We weren't prepared. What if I'm an ingredient in their recipe? Are they preparing to stuff me with crab and then roast me over a fiery spit?

Shouldn't a vampire be able to escape? Am I trapped in silver?

Questions seared my mind as I made headway pulling the strap with my teeth through the loops.

Everything will go as planned, they said. *Nothing will hurt us*, they said. *Drunk with fermented drinks*, they said.

Why did I listen to them?

Khaldon and Harris—they were burning under the water. Did they make it out alive?

What about Briggs? He was unconscious. Did he drown?

The sharks were everywhere.

Where's Torchy? Did he send for help?

Ludovic? Did he—

Footsteps closed in with the acrid stench of disinfectant. A female, disembodied voice threatened. "*Kuthri,* look at this mess. You're making this much too difficult. Hold still."

"Hold Still? Are you kidding me?" I jerked my arms inside their confinement. "Wait—who are you? Where am I? What are you doing to me?"

"You're in isolation." Her words snapped with disdain.

"Don't touch me! Why are you tying me down? Stop it!" I pulled harder on the bonds, and the metal bars confining me groaned and began to give way.

The female voice ignored my question. "Quick, hold her. This won't take but a second."

"Did you dispense the stronger dosage this time?" an agitated male voice hurriedly asked. "She burned through the last one in record time."

Another male voice came from the direction of my feet. "Make sure this one keeps her down for good. We still have fleshy, meaty spots to dig out closer to the bone. I'm not getting another black eye tonight."

For good? Meaty spots? Closer to the bone?

"Get away! Help!" I kicked while rough, wide fingers and hands wrenched my face sideways, exposing my neck. "Khaldon!"

I thrashed my head around and bit the hand holding my face.

"*Kamina!*" the male voice exclaimed and wrenched his hand out from between my teeth, practically yanking my fangs out with it.

Another set of hands held down my legs while an elbow jabbed me in the head. A sharp stab to my neck flashed fire behind my eyes in a kaleidoscope of intense luminescence.

I cried out in pain, arching my back in defiance.

My limbs grew heavy as Aunt Maisie's cast iron skillets.

"No ... stop ... please don't ... eat ... me..."

Far away, the female voice flatly stated, "She's done. Let's get her prepped for Rattanakosin."

There's something ... it's right at the tip of my...

I failed. I should be dead.

The words replayed again and again in the fissure of my memory.

Dakota, my sister?

Oh, no!

Oh, yes ... I should, most definitely, be dead.

Chapter 1

Seven Hours Earlier

The Andaman Islands ~ Indian Ocean

Cheyenne O'Cuinn

"Look right here, Khaldon." I tapped the computer monitor screen and clicked to an article about the Rakshasa. "The Paranormal Wikipedia entry for the Andaman Islands states that North Sentinel is inhabited by cannibalistic, blood-thirsty warriors." I turned in my chair to study his face for a reaction.

He didn't respond, but continued to read over my shoulder.

Khaldon finished the parawiki page aloud in his formal English accent. "With fierce black fangs, they drain the blood of their prey and then roast them over a fiery spit. The Rakshasa celebrate their kill by wearing the bones and teeth of those they eat."

He paused for a moment and made an appreciative noise in the back of his throat. "Right, then."

"So, wait—are you telling me there are different types of vampyre?" Only managing to smear my chocolate-covered fingerprint, I tried to wipe the sugary goo from the screen. "C'mon, is this a load of bunk?" I licked my fingers clean and pursued the sticky smudge again. My blue eyes mirrored back at us in the monitor's reflection as I gazed up at him. "Next, you're gonna tell me there are creatures such as demon fairies, hounds of hell, and black-eyed kids, right?"

He pulled a glass cleaning wipe from the container and scrubbed the computer surface clean. Intently staring at me, his eyes flashed wide and then narrowed again to inquisitive slits. "And if I did, Cheyenne, what then?" His tone was caring, but it had an under-lilt of sarcasm in that *I-told-you-so* kind of voice. "You still haven't read the *Vampyric Canons*, have you? Have you started your training?"

Hoping to find solace deep within the candy bag, I pulled my mouth over to one corner, hid my face, and dug in for another cluster of peanutty goodness. The feelers of a headache were beginning to stab at the back of my eyes. I closed them in favor of a brief rest from the computer screen and the invasive oceanic winds.

Why do I have to embrace anything new? What's so wrong with being human?

He let out an exasperated sigh and kissed me on top of my head. "You're never going to learn how to be a vampire unless you take the time to work through the courses."

Khaldon smiled a genuine smile. The kind of grin where the curve of his lips playfully danced in tune with his green eyes. I had daydreamed about that smile a thousand times, and it never failed to stop me dead in my tracks, turn me around, and make me want him more than I already did.

"Consider your training like a twelve-step program—minus five or six steps. You've got to learn to trust yourself and let go. No matter how much I wish I could, I can't complete this transition for you. Only you can discover what your vampyric dynamics will evolve into." After removing my sweet smudges, Khaldon tossed the chocolate-covered rag into the bin. "Just like you're able to perceive people's emotions through their scents. Not every vamp can do that. We're all different." He evaded my jab to his ribs while I licked my fingers once again. I stared as he walked past the bulkhead and leaned on the ship's railing.

Khaldon's body stood out like a silhouette against the light shining through the yacht's starboard balcony. I studied him for a minute, his chin firm and confident. His five o'clock shadow bristled, entirely framing his mouth, and he had his long, black hair tied back in a jewel-encrusted family heirloom. He seemed very at home within his skin even though at a moment's notice, he could shape-shift into any person he desired.

Indignant, I returned to the monitor. "And when exactly have I had time to read *The Canons* while hunting Dakota and running a multi-million dollar global gaming company with Sheridan?"

Hoping to stave off a headache, I rubbed my forehead, pushing my thumbs deep against the sinus cavities to help relieve the pressure. "My sister is a prisoner on that island. If our strategy works, the Rakshasa won't have anything left to celebrate. They especially won't be roasting Dakota over a fiery spit."

I stood up from the computer and followed him to look out over the crystalline water. He opened up his arms to me, and I leaned in close against his chest, breathing in the warm frankincense he wore. Even if it were just for a fleeting moment, in his arms, I could allow my mind to escape—to pretend we were all alone on a holiday and not faced with this nightmare.

The playful waves mingled with the beachy scents of salt and seaweed while I watched the fish jump out of the water in their graceful aquatic ballet. My fingers twirled the little hairs peeking out from the top of his t-shirt. He wore one of his favorite band shirts with the words "Another One Bites the Dust" written across the chest and the Queen concert tour schedule on the back.

"Breathe, Cheyenne." His lips lingered on my forehead as his hand tangled in among the dark red, auburn curls at the nape of my neck. Khaldon finished his words in a soothing whisper. "Everything is jolly well fine. Our plan is solid. As soon as Torchy and Harris arrive with the final supplies, we'll load up on the beach and take off with the dragons. We'll get her back—tonight. You have my word, m'lady."

I wanted to vouchsafe his reassurance—to stand in his arms and pretend this horrific night was already over, but my doubts consumed me. An inner voice nagged hard at the edges of my gut, pouring acid over an already bleeding ulcer. I was afraid, and everyone knew it. Worst part was, I knew it too. Dakota was my baby sister I'd sworn to protect, and I had to face this fear. There was no going back now—after months we had finally found her.

Dammit, none of us sisters ever broke the promise of our almighty sister pinkie swear, no matter what the cost. Despite the fear, I had even come to terms with the possibility that the cost could be my own life.

⁂

We disembarked from Khaldon's yacht, the *M'lady,* and climbed aboard the skiff toward Jolly Boy Beach about fifty yards from the stern of the ship. We loaded the supplies and trussed the nylon body harnesses around our chests and legs. My feet felt confined in the black combat boots, but from the sound of the creepy crawlies inhabiting North Sentinel, I didn't want to take any chances of bug or snake bites.

I should take a picture of myself in this get-up; Sheridan will laugh out loud for sure.

The sun hung low in the sky as the gulls flew to the beach, finding their mates, chicks, and nests for the night. The waters choppy, we steered the little boat to the shore to meet up with our crew, Ludovic Zyryanov, Tony Briggs, Harris Archer, and Torchy Gravenor. They were to meet us along with an arsenal of guns, ammunition, and various other search and rescue accoutrements.

Khaldon's best mate and loyal dragon ally, Torchy, and my best friend, Harris, were on a final supply run we needed for Dakota's rescue mission. The six of us had rehearsed her forced extrication in virtual simulators, but crossing over into the real world from a cyber-reality was an entirely different story. Unable to anticipate alien factors, we had to expect anything could go wrong.

I spoke over the small outboard engine. "How long do you think we can keep Ludovic alive before the vampyre queen orders Amicula to try and kill him again? Once we have my sister back, won't the queen keep coming after Ludovic to locate Dakota? How can we be sure turning him loose wouldn't endanger us again?"

Khaldon steered away from a patch a kelp. "Well, Chey, I think you've just answered your own questions." His face held a stern frown as if he'd been pondering the same question for a bit of time himself. "We can't risk it any longer. Especially now that Sheridan is going to have the twins soon. It's not right, endangering the children—always having to look over our shoulders. Do you want to spend the rest of your life running? Ludovic is a threat to our family now—more than ever."

I didn't answer him because he was right. Deep down inside, I did know the answers. We couldn't keep Ludovic around us and we couldn't allow him to fall back under the control of the queen. After a few moments, I responded with a surprising sadness in my heart. "Even though I despise him, I guess I never really thought about killing someone just because they were a threat to my family's survival."

Khaldon stared at me possibly remembering an age of his own innocence. Past days when life was simple and fun and not so politically corrupt.

My eyes studied the calm of his face, and I wished I could feel that level of confidence. I ached for the days when I knew nothing about this dreaded paranormal life and I never had to worry about answering the front door. Normal humans don't have to worry about flower delivery guys trying to kidnap them. Why should I?

My life was total shite now and I hated it.

Khaldon pointed to a huge rock on the far side of the beach. "Did I ever tell you how the Andamans got their name?"

I shook my head and gave him a small smile. Not really interested in what he had to say, but I knew he was trying to ease my mind away from the topic of killing Ludovic, so I placated him and tried to give the appearance that I was paying attention.

"It was about the time when..."

Khaldon piloted the boat closer to shore, maneuvering around the outcroppings of Mangrove trees. Even though he talked about the Andamans and their lore, his words faded beyond my thoughts as I preoccupied myself with the reasons I was in this skiff in the first place.

As the boat chopped across the gentle crests, the waves lulled me deep into questions I'd pondered a hundred times before, but never managed to answer.

What would have happened to me if my sisters hadn't have been kidnapped last Halloween? Would I have continued my life as a software gaming designer? Would my days be filled with worrying about the next boss sequence or the mobile roll-out of the game? Would I have gotten a female boxer puppy as a companion for my Beano puppy? Those mundane decisions seem so irrelevant to the ones I was forced to make now.

I reached into my camouflage jacket pocket and took out a picture of me and my sisters dressed up for Halloween Scream Nights: Me as a fifth-century mummified streetwalker, Dakota dolled up as, Elvira Mistress of the Night, and Sheridan, disguised as a man-eating plant in a Ghillie suit. I traced Dakota's face with my finger and bit back a sob in the back of my throat. Would I really get her back tonight? Would she still be the sassy brat I adored?

Talk about a case of mistaken identity. Ludovic was all wrong about us. Why would a vampyre queen want to kidnap us in the first place? The

Irish, red-headed, O'Cuinn sisters—from a royal bloodline? Insanity! I caught the hint of a smile trying to escape my lips and almost laughed out loud dismissing the ridiculousness of the thought.

I breathed in the pungent, salty, seaweed aromas of the beach and sat quietly in the boat trying to take it all in. I stared at the back of Khaldon's head as he pointed this way and that, showing me the what-nots about the flora and fauna of the surrounding seascape. If I were honest with myself, I'd admit to being baffled at how my online boyfriend of two years was actually a different man, and a vampire to boot.

Why couldn't he just've been a normal guy?

I gave him a sweet, simple smile and nodded my head in such a way that showed I was indeed listening, but couldn't help but mull over a new set of questions which would require decision and action soon.

What will our lives be like if we rescued Dakota tonight? What do vampire couples do for an eternity? When forever becomes real, it's seriously intimidating. Would we become dull and boring when the fun runs out? How long does the secret sauce last anyway?

What if I didn't embrace the vampiric lifestyle Khaldon craves? I wasn't sure if I could—or even wanted to embrace it. What would we be doing if we weren't trying to rescue my sister?

If we weren't in the midst of adrenaline junkie acts of heroism, would he grow tired and leave me? Could I handle being a vampire alone if he did?

But I think the most important question was: Did I want to keep around a guy who felt the need to change me? I liked who I was, even if that was a chicken-shit vampire from time to time.

I looked back at the yacht and the comfortable safety of the ship and longed for the happy voyage home. I heaved a worried sigh and tried to unravel the knot of angst in my gut. For now, we were anchored twenty miles east of where my sister was held captive on that island, and I couldn't help but wonder if this was my final chance to find Dakota alive—and would it be Ludovic's last night to live?

Chapter 2

We beached the skiff up on the shore, where Tony Briggs dug his toes into the wet sand. Dragon Mafia hit man and one of the senior programmers for my online role play game, Briggs lifted the wet clumps of sand and dripped them onto the sandcastle turrets he must have built while waiting for us to arrive. Complete with a four-foot-tall dragon guarding the moat, the castle was over ten feet long.

A French, gargouille water dragon, Briggs had the same human muscular build as his paranormal form. Standing over six feet tall, black, both a lover and a fighter, he simply exuded sex. His shaved head and brilliant white teeth showed off his full mouth when he spoke. His voice always reminded me of the singer, Barry White, deep and intoxicating. No wonder my sister Dakota was fool crazy over him.

To add to the overall quagmire of the Dakota love triangle, Tony was madly, deeply in love with my sister and hated Ludovic with every dragon scale of his body. Briggs wasn't taking any chances on losing our sole connection to his true love. Several attempts on Ludovic's life by the vampire queen self-employed Briggs as the Romanian's personal bodyguard and constant companion.

In many ways, I think Briggs missed his calling. Besides putting the squeeze on the paranormal watch in New Orleans, the one oddball thing that stood out was his love for cooking. You wouldn't think such a burly man would care for such a thing, but he held a passion for food. Daily, Briggs goaded Ludovic by reciting scrumptious French gourmet recipes, with Ludovic served as the main course. When we landed on the beach, Briggs was mid-sentence in his thick French accent in what sounded like a tasty marinade.

"*Oui?* Doesn't dzat sound *délicieux*?" Briggs flashed his million-dollar canines at Ludovic and then turned to pull the boat further up onto the beach. The skiff rocked back and forth until it had a firm footing in the sand.

Briggs hollered back over his shoulder to Ludovic in his best Julia Child's impersonation, "How 'bout I use a dzick slab o' organic grass-fed butter with *fleur de sel* and a heavy shake of *herbes de provence*. Dzen I'll simmer shallots and tarragon in a red wine vinegar with a splash of sherry while I braise your tough ole hide in dzhe slow cooker. *Oui?*"

"Sounds bloody delish. When's dinner?" Khaldon asked.

"Tonight, just after midnight." Briggs grinned devilishly at Ludovic seemingly to make him as uncomfortable as possible.

Ludovic rolled his eyes obviously bored with hearing yet another recipe, but still squirmed against his bonds.

Always a gentleman, Briggs offered a hand to help me out of the boat. I managed to step off into the sand without slipping on the wet seat.

Even though I didn't care for Ludovic because he'd sold us down the river, I was able to empathize with him. I stiffened, looked away, and shook my head while Briggs continued to recite human recipes, knowing in an hour, we too, would face cannibals on North Sentinel.

Do the Rakshasa brew up marinade recipes too?

I covered my eyes with my hand and gazed up and down the beach. "Hey, where're Harris and Torchy?" I grabbed my rucksack out of the boat and threw it over my shoulder.

"Not to worry, Chey Chey. Dzey'll be along soon." Briggs unloaded the diving spear gun with extra arrows and set them beside the rest of the supplies we had prepared.

"They're not here? Seriously?" I kicked a broken shell away from my foot, shooting white sand into the air. "How could Harris do this?"

"They'll be here. I'm sure there's a good reason." Khaldon squeezed my shoulders. "We can't leave without them, so let's just take inventory of what we have and go through the checklist and timeline again."

Harris was my best friend, the brother I never had, and the best networking programmer I ever had the courtesy of working with. But he had a chronic issue of always running on the Harris Archer time zone. Despite being chronologically challenged, he also had this curious little habit of turning into a werewolf. A small detail he neglected to share with me while we were college roommates. For three years.

It wasn't until he outed me as a vampire last November that I learned who he really was. All his cyberchrondriac maladies, every full moon, clicked into place, and I understood the drive behind his enormous carnivorous appetite.

I heaved my shoulders round in circles trying to massage out knots of stress. "Dammit, I told Harris not to be late." I cursed under my breath.

"I'm sure it won't be long. We still have time before we're scheduled to leave." Khaldon pressed his talented fingers deep into my neck muscles, rubbing out the tension. Immediately, the pain eased with the touch of his hands as I willed the tightness to dissipate.

"Werewolves are always late, but I'm sure 'arris has a good reason," Briggs rolled his words in his French dialect. "*Oui*, let's just 'ope dzeir tardiness isn't an omen of how tonight will end." He laughed in an evil *muah hah hah* way, which did not help to unravel my anxiety.

My muscles tensed again, spiking a shard of pain behind my lids.

Briggs lit up a cigar, his smoky brimstone intermingled with the sensual scent of warm vanilla in his tobacco. The puff of white clouds contrasted against his chocolatey skin almost concealing him against the white sands.

From a palm tree off to the side where Briggs had tied him, Ludovic chimed in with his husky Romanian accent. "My comrades, I wouldn't underestimate the Rakshasa. If the Lycan is bringing more intel, it's worth the wait. We know nothing about them." Ludovic's tone added a sneer to his words, making me question if he was trying to be helpful or if he was just trying my nerves instead.

"*Maestru* Briggs, what would I need to endure to have a few puffs of that *trabuc*?" A fly landed on Ludovic's nose and he attempted to swipe it away, but with both hands tied to different trees, he had to blow at the bug instead.

Briggs walked over to Ludovic with the cigar. He exhaled a stream of smoke from his mouth and inhaled a dual stream into his nostrils before blowing a forceful plume into Ludovic's face. The fly buzzed away. I couldn't tell who enjoyed the gesture more—Briggs blowing smoke, or Ludovic free from the bug. It was an odd relationship.

No matter how drop-dead gorgeous Ludovic was, he was a walking cliché of a wolf in sheep's clothing. As her vampyric maker, Ludovic was the only one who could mind-message with Dakota. It frustrated the hell out of me because I never knew if he was being truthful with us. Hatred for this man burned through every fiber of my being, but our plan couldn't work without him.

After spending months of time with Ludovic underfoot and even helping to rescue him from Amicula, I had come to understand why Dakota had been attracted to him when they dated. He had bad boy written all over him. His eyes were dark and mysterious, his untamed hair black and short-cropped. His winning smile held a voice that could melt butter with the way he romantically rolled words off his tongue. It was becoming clear the types of male attributes Dakota liked. She had a thing for languages and teeth.

Had it been any other night and under different circumstances, I would have set up my camera and tripod to marvel and shoot the beauty of the sunset, but tonight the twilight colors across the sky became the sands of an hourglass condemning me to my fate.

I heaved another heavy sigh and escaped the testosterone-ladened insults from Briggs by taking a small jog down the beach.

I needed to be alone. To breathe.

To think.

I took off my combat boots and rolled my fatigues up to cuff them up at the knees. I strolled far enough away to talk out loud to myself. "This is crazy." I paced back and forth along the water while my toes sank into the pristine white sands. My calves already ached from the unused muscles pushing into the next step. White and blue crabs, carrying their left claws the size and weight of their scampering little bodies, scurried under fallen palm fronds and wet driftwood.

Outwardly demanding the Gods' attention, I threw my arms up in the air. "Are we insane for doing this by ourselves? Do we need a legion of vampires, werewolves, and dragons to help us?"

I picked up a broken, barnacle-encrusted seashell and skipped it out into the waves. "I'm not sure we're qualified for this mission." My voice trailed off and I hung my head with resolve. "Or, at least, I'm not qualified."

I kicked a weather-worn coconut husk. "I shouldn't go. I've got no feckin' idea in hell what I'm doing. I've never fired a gun. What if I accidentally hurt someone?"

I skipped a shell out over the waves.

Two skips.

My conscience got the best of me. The little angel who sat on my right shoulder tried to talk some sense into me. "What are you thinking? You could totally compromise the mission and put their lives in danger. This is not a place for you. You need to call this mission off or find someone better to replace you."

Throwing it harder, I shot another shell out over the water. Stepping into the water, I embraced the warm waves crashing around my ankles.

Four skips.

The little red demon who lived on my left shoulder and loved to stir up shite just couldn't keep the guilt away. "Yeah, but would you ever forgive yourself if they died and you didn't do anything to help them other than weasel out? Do you really want to be known as the wimpy vampire who stood by and did nothing to save your family and friends?"

Khaldon had walked up behind me and picked up another shell from the sand. "Cheyenne, we're dealing with primitive natives." He joined my game of attempting the most skips over the water.

Eight skips. Damn.

The sun added fiery red to the orange-hued clouds setting over the horizon silhouetting him once again. His sculpted build cut a deep V into his abs peeking out above his fatigues. "Once we swim to shore, we'll navigate to the volcanic caves, we'll rescue Dakota, and fly away on the dragons. Easy-peasy." His voice was confident, self-assuring, as if this were just another day in the life of a vampire. "She'll be safe, and you'll never have to set foot on that island again. I promise."

"Get in, kill a couple of bad guys, rescue the damsel in distress, and be done with it, huh?" I swished my hands together, wiping off the wet sand. "You make it all sound like a Sunday picnic."

Khaldon rested his arm around my shoulders, pulling me in tight. He tilted his head in toward me and whispered into my ear. "Maybe we'll get a chance to snack on a couple of Rakshasa ourselves. Wouldn't that be grand?"

An answer escaped me. I wasn't sure what to think about his suggestion. Could I feed off another person without killing them? Could I trust myself? If I let go, would I become like that horrible bloody beast, the Red Man, who attacked me Halloween night?

I can't lose control like that. Ever.

Avoiding his question, I lay my head on his chest. For the few micro-moments when he held me, all my fears disappeared. He stroked my hair, trying to tame the wind-blown strands, and then held me at arm's length. As though he were capturing my image and hoarding it away into his soul, Khaldon's devilishly defiant, verdant eyes traced every line of my face.

I returned the heartfelt exchange and cupped my hand against his cheek, searching for additional strength to channel and absorb. His black silken pharaoh-like strands spread across my hand as the winds stirred in the ocean breeze. My thumb caressed the sharp line of his jaw and pulled down his lower lip, revealing his intense grin. I tucked his thick locks behind his ear and leaned in close, wrapping my arms tight around his torso. He returned the gesture. I closed my baby blues once again and listened to his steady heartbeat as though nothing in the world could alter the rhythm.

We slowly walked back toward the boat, and I eased into the welcomed embrace under Khaldon's arm. Arriving back at camp, we watched as Briggs held the cigar out for Ludovic and stole it away as soon as the tobacco got close enough to his mouth.

I shook my head again ... boys.

I stepped up to the pile of guns and tools next to the sandcastle and picked up a firearm. Not really sure of what I was looking at, I picked up a sizable pistol. "Okay, gents. I need some help. Who wants to show me how to shoot this thing? I'm not going in there without knowing I can handle the gun and not kill you at the same time."

Khaldon, Briggs, and Ludovic stared at each other, exchanging volumes of conversation with their eyes without ever saying a word.

Chapter 3

After a long period of silence, I broke the peaceful sounds of the surf and nesting birds and defended my request. "Look, guys—I don't want to end up being the *Warning: Do Not Enter* sign to other people who come upon my head impaled on a spike."

They checked one another again to give credence to my concerns.

"Ever since Amicula betrayed us, I don't trust anything that has to do with her or her minions." I studied the weapon in my hands, wishing there was an owner's manual I could download into my brain like in the movie *Matrix*. "Guys, I need to be able to operate this weapon with confidence, or I shouldn't be going. Period."

Khaldon grinned from ear to ear. "Fair enough. You won't see me arguing. Chicks with guns. Totally hot in my book. Let me prep the 9mm for you and we'll do some practice rounds until Torch and Harris arrive."

Briggs pulled out his own 45 auto pistol and showed me the inner workings of the firearm. "Chey Chey, you have a point about dzhe queen's niece, I don't trust her either. But it sounds like you've been watching too many 'orror movies again."

"I think my imagination just has the best of me. I shouldn't have watched that cannibal zombie TV show last night." Why did my sisters and I have to be obsessed with horror movies?

I hugged my arms to my chest hoping to find safety within their grasp. "Impaled meat hooks through women's breasts. Natives hacking through skulls to eat their captive's brains—I just can't handle the imagery."

Intuitively on cue, Briggs' stomach thundered beside me and he licked his lips.

I scrunched up my face, eying him warily. "This isn't funny, and there're sandwiches in the cooler if you're hungry." My hands kneaded my temples once again, trying to evade the headache. "Why couldn't I have settled for watching *Must Love Dogs* or some other romantic comedy instead?"

"*Ma chére,* do not fear. Khaldon's right." Briggs patted my arm and placated me with a *Don't Worry, Be Happy* smile. "Most likely, dzhe Rakshasa will be drunk with fermented drinks praising their goddess tonight. Dzey'll never know we were dzere." Briggs cocked the hammer into place, and then fired at a coconut a few feet above Ludovic's head.

It landed with a thud and missed him by mere inches. "No one is going to pierce your tatas—tonight." He blew the smoke out of the barrel and danced his eyebrows at me.

I shook my head knowing nothing I could do or say would ever make a difference. Dragons were always a seductive show-offy race.

Khaldon wagged a finger of warning in Briggs' direction.

Ludovic turned green and looked as though he needed to change his shorts.

Briggs offered me a sideways wink and nudged me with his shoulder.

I slugged him in the arm. "You say that now, but 'most likely' doesn't cut it for me. I need facts. Remember, we're gaming programmers. The logic has to make sense for me to conclude the program will run." I pointed at the island, which lay beyond the horizon line. "Don't you guys worry about being on tonight's menu?"

"It's a threat I live with daily, Cheyenne." Ludovic's defeated Romanian voice fell flat as though he'd already given up. "What does it matter anymore?"

Briggs heartily laughed out loud and presented a double thumbs-up gesture.

My hands pouted on my hips. "Well, don't you?" I gulped down a hard lump forming in my throat and looked around for a water bottle. Trying to maintain a reasonable sense of calm, I held my chin up awaiting their answer. Secretly, to keep my lips from trembling, I bit the inside of my cheek to restrain my nerves. "Don't you worry about being eaten alive?"

Both Khaldon and Briggs pursed their mouths, looked at each other, and shrugged in a non-committal gesture.

I should have known better than to ask what they thought. "Look, you two might be centuries-old epic war heroes surviving hundreds of battles, but this—this is all new to me. Hell, I don't even like haunted houses in public theme parks, remember?"

Khaldon checked the gun in my hand for bullets and then handed it back to me. I tried to pull on the firearm slide but couldn't see how to release it. "Guys, I just think we need more people with us. None of us have ever seen a Rakshasa, and we have no idea what we're up against. Shouldn't we have more backup in case anything goes wrong?"

"Chey, Chey, when you are working recon, you need a small team. Get in, get out. Otherwise we cannot 'ide an army of people. Too many will jeopardize the mission." Briggs showed me how to release the safety on the gun.

"I understand your logic, I really do. I just feel like we need something more. I'm not convinced we've dotted enough I's and crossed all the T's. I'm halfway expecting to see some kind of run-time error pop up and we have to recode for syntax errors." I easily pulled back the spring loaded slide and cocked the weapon to shoot.

"This is not the same as programming, Chey." Khaldon twirled his firearm around his index finger. "There are going to be unexpected variables we can't predict no matter how many times we try to anticipate what might go wrong. Just relax. We've got this. Breathe in and embrace the vampyric side of yourself. You'll find comfort in your abilities instead of constantly doubting. That comes from your human side." Khaldon tip-toed around his words. "If you'd already gained control over your human emotions, these kinds of situations wouldn't scare you any longer."

I ran a hand through my hair to try and tame the flyaways and looked away from him. I was beginning to get tired of hearing this same broken record again and again. I wasn't in the mood to fight with him on this topic.

"Blimey, Chey. Your vampyric blood should be begging for a little action." Khaldon emphasized the word "begging" probably thinking it was a praise-worthy thing.

Would he give me a high five if I did? Is there a coming of age ceremony for a neonate vampire?

I didn't answer him but instead squared my shoulders for a stubborn showdown. I wanted to give him the what for, but said nothing especially since we both were holding a loaded firearm.

Khaldon checked Briggs and Ludovic for male bonding backup. When none returned, he put his palms up waving the white flag. "Right then, let me build a target and then I'll mind-message Torchy. Maybe I can determine an ETA from them."

The wind picked up, and the waves crashed against the hull of the skiff with a loud *slap slap slap* sound. I placed the pistol aside to dig into my rucksack. After tucking my hair behind my ears, I rummaged for a hair scrunchy. Found, the coveted curl-taming device quickly subdued the mass of unruly auburn curls framing my face.

I snatched up the weapon, a bottle of ice-cold water, and a couple of sandwiches from inside the skiff. Stepping over a fallen palm tree, I offered the drink and food to Ludovic. With a wary eye he nodded but indicated his hands were tied to the trees and couldn't hold the bottle.

"Have you felt Dakota's presence since we've arrived? Anything at all?"

I cracked the seal on the bottle and poured the water into his mouth and waited for him to swallow.

"*Multumesc*, or rather, thank you." He gulped a few more swallows I offered. "Her mind is weak. It's been difficult to keep a connection. She's been unresponsive to most messages today, but she's close." He stared back at me with deepened worry lines creasing around his eyes. From our past conversations, he knew his own life depended on the success of her rescue. "Are you planning on shooting at the coconuts above my head for target practice?"

"No. Definitely not. I don't think my aim is that good, but don't test me."

He looked at the gun and then to me. I fixated on him and then stepped away.

"Please keep trying to contact her. She needs to know we're coming so she can be ready." I untied one hand from the tree and left him the dinner.

Ludovic looked at me as if I'd lost my mind. Maybe I had. Over in the distance, Briggs growled as he finished shaping the bottom fang on his sand castle dragon. I'm sure he wasn't a fan of my decision. But honestly, where could Ludovic have escaped on this deserted beach?

From back at the skiff, I regarded his reactions. I didn't want him to know that I had to trust him. That I needed him. He detested Amicula just as much as we did after she'd deceived him. Leaving him for dead by the dhampir army. Would he betray us again?

Truthfully, I didn't care if Ludovic blew up into a million bits after tonight, just as long as I had Dakota back. Nothing else mattered anymore.

I checked my dive watch again, and we practiced shooting until I had a bullet grouping the size of a fifty-cent piece in the side of a coconut shell. We celebrated the sharp-shooting with a toast of the raw milk.

"Damn good shootin', Tex." Khaldon swiveled his pistols around his index fingers again and shoved them deep into his hip holsters.

"Dzat'll kill anything dzat comes near us, *oui*?" Briggs smiled, his face bright and excited.

I was beginning to get the feel of the firearm and was ready to confidently reload the magazine again when Khaldon shouted.

"They're on the way," He pointed toward the Eastern sky. "They'll be here presently. Torchy says Harris found out new information and they had to fly to Malaysia for different supplies, and that's why they're delayed."

Briggs patted my arm once again. "Everything will go as planned, Chey Chey. I'm proud of you. I know you're scared, but dzis is 'ow you play dze game."

Knowing I could hold and shoot a gun properly now, an enormous sigh of relief escaped my lips. Tense anxiety uncoiled from around my shoulder muscles like a braid let loose from its bindings.

I can do this!

Khaldon joined me beside the skiff and turned me to face him with a piercing gaze. He held my hands and pressed his forehead to mine. "I promise, nothing will hurt any of us." He ran a finger down my nose. The crook of his mouth revealed a naughty smile, and a quick flood of warmth escaped from under my shirt and up my neck.

When the cascade of calm flowed over me, I broke the stronghold he employed. "Why are you trying to control my emotions? I don't like it when you do that—it makes me feel all weird inside." I took a step backward out of his grasp and nudged a broken piece of sun-bleached coral with my toe and remembered to breathe.

"I'm not trying to control you, I am just trying to protect and help you handle what we might find on that island. My apologies. I should have asked." Khaldon moved in and cupped my cheeks. His whisper tickled the fine hairs in my ear and I returned his smile. "*And* no one is going to hang you by your breasts, m'lady. I'll guard those with my life if I have to."

ஐலை

Torchy landed with the grace of an elder dragon and with Harris holding on for dear life atop his back. Crimson spikes ridged up Torchy's sides, and his teeth glistened with a frothy mist. His fiery orange lava-quartz eyes frightened and mesmerized me at the same time. Those vertical slits for pupils stared through me, dissecting every thought in my head. The weird thing was I wanted him to see inside. I shook my head to clear my thoughts, pulling from the enthrall. Must be a draconian hypnotic trick.

What is it about everyone trying to mess with my mind today?

From our harrowing flight a few months ago, I knew Torchy's dragon tail, now docile and calm, could instantly change to any shape and size he desired to thwart an oncoming attacker. It was a formidable weapon and one I steered clear of. I ran my hands over his neck and chest as though I were petting a mythical beast. I supposed, to most of the world, I was.

Torchy Gravenor, Khaldon's best mate, was the opposite of Harris. Clean-shaved, well-kept, Torchy was a Welsh dragon but preferred the rocky crags of Northern Scotland. Befitting of his name, Gravenor was ancestrally known as the great hunter, and Torchy had most definitely lived up to that namesake. A prompt fellow, and he seemed to be one of those gents who was always in the right place at the right time.

The human persona he wore was a self-made billionaire catering to the every need of paranormal entities. The owner of the international retail giant, *The Super Market,* Torchy was a resource of connections and solutions. If one had a problem, Torchy's interests would most likely have a way to procure the solution. He and Briggs seemed to have hit it off—both being in the providing of services sort of work. However, Briggs' services were more in the realm of extorting ... or rather ... protecting retail establishments, whereas Torchy's interests were the retail establishments themselves.

Harris jumped from Torchy's back and landed face first into the shallow waves, spraying all of us with salt water. Scurrying out of the waves he shouted, "Sorry, I'm late."

Khaldon helped Harris stand up and gain his footing in the wet, uneven sand.

Harris spoke faster than we could understand him. "We got here as fast as we could. Torchy flew like his ass was on fire. I could barely hold on. You should have seen him. We found out more info. They use arrows and spears. We need to be ready or we're dead meat for sure."

As when he in his werewolf lupine form, Harris shook his body from his nose to tail, covering us again with salt water.

"*Idiot!*" Briggs wiped his face.

It looked like Harris had splashed him on purpose. Knowing Harris and the pranks those two played on one another, anything was possible.

Harris grimaced, furrowing his brow, screwing up his face. "Sorry, I sometimes forget I'm in human form. I'm all amped up." He wiped his brow with his sleeve and continued in his hurried explanations. "Anyways ... since the reef sticks out, boats crash on the coral. So no one can get to the island without the Rakshasa knowing they're coming. They're armed."

"What do you mean—armed?" Briggs crossed his arms over his puffed-out chest. "Next you'll be telling us dzey 'url bananas and coconuts from catapults."

"Whoa, whoa. Slow down, Harris." I handed him a towel. "You're not making any sense. We already knew about the boats, that's why we're swimming to the island. Stealth mode, remember? Why are you so worked up about this now?" I crossed my arms, mimicking Briggs' posture, but mine radiated with confused impatience.

"Yeah, but what we didn't know is that a couple months ago *Nat Geo* tried to film a documentary on North Sentinel. The Rakshasa shot poison arrows at them when their boat crashed into the reef. One of the cameramen died the next day. To get the crew off the ship, they had to Medevac them using Kevlar body armor."

Harris pulled a backpack and another long rifle bag from Torchy's back. Torchy flew off again toward the ship.

I knitted my eyebrows, trying to read between his words. "So you're saying that even though the Rakshasa are primitive, they're deadly?"

"Exactly!" He pointed at me and slapped his hands together as if I'd successfully guessed his charades game. Harris dabbed his face and then draped the towel over his shoulder, beaming with his news.

"Might I inquire, aren't *most* cannibalistic cultures considered deadly?" Khaldon's sarcasm drained the proud smile from Harris' face.

Harris bantered back. "Whatevz, hot shot. They use poison. Just thought we should know. Torch and I tried to change our defense weapons to counteract their tactics."

"Okay, show us what you've got." I flipped off his Chicago Wolves Hockey cap and tousled his sandy brown curls. "We're running out of time."

"My bad, Chey, but I couldn't ignore it. We were about to leave when I overheard these merchants talking about it, so I had to check it out, ya know?"

"Uh huh, ever hear of a cell phone?" I splashed wet sand and water onto his legs. "Did you learn anything else? Did you bring any bullet proof vests after learning this?"

"Hey..." He squatted down in the salt water. "Negatory on the Kevlar and the cell phone. No service. Torchy wasn't able to score any vests until next week and we didn't want to delay." Harris pulled off his shoes and swished them in the shallow surf.

"What about the ammunition? I've used up some rounds learning how to shoot. Check out this grouping." I handed him my mutilated coconut.

Harris eyed it and grimaced. "Just be sure you're not aiming at my head, okay? So yeah—we got the ammo—the colloidal silver ones. I have to say, Chey, you're looking kinda badassed in that outfit. Camo goes with your red hair."

He laughed out loud and then sing-songed his words. "I'm sure we've got what we need for the rescue, but you're not gonna like what's in the water." A stupid grin smeared across his face.

I studied him, thinking of monstrous water creatures. Orcas? Kraken? Piranha, maybe? No—those are in the Amazon. "What do you mean—monstrous? Is there a storm coming? Genetically engineered squids or something?" I took a few steps up toward the beach and stood in ankle-deep water.

Harris ran a hand through his wet curls, pushing them back off his face, and replaced his ball cap. "The reefs are teeming with sea life. Because of the volcano eruption and tsunami a couple years ago. It raised the entire island by two meters, making the coral reefs even deadlier than they were before."

I stole a glance at Khaldon and Briggs. Even Ludovic was listening intently on what Harris was describing. "The warm temperatures have fed the ecosystems around the island, and they're infested now with hammerheads, silver tips, and gray reef sharks. There's loads of barracuda, jellyfish, and manta rays. Oh, and poisonous sea snakes too." Harris stood up and joined me closer on the shore and pointed out toward North Sentinel. "Wouldn't it be wicked to see a man o'war jellyfish with thirty-foot tentacles?"

"Umm—that would be a 'no.'" I stepped out of the water and higher onto the beach. "Sharks? Barracudas? Tentacles?" I gulped as the theme from *Jaws* played in my head. The lump in my throat felt big enough to choke Briggs in dragon form several times over.

"Seriously?" The pangs of tension reemerged, and my shoulders seized up into my neck. "I hate swimming in water I can't see through. Dark, scary water with slithery things that want to eat me—no way—count me out. I'll ride Torchy."

"But, of course, *ma chére*." Briggs patted my arm again as though that was actually going to help me feel better. "*Oui*. We're in dze middle of dze Indian Ocean, deep into dze Bay of Bengal. But not to worry, my draconian sonar will jam their frequencies. We'll be finer dzan frog 'air. You are safe with me."

Draconian sonar? Frog hair? Would that be in the Paranormal Wikipedia or The Canons?

A cloud of fog engulfed us, and Torchy emerged in his human form beside the skiff. His coppery hair spiked up, and he was clad only in his kilted plaid. He was lean, abdominally chiseled, and one of the hairiest chested men I'd ever seen in my life.

Salt water dripped from his day's beard growth while Khaldon handed him a towel. In a thick Scottish accent, Torchy said, "Winds and waters are calm. We shouldna be seeing any issues with Poseidon tonight." He wiped his face and tossed the spent towel into the skiff. He scratched his fiery red goatee, and I noticed specks of blond interspersed among the deep mahogany colors matching his chest hair.

Khaldon dug into the boat and pulled out a leather flagon. "What about the cyclonic system to the south of us? Did it turn inland?" He uncorked the pouch and handed the whiskey to Torchy.

Torchy nodded and accepted the offer. "Oh aye, it did. We had to alter our course to go around it. I dinnae spot any cyclones in the forecast up here, but rumor has it this season be a damned wicked time for the seas. Nay sure I want to be moored here for long." Torchy drank deep without taking a breath and tossed the empty container back into the skiff. "We shouldna have any surprises tonight." He continued to run his hands through his hair until it was almost dry. "I'll be a damned sight happy when this is over. I've 'bout had it with salt up me backside, ya ken?"

Khaldon nodded and shot me a wink. "See, m'lady, nothing to worry your bonny self about."

Briggs removed a couple of automatic rifles, with several magazines full of ammunition, and inspected them before adding them to the pile of increasing firearms.

Harris pulled out a waterproof pouch from his back pocket and removed a global positioning device. "I found that blackout shield for the mobile GPS. Unless you're standing right in front of it, no light escapes." He snapped on the blackout cover and duct-taped it to the AR-15 rifle slung across his shoulder. "We'll be able to know within one klick of Dakota's location when we reach the shore."

I picked up a box of what looked like regular bullets and opened them to examine the death-eaters. "Are bullets really going to be effective? I've seen it a thousand times in movies, like *Blade*, where vampires and werewolves heal themselves and the fired bullets push out of their victims and clink to the ground. Is that true?"

Khaldon stared at me from the sides of his narrowing eyes. He arched his brows pondering to answer my question, but his flat-pressed lips told me otherwise.

"I know, I know ... read *The Canons*."

Harris slammed a loaded magazine clip into his Glock 9mm pistol and holstered it into his leg harness. "That's why these are pure silver, Chey. Torchy had a stash of these at his Malaysia Super Market. Not just colloidal silver, but the real stuff. Nothin's gonna hurt us tonight with these babies."

I eyed Torchy and wondered why he would have a secret stash of silver bullets. I guessed even dragons were preppers, but most likely "hoarders" was the more appropriate term for dragons.

Harris pulled on a leather glove then pulled a small object from inside his jeans pocket. He held up and flashed a single silver bullet and rotated it in the light. "I'll admit, it's not easy carrying something that can kill me just as much as it can kill others, but it has a certain power to it."

The radiant setting colors of the sun shimmered off the bullet in a spectrum of orange and red. He tossed it up into the air, breaking the spell it had me under. Harris took off his hat and slid the bullet under the brimmed edge. Slapping his cap back onto his head, he adjusted the fit and then pocketed the glove once again. "C'mon, Chey. Let's go blast a couple more coconuts before we go." He gave me a confident slap on the back. "I can't wait to see you shoot. Can I call you Annie Oakley from now on?"

"That's a tall order to stand up to. Give me just a sec, H. I've gotta talk to Torchy for a moment." Turning my attention away from the guys and their preparations, I surprised Torchy from behind and hugged him tightly around the neck. "I'm so glad you're here. Have you heard from Sheridan? Is she feeling okay?"

"*Aye*, she tells me all's well, but I dinnae think the lass is entirely forthcoming. Yer father has shared his concerns with me, but says he'll ring us if something comes up." He handed me another knife sheathed in a leather pouch.

"I'm glad she decided to stay home this time. I'm not sure she could've taken much more of the open seas with her pregnancy. I know Sheridan wants to find Dakota as much as the rest of us, but if the storm weather predictions hold true, then she definitely doesn't need to be on the ship."

"*Aye*, I'm a bit unnerved about her giving birth to the twin bairns before we return. But if all goes well, we'll be back before the fortnight." Torchy checked the straps on the back of my shoulder harness and cinched it up tighter. He smacked me on the ass. "There ya go, lassie. All set now."

I shook my head. *Dragons.*

We were as ready as we were going to be. Studying the wall of men in front of me, I ran the gamut of emotions from loathing to lust. Ludovic, Briggs, Torchy, Harris, and Khaldon. If I was going to win back my sister tonight, I needed to trust these men with everything I had. I needed to invest in their skills, their expertise, and relinquish my anxiety, or I wouldn't be of any use to them. Still, something inside me said we weren't prepared, we needed more people.

Should I call this mission off? Should we arrange for backup?

Khaldon clapped his hands. "All right, mates."

I jumped at the sudden sound.

He eased a hand down on my shoulder and arched an inquisitive brow. "We've discussed the drill. Try to use hand signals as much as possible once we land. We're not going to be the Rakshasa's celebratory dinner tonight. We're bringing Dakota home."

Everyone nodded and set out for final checks of lock picks, ropes, carabiners, and bolt cutters. There was no telling what we would need for this mission.

Briggs called out a French historical battle cry. "*Montjoie Saint Denis!*"

Torchy cried out in Gaelic, "*Eigfte Co'raig!*"

Harris hollered out in his Southern all-American, "Oh, hell yeah!" He then untied Ludovic and tethered him to his leather belt loop.

It was Ludovic's turn to say something, and he studied all of us for a long moment. He raised his bottle of water. "*Salut.* It has not been a pleasure, but it is my sincerest desire tonight to end this chapter and remove Dakota from the clutches of Amicula and Queen Civetateo."

The rest of us also raised our hands in a silent salute to his toast.

After we popped off a few more rounds for equipment checks, Ludovic cracked his knuckles and stretched out his hands. His fangs lengthened and the hair on my neck prickled. Harris stared at Ludovic, and his skin sprouted with the fine underfur that would make up his Were presence.

Ludovic patted him on the back and pulled in his fangs. "Just stretching, my comrade. Let us go and find Dakota, shall we?"

Harris relaxed back into his human form and punched Ludovic in the shoulder. "Dude, you almost became a Scooby snack."

Khaldon pulled out a painful looking sword with spikes on the handle. He held it up over his head and then released a vampyric shrill of a growl, revealing a full mouth of bloody, sharpened teeth. His size grew a couple inches and veins popped out on his arms. I took a few steps backward from him and my eyes grew as wide as silver dollars. I'd never seen him shift into anything that wasn't his gaming avatar, Roxas Morgwain. This was a beastlier side of him, and I wasn't exactly sure I wanted to experience it. He was downright scary looking.

Hmmm ... wonder if I can shift into something?

Briggs stretched and cricked the bones in his neck, back and forth, and then stepped into the night's water. Fog enveloped the beach, blinding me so much I couldn't see my hand in front of my face. Briggs morphed into his fantastical dragon form of shimmery black scales. So deep in color, they luminesced in purple. I would never tire of watching a man disappear into a fog bank and emerge a massive creature. One who breathed fire and could cremate living flesh on a mere whim. I was glad Briggs was on my side. I'm sure Ludovic was a tad bit more careful around Briggs when he was in drag.

When Briggs stomped into the waves, his scales glistened in the water, making them even shinier than the glass scales I'd seen in the daylight. His ochre talons dug into the sandy beach while fiery brimstone plumed from his nose. He stared intently at me with those hypnotic, opalescent eyes.

I found myself swallowing down the lump forming in my throat. Was I really going through with this? I checked my waist harness for my firearm again and held onto it.

Torchy laughed and patted me on the head while I stared at both Briggs and Khaldon. They were quite intimidating. "It's all right now, lass. Hesa crankin' up the juice. No need to be a scart of them." He turned to Khaldon. "I've got yer back, mate, and I'll be yer watcher in the stars."

Khaldon nodded, and I noticed an almost imperceptible understanding between the two men as if to say, "Stay safe, my brother."

Torchy waved to the lot of us. "*Aye*, listen. Try not to get yerselves kilt, will ya? I cannae do this all by me self."

Everyone was silent, but my ears tuned into their heavy heartbeats over the breaking waves. Even though the guys offered a confident façade on the outside, I still didn't trust we had covered all the bases.

As I climbed aboard Briggs' back, I could have sworn I heard a voice deep within telling me to stop and go back.

Unholy hell, why'd it have to be sharks and cannibals?

Chapter 4

B riggs had no issue gliding us through the currents of the deadly undertows which swirled and whirlpooled around the island. Opaque waters was home-field advantage for him but a nightmare for me. I watched for fins and slithery creatures breaching the waves and prayed Briggs was using his dragon sonar deflection distraction system thingy or whatever it was. I didn't care as long as it worked.

Torchy hovered above us, his red spikes reflecting the water's glossy surface rendering him virtually invisible to the naked eye. The moon goddess, Diana, didn't provide us much illumination since she was just coming off her new phase. In some ways, the lack of lighting might have been to our advantage, but we had no idea how well our adversaries could see in the dark.

The seawater was warmer than anticipated as it spewed salty sprays across my face. The briny waters stung my eyes, but it was only a momentary dis-ease, as my vampyric body healed itself almost instantly. The crashing, rhythmic pulse of the pounding waves on the beach rocks reminded me of my interactive bedroom wall which lulled me to sleep each night. Every unwelcome spray of the water confirmed my desire to be safe at home, tucked away in my bed, with my Beano boxer puppy, and far away from this insanity.

With the stealth of an octopus, we dismounted Briggs about three feet from the edge of the coral reefs. Razor blade coral outcroppings threatened to slash us to pieces while we skimmed close to the surface. We wore gloves and other impervious clothing to protect us from the poisonous barbs. The last thing we needed was to come all this way and to be shredded by the sharp rocks before we ever set foot on the ground.

The beach was a welcome relief as we scrambled out of the eerie water. I fisted handfuls of the sand, thankful to be on land once again. Heat spread through me, instantly drying my clothes, but my feet sloshed in my boots.

The haunted thundering cadence of drums pounded against the night, warning us we were not alone. We crouched low to the ground to avoid being seen. Shifting back into his human form, Briggs dressed into his warfare clothing Khaldon had packed from his cargo bag. It was hard not to peek, but I knew if I did, Briggs would catch me and that was the last thing I needed.

In the far-off distance, troops of macaque monkeys shrieked their nighttime rituals in time with the percussion clicks of man-eating beetles. The macaques' shrieks crawled under my skin and made an itchy nest just waiting to hatch and eat their way out.

The hairs on the back of my neck stood up in quick succession as I tensed, not only with visions of screaming baboons with five-inch tusks and pink butt-cheeks attacking us, but the Rakshasa throwing our bones into a pit of deadly fire ants to strip off any remaining flesh.

Get a hold on your imagination, Cheyenne.

We had timed Dakota's rescue on one of the Rakshasa's most sacred nights. An evening when the natives thanked their gods and goddesses for dry days. Monsoons pummeled the island for ten months out of the year. I supposed I would raise my hands to offer thanks for sunshine and preoccupied monkeys as well. I prayed the Rakshasa would be distracted enough with the rituals to provide us the opportunity to move undetected. Who was I fooling? The Rakshasa or myself?

Silent as a naval SEAL team, we performed a weapons inventory check and Ludovic homed in on Dakota's location. Khaldon removed the shotgun from its holster behind his shoulder.

The plan was for Torchy to stay above us in his dragon form, circling the island, and maintain mind-message communication with Khaldon in case we needed to make a hasty retreat. Our only escape was to fly off the island after we rescued Dakota.

We checked our position against the GPS, and the device confirmed we were only about .10 klicks off from our landing destination. The blackout screen worked, as I could barely make out the map screen simply standing beside Harris. We adjusted our course and gingerly walked into the thick canopy of trees.

The jungle's leafy maw swallowed us barely five feet past the beach. The air was thick with the rotting vegetation littering the ground. Hanging moss dripped out of the trees, giving me cause to consider what evil insects might be lurking and waiting to feast upon us. I remembered my Uncle Charlie once said chiggers lived in moss and not to use it if you couldn't find any toilet paper.

Could chiggers have tropical bloodthirsty cousins?

We couldn't afford the luxury of the *thwack thwack* sounds a blade would make against the trees, but we desperately needed a machete to clear a path since the lush foliage and ferns covered the gnarled roots making it impossible to see. A snare trap lie in wait for every step, waiting to break an ankle and face plant us into the detritus. An ambush built by the man-eating fire ants, I was sure.

Painstakingly, we moved each palm frond and leafy blade as quietly as possible while we trudged deeper into the unknown. I found refuge by grabbing onto the ropelike vines choking the tree trunks. I prayed I wouldn't accidentally grasp onto a snake instead of one of the tree vines, leaving it to coil around me like an appetizer.

My hands slipped on the green moss growing on the thick vines. The moss slimed into a black, gooey substance, caking my hands in an oozy sludge almost to the point of not being able to hold on. I gathered wet leaves off the ground and tried to wipe it off.

Lifting a palm frond leaf revealed a foot-long red and yellow centipede. It skittered across the back of my hand and up my arm. I smacked at the damn thing and we both fell to the ground. It reared on its hinged body to attack me. Eye to eye, its pincers opened and closed. I crab-walked away from the disgusting, alien creature and wondered if my odds might have been better back out in the water. The centipede stared at me, daring me to attack. It pinched its jaws closed and open several more times and then lowered itself back to the ground. I guess the creepy-crawly thought I was no longer a threat. My heart beat in relief when it skittered back under the leaves.

Where was my keychain of mace, bug, grizzly, sunscreen, and rabid wild animal sprays when I needed it? If the critter had more than four legs, it was not a friend of mine.

My skin shivered with heebie-jeebies as I began to scratch and slap at anything that didn't feel normal. You would think a vampire wouldn't care much about these kinds of nuisances, but dammit, I was still part human, and vampire or not, I still didn't like bugs.

Khaldon led the pack of us closer to the caves. I smacked an enormous mosquito biting my cheek. The monster bloodsucker reminded me of how Dakota appeared as a blood demon with her long, outstretched serpentine tongue. I hoped it wasn't the kind of mosquito that carried the malaria virus, which killed hundreds of thousands of people each year. Suddenly, it wasn't the cannibals I was afraid of, but the myriad tropical creepy-crawlies I had encountered.

Can a vampire die from malaria?

Up ahead, fire-lit torches surrounded the underground tunnels where Dakota had mind-messaged Ludovic she was held captive. We spread out, each searching for the best entrance. The faint rat-a-tat of nervous heartbeats pulsed around me. I was able to home in on each of the guys and feel their levels of calm. I could smell any hints of fear. I took a good whiff under my own arm and learned the only fear I sensed was my own. I was able to discern other heartbeats from the Rakshasa farther away. The natives seemed to have quiet rivers of blood pulsing under their skin, which gave me a false shred of hope we were safe to move forward.

Khaldon whispered in my ear, "Torchy says it's clear from his vantage point. He says most of the natives are on the far side of the island."

"Can Torchy talk to all of us?" I asked. "What if we get separated?"

"Indeed, we should have thought about that earlier. I wish I could mind-message with you, but maybe that would get me in trouble." He winked at me. "I'll let him know you want to hear." Khaldon squeezed my shoulders and offered a quiet reassurance in the tone of his voice. "Relax, love—we're on task."

Torchy glided in stealth mode high above us to sustain our intel. I noticed his dragon scales were now non-reflective, and unless I knew to look for him, he was simply invisible. I nodded and advanced the message to Harris and Briggs. We crouched in a single-file formation and sprinted to the torch-lit entrance.

At the bottom of the steps leading to the caverns, an arched opening cut into the volcanic rock. We gathered in a small alcove and assessed our situation. Torchy gave Khaldon another "all clear," and we tentatively descended into the cave.

Water crashed inside the cavern, echoing somewhere off the dank, moss-covered walls. The noise of the cascading water provided a solid cover from our echoing footsteps against the flagstone. However, the falls might also defeat our leverage since we wouldn't be able to hear any of Amicula's monsters coming up on us either. To give us as much advance warning as possible, I homed in on my hearing and tuned in for any unusual sounds.

As we advanced three more steps, the putrid stench of sulfur curdled my desire for eggs anytime soon. The dense moisture soaked me as if I'd walked into a bacterial sauna bath. Since it was difficult to see through the steam, I reached out my hand to hold Khaldon's satchel he had draped over his shoulders in order to maintain my sense of space. The heat escalated to nearly stifling degrees. Could we be in an underground waterfall? Or is that water boiling up from the volcano?

A few more tentative steps in, and the heavy water vapor dissipated, leaving us with the unmistakable permeation of rotting flesh and ankle-deep water. The stench cloyed in my mouth as eidolons of past prisoners were reduced to macabre rag dolls, their rotting bodies hanging forgotten from the shackles.

Something scurried over my foot as I squeaked out a scream. I cupped my hand over my mouth, hoping to stifle my nerves. Skittering paws rummaged around us.

Unholy Hell. There had to be rats. Why didn't we consider this?

Red eyes peered out from behind the imprisoned, shackled bones hanging on the wall. I'm sure they were eagerly licking their lips to get a bite out of the fresh meat that had just waltzed into their haven. I took in a deep breath of the soured air, regretting it immediately.

It's okay. They're much smaller than you and they have four legs. You can do this.

I sipped in short breaths to keep from passing out. Thoughts of traversing an underground sewer system laden with rats made my skin crawl and reversed engines on my stomach.

Oily torch lamps cast eerie shadows on the cracked, seeping black walls as we crept deeper into the island's belly. We sloshed forward.

Could the echoes against the cave walls make it sound like there were more critters?

Maybe it's only a few.

My logic was discredited by the amount of little, glowing, beady demon rat eyes staring back at me. Something told me that was simply wishful thinking.

My foot slipped sideways on something mushy and slimy, and I didn't dare look to see if we were already walking in the cesspool of waste. Each tiny prison cell contained a table with a bucket and ladle of fetid water lined with scummy slime. Upon closer inspection, each bucket teamed with little creatures as though it had its own ecosystem.

This cave of horrors was the real deal. The haunted houses at Global Studios Halloween Scream Nights in Orlando had nothing on this creepy island. Given I hadn't yet gotten over my case of oldhouseophobia, this cavern proved to be the scariest place I'd ever encountered on the planet or in any virtual simulated environment.

Resting against the side of the cave was a wooden staff about seven feet tall with a green glowing orb in it. I picked up the staff and inspected the intricate wooden carvings in the handle. As I moved the stick, the orb glowed brighter. We continued down the steamy hallway, but Dakota was nowhere in sight. I picked up on two very faint heartbeats.

She had to be close.

"Where is she?" I grabbed Ludovic by the shirt and hissed.

His voice vibrated with uncertainty. "I ... I'm not sure. I haven't felt her presence since we landed."

I glared silver daggers at him.

Briggs pushed him forward and raised his hand to strike.

Sweating profusely, Ludovic flinched backward and raised his arms to shield his face.

Khaldon held up his hand in the universal gesture for *stop*. He sliced his throat with his finger indicating everyone to calm down or he was going to let loose. He then moved his index finger in front of his lips and tilted his head toward the direction to keep moving.

After the five of us exchanged heated glances, heads nodded and we set off again. About ten feet ahead of us, we turned a ninety-degree angle to the left, which led up a set of narrow stone stairs and out of the water. I was thankful to get out of the filthy slime, and my shoes sloshed with each step.

Khaldon immediately stopped and stiffened, and I ran into the back of him because I was shaking the water out of my boots. Ludovic bumped into me and I envisioned the rest of the team crashing into one another like a five-car pileup on the highway. Khaldon turned to face me and slowly exhaled. He fixed on me and reached out a hand, slowly walking us another three feet into an open cavern.

Afraid to learn what was in front of us, I fiercely conjured up the courage to engage. I stumbled back a couple steps at the horrific sight.

My knees instantly wobbled.

Briggs cursed something in French and crossed himself.

Ludovic outstretched his hand toward her. A gasp fled his throat.

Harris bent to one knee, whispering a prayer, and kissed his Saint

Francis medal.

Pulses raced and hammered in my ears from everyone, including my own. Our heightened sensitivity solidified that the death scene in front of me was anything but a phantasm.

Torch lights illuminated the cell. Dakota hung limp in chained manacles by her clawed hands and at the apex of her wings. Iron shackles had worn deep bruises around her neck. Leather straps at her waist and ankles further immobilized her with no chance of escape.

Trying desperately to steady my legs, my body shook while my hands cleaved tighter onto Briggs and Khaldon's shoulders. Intense, the odor of infection snapped my brain to attention.

My vampy sense indicated she was alive, but her body was filled with pus and putrefaction. I slammed down my eyelids, praying the heat was causing hallucinations.

Dakota's head had sunk forward onto her chest. Her own heartbeats were very far apart and faint as a butterfly's whisper. Her scarred back faced us. The distinct odor of smelted silver hung heavy in the air.

My lips quivered as her name barely escaped. "Dakota?"

Are we too late?

Chapter 5

Monsters! What did they do to her?

My hands flew to my mouth as rivulets of bloody tears escaped over my cheeks. I gulped at the sight of Dakota's emaciated body left to die in those iron restraints. Her once beautiful auburn hair hung limp in a matted rat's nest. This scene was so far removed from the ever vivacious sister I'd known growing up.

No amount of therapy will ever heal this. Dakota will never be the same.

In the corner slumped the remains of what might have been Dakota's last meal. By the appearance of his decomposing flesh, it looked like days had passed since she'd last fed. The rats busily ate what remained.

Khaldon clutched my arms and steadied me. He whispered, "Cheyenne, we've found her." He kissed me hard and fast on the forehead, releasing me with a look of worry I'd not seen before. His auric energy had changed. Khaldon was no longer calm and collected. His heart beat faster than I'd ever heard and he excreted a strange pheromone I'd not smelled on him before.

What isn't he telling me?

Harris roughly held my left shoulder, grabbed my face by the chin, and forced me to look away from Dakota and straight into his eyes. "Deep breaths, Chey. Stick to the plan. Ludovic and Briggs will get her out of those chains." He hugged me with the fierceness as though it could be our last. His heartbeat also ran a mile a minute. The fur on his arms had sprouted, and the nails on his fingers had elongated into sharp, black claws. "Keep calm. Stay vigilant. We're taking her home."

The electricity in the air was palpable. I leaned the staff with the green glowing orb against the prison cell wall. Forcing down the contents of my stomach, I focused on the task at hand and tried to check my emotions at the door. "Can we get her out of this contraption without killing her?"

Briggs moved quickly in front of Dakota but was careful not to touch her. He spoke in kind, gentle, and endearing terms in French that I couldn't quite understand. I caught the words, *mon cheri, je t'aime, and je suis désolé* among the words he spoke quietly into her ear, and I knew his heart was aching as much as mine. He kissed her cheek and studied the iron chains. He removed the bolt cutters from his backpack and set out to free her.

Harris handed me a second pistol he had tucked in behind his back. "Shh. Take this and pull the trigger on anything that isn't us, okay?" It wasn't until he handed me the gun that I realized how much my hands were shaking. I fumbled with the pistol, almost dropping it.

"Be careful. The safety is off. Just point the red laser where you want the kill." He unholstered his rifle from his shoulder strap and aimed for a rat crawling along the far wall. The red light shined on the fat rat's belly.

"Ok—kay." I nodded and tried to swallow the thick bile congealing in the back of my throat. I pinched my lips closed with my teeth, biting back the emotion.

Harris let go of my hands. Both he and Khaldon returned my worried glance as I watched them disappear down the corridor, searching for any other survivors.

I shook my head and pushed the torrential terror deep down into the crevices of my mind. I had to turn off my emotions or I was going to fail.

Stay strong for her. You can crumble to pieces later.

Gun in my hand, I stood attentively for any Rakshasa while Briggs and Ludovic disconnected Dakota from her living prison. Stepping closer, little rat feet scampered away and ran across the room. I was tempted to shoot anything that moved, but didn't want to cause any unnecessary sound.

Briggs was making headway on cutting through a chain that suspended her wing.

I held the gun at my side and brushed Dakota's filthy hair away from her ear with my right hand.

Gently, I touched her. "Dakota. Sweetie. It's me, Cheyenne." I steadied my voice as it croaked with hoarse words. "Stay calm. We're getting you out of here."

Her hair was a tangled, gnarled mess around the buckled clasps of a mask fastened behind her head. The face mask reminded me of the one Hannibal Lecter wore. If she were this far gone, could she become disoriented and think we were the bad guys? Remembering the deadly damage Dakota inflicted with her tongue, I thought better to leave the muzzle on.

Dakota's entire frame shuddered with each breath, enticing consciousness back into her physical body. Incoherent mumbling, she tried to form words. From the crooks of her elbows, festering wounds oozed where rubber tubes had been inserted. The plastic tubes dripped her blood into jars on the floor.

They're draining her?

Ludovic gingerly removed the blood shunts, and she pulled away wincing. I pulled the other end of the hose and removed it from the jar.

A loud cracking sound echoed down the hall, possibly an old, rusty-hinged door opened.

I turned, held up the gun, and tried in vain to keep a steady aim. The red laser light bounced against the wall, reminiscent of playing *catch the red dot* with a cat. Not sure if a nest of them had been disturbed, more rodents scurried about the floor and along the walls. Some even crawled up on the iron bars of the cell and swung on the door. We stared at one another for a brief moment and then resumed our work.

Briggs cut the manacles with the bolt cutters, releasing one side from the wall. After laying the gun on the floor, I helped ease her right wing down to her side. Dakota was covered in layers of mildew and crud. She groaned with ache as she folded the other wing up into her torso. Her arm hung limp by her side. Her muscles twitched and spasmed with the movement. How long had she been suspended?

Down the hall where Harris and Khaldon had disappeared, chains rattled. It sounded like chairs scooted across the floor. They must have been closer than I'd perceived.

My fingers slimed over incongruent bumps under her skin. The goo sloughed off onto my fingers in a mucousy mass. The fevered, viscous feel to her skin stung and I immediately wipe the ick on my pants. I wriggled my fingers to shake off the tingling sensation.

What is on her skin? Is she growing poisonous dragon scales?

"Go away. There's no escape," Dakota hissed in her demonic voice.

I jumped at her words and then breathed a sigh of relief that she was conscious.

"Shh. Stay quiet. It's okay—we're getting you out." I whispered in her ear. "Stay calm. We're flying out of here." I picked up the jar of her blood and tried to close the rusty cap onto the rim.

"What's this?" I held up an ornate key hanging on a chain around her waist. It held an evil eye encrusted in the blood, daring me to use it. It glowed the same green as the orb in the staff, and I sensed the alluring relic had some mystical energy. My hand seemed overtaken by a cryptic pull beckoning me to insert and turn the ornate bobble. Straight away my gut told me not to fall for the trap. I lowered the key closer to my side.

Ludovic stepped closer to Dakota and snatched it from my hand. "Give me that!"

"Wait, Ludovic, stop. This is too easy. Somethings not right."

"Don't be ridiculous. Time is of the essence, *vrăjitoare*."

Briggs stopped his cutting and stared Ludovic straight into his eyes. "Did you call 'er a witch?"

Ludovic challenged Briggs' eyes and ignored his question.

He called me a witch?

Before I finished my protestations, Ludovic inserted the ornate key. The lock clicked, unlatched, and released four chains holding together a hanging metal cage around Dakota's torso. The chains fell to the floor in heavy thuds, but the metal cage had embedded into her skin.

Ludovic moved in closer examining how to remove the cage, but his left foot stepped on something with a loud crunch. Immediately, a resonant series of clicking echoed off the walls of the cell.

"What was that?" Briggs asked as he smacked an unusually large critter crawling toward his leg.

Ludovic stood frozen. His lips thinned and whitened. Stepping backward, he cleared away the tangle of chains and filthy straw, revealing a small, crushed wooden box with wires running out of it and up her leg.

Dakota's heartbeat sped up.

My mind tried to reconcile what I'd seen against what my ears registered.

"Hurts—trap," Dakota grunted a pained wheeze. "Not what you think."

My eyes closed in defeated understanding. She was wired!

Her heartbeat gained speed as she panted.

"They know we're here," I gasped.

A flush of adrenaline ran icy through my veins. The three of us stood looking at one another as Dakota moaned out again in agony.

Blood pooled in her mouth and ran down her chin.

I frantically signaled the *hurry up* motion with my hands.

Briggs continued to cut through the iron chains holding her legs to the walls.

Dakota's heartbeat sped even faster when a timer started to count down.

The vermin nestled in the straw took flight and ran toward the door and out into the hallway, away from where we stood.

Ludovic tried to quiet Dakota. "Shh—take slower breaths. We're getting you out of here, *iubirea vieţii mele*."

Briggs leaned down to cut the last two shackles from Dakota's left ankle. "What dze 'ell?"

In my mind, I screamed *Stop! Run!* But my synapses eclipsed my brain signals, disabling my voice.

Time slowed to a snail's crawl as I watched in hideous slow motion.

Dakota screamed as she grabbed Ludovic and yanked him to her chest. Her tongue slithered out through the mask and stabbed him in the throat. Her grip on him was that of a vice. She sucked him dry through her straw-like tongue wrapped around his neck.

My fangs inadvertently dropped in primal protection not knowing what she was capable of next. My mouth let out a hiss of defensive posturing.

Briggs stared at me, his eyes wide. "Chey Chey, you 'ave never done dzat before."

I covered my mouth with my hands. My eyes widened with the realization of what Briggs had said and also from the hideous scene which stood in front of us.

Dakota turned her neck toward us and grinned with a mouthful of bloody, razor blade teeth.

Both Briggs and I had stepped several feet away from Dakota while we watched my baby sister claw and decimate Ludovic with her newly freed hands. She began to eat the torn muscles from where she had bitten him.

Briggs' body started to shimmer in black scales which covered his arms and legs. He must have been as alarmed as I was.

I listened for the clicking noise once again. It had reached a crescendo and then stopped altogether.

There was a moment of utter silence.

Dakota turned once again and stared me in the eyes.

The only sound was a water drop.

I held out my arms toward her and mouthed the words *I love you*.

With one last click, Dakota's body exploded into nothingness, taking Ludovic with her.

Briggs was smashed hard against the ground.

I flew backward, slamming into the slimy cave wall from the massive percussion blast.

Glass shards of the jar exploded, covering the heart region of my chest.

I slid down the dank, wet stone as every inch of my body smoked with embedded silver buckshot.

"My eyes!" My face scorched with the precious metal digging deeper into my flesh. In desperation, I squeezed and pushed at my eyes, blinking to dispel the silver, but only managed to embed glass shards into most of my face.

My vision irised in as if it were a camera lens and blackened around the edges. The scalding metal ate away at my sight. Bloody tears flooded my eye sockets.

Breathless, I reached out shaking hands squinting back at the hideous scene where my sister had stood just an infinitesimal moment ago. The last image of my sister was Dakota's feet standing in the iron manacles from the ankles down.

Hands gripped me and yanked me to my feet. "Cheyenne, we're getting out of here. Now! I've got to get Briggs. I'll be right back." Khaldon propped me against the wall, but my legs caved in on me. I didn't have the strength to stand.

Dakota wasn't growing dragon scales. They'd buried silver under her skin.

My breath sawed in and out of my chest with each intake of breath. The poisonous metal lacerated every inch and scalded me from inside out where it had embedded itself deep into my muscle layers. The silver pellets scraped against my bones. My mind grew clouded and muted as though I were underwater. Unconsciousness pulled me under with a thick, heavy rope weighed down by an old rusty anchor.

Trying to shake off the inky blackness of passing out, I attempted to rub chunks of metal while it ablated my skin. The silver and glass eroded more skin with every swipe. My vision grew darker, and I didn't dare move anymore for fear the agony would escalate beyond my pain threshold.

"Dakota?" I struggled to form words. Blood pooled in my mouth.

Touching my fingers to my lips, I realized most of my lower lip hung from my mouth as if it were fabric dangling off a curtain rod.

Mostly blinded, I saw a fuzzy mass struggling to stand as another bent down over it. My head reeled and pounded from the blood forcing its way through my body to send healing nutrients to the caustic burns. Through dark, hazy vision, my eyes lied as I strained to see my sister's shape and only found an empty wall. The sounds of blood, flesh, and bone plopped to the floor.

A conch shell bellowed out through the cave, rattling my eardrums.

The Rakshasa ... they knew we were here.

I sensed something in front of me.

"Grab her. I'll run interference," Briggs gruffed out in a labored breath.

"Torchy's on his way." Khaldon picked me up and threw me over his shoulder. The fireman's carry almost proved to be more than I could handle. I cried out with every step as it forced the silver deeper under my skin.

Khaldon ran us down the corridor, but he abruptly stopped.

I screamed as razor blades sliced into the backs of my legs. Khaldon swung us around, and my head slammed into the side of the cave wall. Blinding colors fireworked inside my head. My calves were gashed open.

"He's clawed her!" Briggs hollered.

My mind fuzzier than before, all I could imagine was a behemoth of a Rakshasa with my calf muscles impaled on his sickle-shaped talons. A swoosh of air cascaded over me, and I heard a thud land at my side.

Khaldon called out to Briggs, "Behind you, there's another one. Here, grab my knife."

My ears registered a grunted wheeze, a bone-ripping, wet sludgy slice, a metal clang, a gun blast, and then a solid thud.

"Harris, get in here. We've got to go!" Khaldon yelled and placed me on the vile floor. His footsteps left me.

I crouched up into myself cradling my body. Squeezing my calves, coppery wetness saturated my hands and pooled in my boots. My wounds weren't healing.

Briggs hollered, "Dzere's more coming."

Sounds of the fighting cascaded all around me. The only way to describe it would be if I were sitting in the middle of a professional, concert surround-sound stereo system. Every crunch, punch, fall, kick, groan, stab, and jab amplified the tearing flesh all around me.

I ducked my head and heard Khaldon grunt after a solid punching blow. Was that a blow he gave or took?

"Watch out! It's gonna spew 'is guts!" Briggs shouted and then it sounded as though he fell to the floor.

A splash of repulsive, toxic liquid cascaded over the ground and pooled around me. The smell was even more hideous than the stench we'd been breathing, if that was even possible. I gagged at the acrid odor of the eviscerated bowel.

Briggs let out an uproar.

"You all right, mate?" Khaldon's voice edged with high alarm, and I heard more gun shots explode over my head.

"Is he ahwight?" My words were a jumbled mess with my lip dangling off my face. I coughed and choked on the sticky blood pooling in my mouth.

We must have been closer to the entrance than I realized. More mollusk horns broke the night's drumming.

I looked up, but only masses of light and darkness were visible through the bloody rivulets.

Thunderous footsteps poured in all around us. Khaldon cursed under his breath. "Just feckin' lovely."

"Khaldon, get down!" Gunfire shattered against walls and their reports filled the chamber. When the spray of bullets was over, nothing but the echoing sounds of bodies fell to the floor while the remains of Harris' voice punctuated the air.

Khaldon hollered, "Torchy's ready to land. Let's go."

Harris asked, "Where's Dakota and Ludovic?"

"Harris, they're gone. We have to go." Khaldon's voice was across the room. "Can you lift her? Cheyenne is covered in silver and glass. Be mindful of the silver burns."

"Gone? Burns?" Harris questioned. The tone of his voice unbelieving.

"No time. I've got to help Briggs." Khaldon yelled back.

"I found another girl," Harris hollered.

"Pull the twist outta yer bloody knickers and move yer arse!" Khaldon replied.

Harris grabbed my arm and yanked me up to my feet. "Sorry, Chey. We seriously gotta move."

There was zero time to think about pain or the shocking reality of what had happened to my sister. We had to get everyone out of this hellhole before we were all dead.

The drumming outside echoed through the cavern. It grew in depth and tempo as we approached the entrance. More mollusks reverberated and sirened through the island.

They were coming after us.

The fresh night air was a welcome relief, but the macaque monkey screams and deafening drums unhinged me further. The wind from Torchy's wings toppled me over into the cool dewy grass.

Khaldon cried out, "Oh shite, Briggs. Harris—he's collapsed."

"Chey, can you see at all?" Harris asked.

I shook my head, which seemed to throb in sync with the pounding footsteps running through the jungle. My stomach roiled with nauseating pain from the silver as it continued to send waves of scorching spasms. I rolled over onto my hands and knees. The next thing I knew, strong arms hoisted me into the air. I landed with a thud onto Torchy's back.

"Hold on to this girl. I don't think she's conscious." Harris threw a limp body in front of me.

"Briggs has been stabbed," Khaldon hollered while they heaved Briggs in behind me.

Rakshasa erupted out of the jungle's lush undergrowth and ululated their hungry battle cries.

Gun blasts cut through the night, and I covered my ears from the deafening reports.

Torchy's neck grew hot. I imagined it like sitting atop of a chimney flue. Just when I couldn't stand the pain of the searing temperature, Torchy blasted fire from his throat, unleashing his liquid fury.

I squinted hard as the powerful bright light erupted, searing my sight even more.

Torchy's vengeance scorched vegetation and bodies. Charred aromas wafted in the energized air, while natives screamed all around us. Many cries raced away.

I prayed his blistering flames were cremating everything within range, awarding us precious moments to escape. Torchy revved up his pipes once again, and the blaze built in his belly.

"Jump on, Harris," Khaldon bellowed over the loud flame thrower. Another massive intake of air and I braced myself for the next flame blast, but instead we were airborne.

"Watch out! Ten o'clock," Harris shouted. "They've got blowpipes and spears."

I instinctively tried to look, but all I could see was the faint orangish glow from the fire while the sound of poison darts whizzed over my head.

Gunfire exploded again.

I flattened myself closer to the girl and deeper into Torchy's back for fear of being hit by either the poisonous darts or the bullets.

Harris screamed, "Ahhhhggg! Dammit, I'm hit!"

I looked back over my shoulder and yelled. "Hawwis, hang on!"

The air pressure increased as Torchy's wings climbed higher and higher, up and away, hopefully out of range of the deadly barbs.

Torchy mind-messaged, *Watch out—they have flaming arrows. I'm gonna blast them again.*

The furnace released once again and my legs closed in around his abdomen tighter.

Bolts zoomed overhead.

Arrows clinked against Torchy's scales. One of them nailed me in the calf and embedded itself into Torchy's side. I felt him moan at the embedded projectile.

"Arrrgh!" I screamed and reached to pull at the arrow, but it was too far down for me to loosen my grip on the girl. With every heave of Torchy's wings, his body flexed the arrow inside my leg. It was all I could do not to black out.

It sounded like a shotgun blast erupted from Harris. A deafening crack, and then a quick succession of the reload, and then another explosion.

The rushes of flames whizzed past my ear and clinks of spears bounced off Torchy's hide at this height.

"Bloody hell, Torch—I'm hit! Get us to the water!" Khaldon called out.

"Chey, your hair is on fire!" Harris yelled.

Harris banged on my head, patting out the flames. The pressure from his hands pushed my face deeper into Torchy's neck, which in turn heated the silver burning deeper into my face.

More quills whizzed past us through the night sky as Torchy flew our injured load higher away from the onslaught.

"The fire! I can't get it out. It's spreading! It's—it's—" Khaldon's voice escalated, "some kind of silver oil mix." He screamed in a voice I'd never heard. *"AHHHHGG!"*

Harris cried out, "My hands—I can't feel my hands! I can't get the fire out!"

Torchy abruptly changed his direction from going upward to a fast forward motion that threw me off balance. I barely hung on, the change in direction leaving me gasping for breath. Torchy maintained his forward inertia. We plunged into the water. Our crash landing felt as though I were ensconced in a full body seatbelt. Torchy held us on with his gluey type dragon essence, and we managed to stay attached to him without being thrown into the salt water.

Seconds later, watery plunges indicated Khaldon and Harris had dived off Torchy to squelch the flames. I squinted, barely able to see the orange glowing masses under the water.

They're burning? Under the water?

I reached for my calf. "I can't get it, Torch!" I tried to remove the arrow pinning me through the calf and embedded in Torchy's side. The head of the bolt was too close to the bone. My fingers wrapped around it, but the slick blood didn't help to capture a firm hold. I rocked it back and forth almost blacking out. Torchy and I both groaned at the failed extrication.

"Torchy are you aw wight? Can you see 'em? Are 'ey okay?"

Aye, I'll be fine, lass. I see them. It looks like the flames are dying down. I think some of that fire is laced with a silver compound, and they're gonna be in worse shape than you. We'll get that bolt out soon enough.

I couldn't imagine worse pain than what I was already experiencing. The saltwater scalded my open wounds where the chunks of silver refused to allow the sores to heal.

Will the sharks be attracted to the blood and flames?

After what seemed like an eternity, finally Harris and Khaldon breached the surface. Their heavy breathing told me just how ghastly they'd been injured. They had never sounded like that.

"How 'ad is it?" My bottom lip throbbed with every new splash of the ocean water.

There was silence from both Harris and Khaldon. Their lack of speech told me volumes more information than if either had uttered a single word.

Briggs and the girl hadn't moved this entire time. If it weren't for their faint heartbeats, I would have sworn we had lost them, too.

Waves of nausea roiled through my guts with the knowledge that the burnt stench came from Harris and Khaldon. The scent of my scorched hair and their charred flesh amplified the qualm.

"Hey guys, can one of you help me remove this bolt out of my leg? I'm pinned to Torchy's side."

Khaldon swam over to me, and before I knew it, had yanked the bolt out. I screamed in relief, but the overwhelming pain finally took its toll and I retched over the unknown girl's body.

Torchy mind messaged, *Oh, for chrissakes, mates. We've got company. Jump on now, will ye? Sharks are schooling and bloody hell if they don't look hungry.*

Chapter 6

Phuket Hospital - Thailand

Twelve Hours Later

Cheyenne O'Cuinn

I failed. I should be dead.

A familiar schism of words replayed again in my head. This time the repeating scratch on the record fell to the end of the vinyl in a muffled vacuum of white noise.

The percussion section of hums, beeps, blips, and pings harmonized the soundtrack of the intensive care unit behind my head. I grew aware of my body, and consciousness flowed into the empty vessel reanimating me back to life.

My right hand reached for my head to cradle the weight of it. It weighed as much as ten bowling balls and pounded as members of a rock band were testing their amplifiers between the cranial walls.

Suddenly remembering the last time I awoke, I opened my eyes and shot up in bed, ready to fight off anyone who came close to me with another drug. But instead of being blinded and tied to the bed frame, I found myself in a room with blurry faces of loved ones who looked worse off than me.

"There now—slow it down, lass. You're all right. It's been a good while since you've been out." Torchy's strong Scottish accent punctuated the air. "Easy, now. We're here. Just take a deep breath and relax yerself."

I looked around, blinking and amazed I could see again. Khaldon and Harris were across the room, both in beds with bandages taped to their faces, necks, and legs. Briggs lay in a bed beside me, surrounded by an army of white coats and nurse uniforms.

I tried to croak out words. "What time—what day?"

"Relax, it's all right." Torchy eased his hands down on my shoulders and gave me a slight squeeze. I winced at the pain and he released.

"You've been out for nearly twelve hours since we left the island, Cheyenne. We're damn lucky we made it out of there with only the pains we have."

"Where?" Remembering it was severed, I reached for my bottom lip and was relieved to learn it was reattached. Faint stitches lined the entire bottom lip.

I guess they weren't trying to stuff me and roast me over the fire.

"We're are in Phuket. About five hundred miles from the Andamans."

I leaned back in my bed. Khaldon and Harris waved at me. My fingers wiggled back at them, and instantly my anxiety lowered a few notches.

The stench of burned hair permeated my nose and a slight moan parted my lips. How long would it take to grow back?

I closed my eyelids, still so exhausted from the mission. "There were sharks." My eyes flew open and I sat up bolt-right. "How did we get here?" My heart raced, and I pointed. "They—they were burning under the water."

"We were saved by Merfolk. They surrounded us and the sharks swam away. We have them to thank for escorting us here to this hospital. Would ye believe there's a specialty unit for supernaturals and their ailments all the way out here?"

I blinked at him, not sure if I'd heard him right. "Merfolk?"

"Oh, aye." He nodded, and then he looked at the rest of the team.

"Dakota? We didn't have time—she blew up—" I could barely choke out the words. "She's gone."

"Don't be worrying yerself right now, lass. You need to tend to healing, ya kin? Be minding yer lucky stars above for these folks over there." Torchy waved his hand to the nursing staff. "They saved yer vision, and they say after a few more pints of blood, your sight should be fully restored."

I looked across the room to Briggs, and the four hospital staff members turned to stare at me. One guy had a deep purple black eye. Another orderly had several bite marks on his arms and hands. The woman, whom I suspected was the disembodied voice, held nothing but disdain on her face.

Well ... maybe they deserved it for not explaining things to me.

There was nothing more I could do. Torchy was right. I needed more sleep, and the only thing to do was to heal.

I rolled away from him and faced the wall. Privately, I cried myself into oblivion. I had failed my sister, my family. It should have been me who died in that wretched cave.

Even through the tears, there was no peace in the escape of sleep. Only nightmares that had plagued me since Halloween.

જીભ્ઝ

Hauntingly familiar, the creature's hideous, maniacal laughter crawled a frigid, wet, dead finger up my spine. He forced his hand around my jaw and smashed my lips with his fingers.

The beast bit into my cheek and chin.

I kicked, screamed, thrashed, and struggled in vain to wrench away from his vice-like grip. His hand clamped on my face and sent shattering fractures of pain through my jaw.

Flight or fight. Self-preservation time.

A guttural wail escaped my throat. I pulled my hands free and gouged his face with my fingernails, trying desperately to dig into his eye sockets to blind him.

The cretin's hands gripped like he wanted to rip off my jaw. He shoved his fingers into my mouth for a better hold. I grabbed his hand and pushed his fingers in deeper. My back molars crunched hard. I ground my jaw back and forth, stripping off flesh between my teeth. His blood gushed into my mouth, filling it with hot, coppery spurts. The beast relinquished his hold with a grunt of pain and let go of my face.

I fell backward, away from him. In an instant, he yanked me up by the arms and shook me like a rag doll. He held me there, panting. Face-to-face.

Time stopped.

For a split moment, milliseconds of reality, his eyes softened. Spider web creases around his eyes made him seem almost human. Glowing vermillion, an intense fire filled them with hatred.

I froze, cemented to the ground.

His eyes met mine once again. They were wide and conscious. At that moment, I emblazoned his image forever on my soul. It was the Red Man from my nightmares.

He seized me by the hair, and his hands stretched my neck in an unnatural arc to the left.

All I could do was watch him in paralytic horror, my heart pounding out of my chest. Black dots clouded my vision. He held my neck on display, his bountiful banquet awaiting him.

I watched as he licked his lips. He tenderly lavished my neck, stroking it, kissing it, basking in his sumptuous feast. His eyes danced time with the throbbing artery pulsing viciously under my skin.

"911—is this an emergency?" The voice from the phone came just in time to hear the devil sink his teeth deep into my neck and attenuate the life force out of me.

⪘⪙

"We're losing him! We need a dragon donor for adrenaline, or he's not going to make it."

I awoke to the anxious voice of the physician treating us at Phuket Hospital. My heart skipped a beat as I listened to Dr. Rattanakosin behind the hanging sheet between our hospital beds.

I tried to sit up, but the silver embedded in my skin had weakened me to the point of exhaustion. We were still in critical condition, even though we had been in the hospital for close to sixteen hours treating each of our specific injuries. Thankfully, my vision had fully returned after I had been given several pints of whole human blood. My head continued to ache from the silver poisoning, and I prayed the dreaded metal hangover would subside soon enough.

I croaked out words to the closed curtain. "Can Torchy donate the adrenaline?"

The curtain inched aside and revealed the doctor who had been treating all of us. Dr. Rattanakosin peered at me through his pop-bottle eyeglasses. His brown eyes were magnified as if they were four inches wide, and his eyebrows bushed out over the top rims. Some of the hairs over three inches long. The doctor opened the flimsy privacy curtain farther.

I urged on his curiosity. "It's true. The gentleman who brought us in here is another dragon. Can he donate, or do you need a family donor?"

The doctor nodded at his nurse. "See if you can locate Mr. Gravenor."

Briggs moaned, grinding his teeth against the pain. He looked terrible lying in the fetal position with his nostrils flaring and his jaw clenched. His labored breathing spewed thick spittle across his lips. The bleeding had slowed from his abdomen, but his color was awful. He was beginning to turn shades of green.

"Can you give him something to help him change into his dragon form, so he can heal himself?" I asked the doctor.

"I'm afraid it isn't that easy, Miss O'Cuinn. You see, he has been gouged with a dragon scythe. These are elusive, magical blades. I've never seen one until tonight, but I've read about them in my medical journals."

"What does that mean? That the scythe blade took away his ability to shift?" I heard Harris ask from across the room. His voice thick and labored since his lips were swollen.

"What it means is that the magical scythe has damaged his internal energy core vortex, which impairs the power source needed to transform. The injury looks to be remarkably precise. The creature who wielded this weapon knew exactly where to make the blow. Until Mr. Briggs has renewed strength, he cannot complete his healing. We have stopped most of the bleeding, but we need the dragon adrenaline to help him overcome the fatal damage of that magical blade."

Briggs bunched up his fists to combat the pain. Utterly helpless to take away his agony, he never would've been in this situation if it weren't for Dakota.

"Can't you give him something for the pain?"

Dr. Rattanakosin replied, "We've maxed out the morphine dosages for him. His body is burning through it and is unable to provide relief."

I slid off my bed and reached for his hands. "Hang in there, Briggs," I whispered. "We'll find you the help you need. Is there anyone you want us to call—someone you might know on this side of the planet who can help?"

His skin felt clammy under my palms. He swallowed hard as even more color drained from his face. He choked out the words. "Sister, father. I've sent for Kalina. Here, soon."

"Good. You rest now. I'll let the nurse know she should let them in as soon as they arrive." A faint, anguished smile crossed my lips, and I kissed his forehead. His skin was hot as the asphalt of Disney World's parking lot in August.

A slow tear caressed my cheek as my grief over Dakota overwhelmed me once again.

I am to blame for his pain.

I turned to walk through the hanging curtain to check on Khaldon and Harris. Still weakened, I tripped, fell forward, and caught hold of my IV pole to keep from crashing to the ground. I took the privacy curtain down with me in a clang of metal, spasm of pain, and tangle of canvas.

Khaldon leaned forward to help me, and I raised my hand to signal him to stop. The nurse grunted and *tsked* at me. She helped me to my feet, untangling the curtain from my blood line. She yanked the privacy sheet out of my arms, offering a *thank you very much* look, and she whisked it away into a laundry hamper.

I was pretty sure the nursing staff was still mad at me because of the way I kept biting them while they dug the silver out of my skin and muscles. I tried my best to not bare my fangs at her through most of the extraction, but I found it harder than I could manage. To finish removing the deeper pieces of silver embedded in my bones, the hospital staff had to secure me to the bed and sedate me several times. When I came to, I wouldn't remember where I had been or what had happened, even though it had been explained to me several times prior.

Overall, I was lucky to be alive but the whole blood transfusions were taking longer than expected for healing. Dr. Rattanakosin had explained how after a severe silver breach, mending always took its toll and time on unlucky victims, especially newbies. Bagged blood was sufficient, but I needed to live-feed. We all did.

I took a step toward Khaldon and glanced over at Harris and the girl. She was conscious and drinking water. None of us presented much better than Briggs, but at least we were alive.

Khaldon sat on the edge of his bed across the narrow walkway with silver thermite oxide burns deep into his legs, hands, chest, and face. His skin had blackened from the third-degree burns. He also had a pint of whole blood draining into him, but his wounds were healing slowly due to the extensive damage from the silver poisoning as well.

I picked up the weapons lying on the sheet and then sat on the bed beside him. "Where did these come from?" I examined the dragon scythe blade, burnt metal arrow, and a crossbow bolt.

"This is the blade the Rakshasa used on Briggs. And this—" Khaldon plucked the arrow from my hand. He centered it over his left thigh. "This was the flaming silver thermite arrow I dug out of my leg."

"Masochistic much? Do you like being reminded of horrible things that have happened to you?"

He shrugged and then winced at the effort. "Warriors historically keep their battle implements." Khaldon handed me back the arrow and gingerly picked up the blade. "Figured Briggs would like to have this one, especially since it has caused him so much strife." Khaldon grimaced as he tried to sit up straighter then leaned back against the pillows.

"So you're going to give it to him as a souvenir? You want to keep the thing which almost burned you alive?"

"Indeed. And just for the record, the silver thermite did burn me—while I was alive." He tried to dance his eyebrows at me, but failed miserably. "I have a couple of souvenirs for you too."

I tilted my head in interest, wondering just what in hell he would take from that gawd-forsaken place—especially something that *I* would want to remember.

He leaned forward wincing and whispered close to my ear. "It's in my satchel, but I don't think you should take it out in here. Just open it."

Intrigued and a little worried, I was hoping it wasn't a severed head of a Rakshasa. I picked up the leather satchel stowed under his bed, carefully looking for any puddling body fluids. When the bag seemed innocent enough, I brought it up top and unbuckled the leather strap containing the elusive contents.

My eyes narrowed in disbelief. My hand flew to my mouth and immediately the pace of my heart jumped tenfold.

Khaldon covered my other hand with his and squeezed. His quiet reassurance helped me to catch my breath. "I noticed for some reason it glows more when it's close to you, so I snagged it." His devilish grin revealed *secret mission accomplished* all over his face.

Inside the bag, the green orb from the staff I was carrying in the cave was wrapped in an oil cloth. The staff had snapped in pieces, but the ornate carvings in the wood held the orb in place. I stared at Khaldon in disbelief. He guided my hand to touch it and I ran my fingertips across the runes carved in the wood. A zing of tingle rippled across my fingers when my hand caressed the cool gem. The warm green glow of the orb purred a connection between us. I could feel it humming.

Removing my hand, I re-covered it with the oilcloth. I hissed in a rushed whispered and looked around the room hoping nobody was paying any attention to us. "Are you insane? Haven't you ever watched *Heavy Metal*?" I quickly closed the satchel and stowed it back under the bed. "That thing could represent all the evil in the Universe and be the demise of us all!"

He smiled as best he could and pulled me in close. "Who knows, maybe you're the new Taarakian, ready to defend and protect us against the evil of the Loc-Nar."

I shook my head again in disbelief that he would remove such a relic from their island. "In your dreams, Bucko. You must be feeling better." I grinned a small smile and my heart sighed a tiny amount of relief knowing, in time, he was going to be just fine. "I think you just want to see me dressed up in red, thigh-high leather boots." I checked his eyes for acknowledgment and they beamed with devious intent. "What in the world am I going to do with that thing? We have no idea what it is. Seriously, you may have just opened up the wrath of Sekmet or something on us."

Khaldon made an erotic, appreciative noise in the back of his throat. "Right, leather boots ... I think you should dress as a Taarakian for the next Comic Con."

I would have punched him in the arm if we all weren't still in so much pain.

"But not to worry your bonny head, since Sekmet is my direct ancestor, you needn't worry about her wrath anytime soon." He sat up a little straighter on the bed. "If you want, we can keep the orb at my house. I'm just trying to think how I'm going to get it past customs."

"Yeah, well I'm just waiting for the Rakshasa to crash through those doors to recover their ancient relic." Feeling an imminent sense of foreboding, I peeked over my shoulder toward the door. Just in case.

"I've the perfect place for the orb next to our crossbow bolts. I'll hang it next to the one I dug out of my shoulder in the Civil War."

"Our bolts?"

"Indeed, m'lady." He flipped a bolt into the air and caught it. "This is the one I dug out of Torchy's side and through your calf. I guess technically, the bolt is both of yours."

He picked up the dragon scythe and pointed it at me. "That silver thermite arrow will make an excellent addition to my gallery."

A humble smile emerged through the pain as flakes of ash fell from above his eyebrow. "Keeping mementos like these helps me to appreciate the days when life is simple." He whisked away the ash with his hands.

"Never expected such exciting adventures when we started to date, huh?" I ran my hand down the side of his cheek where there weren't any burns.

"Blimey, Chey, you do manage to keep things interesting. I'll give you that." He tried to wink, but winced in pain as scorched flesh fell off in chunks, revealing pink shiny skin underneath. Even though he looked as though he would never recover, it was miraculous to watch how his skin repaired itself.

"Looks like you're going to need more blood. Is there any way they can bring us live donors?"

Khaldon shrugged and reclined back on the bed, slowly closing his eyes obviously still too tired to care.

"I'll ask and see what I can find out." I stood and tentatively stretched my newly formed calf muscles and leaned up against the windowsill beside Khaldon's bed. It looked as though we would have a shy pink and orange sunset in a few hours. In some oddball way, the setting sun offered a renewed hope that we might live to see another day.

I picked at a silver scab pockmark on my elbow, not trying to think about why we were here recovering in the first place. "Ya know, it was really weird. Right before the explosion, I found a key around Dakota's waist. It glowed the same as the green orb and it had a serpent's eye in it. It was so *Lords of the Rings* cliché, but the weird thing was, the key actually called to me. It wanted me to insert it into the lock. Like it was enchanted or something."

"What did you do with it? Do you still have it?"

"I didn't do anything with it. Ludovic snatched the key out of my hands and called me a witch. The next thing I knew—Dakota and Ludovic were gone."

"Wait—what? He called you a witch? Are you sure?"

I tilted my head from side to side, not saying yes, not saying no. "No, not really. I'm not sure. But Briggs accused him of calling me that and I'd never heard the word before." I shrugged. "It's no big deal, it just made me wonder who planted that key as the trigger for the countdown. Someone spent a lot of time planning to kill us."

Khaldon breathed in as deep a breath as he could. "This whole shite show is nutters, but are you all right? This has been very difficult for you." His voice was kind. So kind, it made me feel guilty for focusing my own needs and not paying more attention to him. He was hurt just as badly as I was.

"Truthfully?"

"No, please, lie to me," he teased. "Of course, tell me what's going on in that burnt, red head of yours." His grin reached his green eyes, and I hoped he really didn't care what I looked like after what we had been through.

"Please don't remind me. It's going to take forever to regrow at this point." I shook my head. "Physically, I'm better. But earlier, I thought I would lose my mind when I couldn't see. I still just can't believe we failed."

Khaldon reached out a hand to me. I accepted it and ran a finger up and down where the skin had grown back. My own hand was pink and rosy with renewed flesh.

"Mentally, I can't wrap my head around who would want to do that to Dakota. To any of us. They used her as a lure to kill us." I looked at our hands once again. My breath hitched in my chest as emotion swelled. My words were thick with shock. "I feel like my mind is refusing to believe how my heart is breaking. My brain is in complete denial of what happened. Everything I remember happening on that island was true. I feel more numb than anything and I want to crawl into a hole and hit the reset button on life."

Harris reached over and held my hand. "Ctrl-Z, Chey." Even with a pint of whole blood and two IV bottles hanging above him, his face, hands, and arms were still bloated as though he were a corpse pulled out of a lake several days after drowning. His hands and arms spidered out with angry punctures of red lines radiating from the dart's impacts.

"Guys, how can we go on knowing our rescue attempt is what ultimately killed her? We weren't prepared. We should have done so much more to make this successful, but we didn't. We needed back up. I—I can't handle it."

"Chey, it's not our fault. Don't you dare think that way." Harris sat two chairs down from Khaldon, so I sat in a chair between them to talk to them both. "We were set up. There're no two ways about that. But there's one thing I do know." Harris pointed directly at me. "She wasn't going to be alive much longer if we hadn't of shown up. So you need to get that kinda crazy talk outta your head."

"I understand it was a set up. The Rakshasa were expecting us. But we should have had more people, more ways to defend ourselves. How am I going to tell Sheridan and Daddy that Dakota is dead?" My chair creaked under me. I was convinced it would collapse if I moved or adjusted wrong, so I sat perfectly still for fear of another floor debacle.

Harris sat up and tried to stand. I stood to help him steady his balance.

"Damn, Chey, I'm sorry and you're right. We should've been more prepared." Harris pulled on the back of his pants trying to remove a wedgie. He leaned down to whisper in my ear. "I've got a rotten case of monkey butt. I'm in desperate need of a shower."

"Gawd, a shower would be fantastic," I agreed.

Torchy had walked back into our room and he picked up a chair seated closer to the door and brought it over to me.

"Thanks, Torch. Have you spoken to Dr. Ratta ... Rattoko ...Dr. Raattatakosin... Dr. Whateverthehellhisnameis. Have you spoken to him about the dragon adrenaline donation? Are you compatible?"

"Dr. Rattanakosin? Oh aye, they're prepping for the procedure now. Tis very simple, but we willna be able to fly in our dragon forms for a couple of fortnights."

Torchy picked up several bamboo darts that Harris had on his bed stand. "Starting yer own collection, huh?"

"Are those the wolfsbane darts?" I pointed toward sharp, angry shivs still dirtied and bloody.

Harris nodded with an uplift to his chin, most likely proud of the awful things. "I figured I'd take them back to my pack and tell war stories. I'm sure my Cub Scout troop will think they're awesome."

After running the allergen tests, we learned how Harris had been poisoned with wolfsbane in the blow darts. In the United States, wolfsbane had become a non-existent weed. But on this side of the planet, werewolves take special precautions against rarer species of the weed to avoid these kinds of poisonous reactions.

It never occurred to me that werewolves might need allergy shots. Dr. Rattanakosin said the allergy medicine would take much longer to work against this type of plant because it was so rare. The known antidotes might not be sufficient.

The nurse came back in the room and asked for Torchy to begin his prep. I asked her to please be on the lookout for a woman and an older man who were family members of Briggs. The nurse acknowledged my request with a nod and a grimace, and then she quickly left again.

"I bet she'll be happy when this shift is over," I muttered under my breath.

Harris tried to smile and nodded his head. "Yeah, I'm sure they'll claim worker's comp from you biting them so much."

Khaldon sat up a bit. "Do they have worker's comp in Phuket?" He tried to smile, and more ash fell away from his face as layers of pink skin shined through the charred crust.

Normally, I laughed at his jokes, but today I wasn't in the mood. Little black spots still floated across my vision. I deliberated the situation we were in. It didn't make any sense how each of us had been uniquely injured.

"Just look at us. Who could have known what weapons to provide the Rakshasa to mortally injure or kill each of us?"

"Isn't it obvious? Who other than Amicula and her crazy aunt?" Harris said as he reached for a glass of water. He knocked it over with his swollen fingers. "Dammit."

"Do you think Ludovic got a message out to her somehow?" I asked.

"Why would he take that chance when he was trying to save Dakota?" Torchy asked.

There were no answers to our questions. Only silence.

Since Harris spilled his water, the unnamed girl sitting next to him sat up in her chair and offered him sips from her cup. She also had an IV stuck in her arm to help replenish fluids.

"Thanks for helping him," I said. "You're very kind. What's your name?"

The girl pulled the water cup into her lap and glanced up at me under dirty blond hair, which hung limp over her shoulders. She was filthy from being held captive in that pit.

"My name is Tiffany—Tiffany Miller." She looked at Harris once again and gestured in his direction. "He saved me. I owe him my life. It's the least I can do."

Her voice was whisper quiet. It was fortunate I had what I called vampionic hearing. One of the perks of vampirism I had learned.

"Are you hurt, Tiffany?" I asked. "Can I help you with anything?"

She shook her head and stared at her feet.

"Do you know why we were there on that island?"

She shook her head again.

"We were trying to rescue my sister Dakota, but—" My voice trailed off as the explosion of my sister's body played over and over in slow motion, in black and white until I was sure I might pass out again.

She wiped her nose, her slack expression mimicking my own. "I knew her. She was nice to me—until they took her away."

Tiffany's hazel irises barely encircled the black holes of her pupils. Her eyes were dull, mostly lifeless, utterly defeated.

My own bloodshot blues stared back at her. "Do you know why you and Dakota were on that island? When did you get there?"

She shook her head possibly trying to erase painful memories. Her face was haggard and beaten with time. I noticed she had a nervous twitch to her left eye. She sighed a heavy breath, and her knuckles turned white from holding the cup so tight. I was sure she was going to shut down again.

"Hey, hey." I reached for her. "Shh—you don't have to go there. I'm sorry for asking."

She shook her head again, "No. I'm okay. Beyond fine. I'm downright pissed, that's what I am. I'm thankful to you for saving my life, but I want to go home."

Her unbridled outburst startled me. I pressed my back against the chair and stole a glance over at Khaldon. His eyes shot open. The scent of curry and turmeric filled the air. The nurse escorted a woman with long, brunette hair and an older gentleman dressed in a long-sleeved blouse with lacy cuffs, reminiscent of a pirate. He held a top hat and coat tails over his arm.

Khaldon sat up straight and reached for the dragon scythe. He pulled it up close to his chest and then tried to conceal it under the sheet.

The brunette had elaborate, ornate tattoos all over her body, or the parts visible. She swept the room with her eyes, and I saw Briggs motion to her to come to him. She walked at once to Briggs and gently took his hands. The man looked about the room and glared at the place in disgust. His lips pursed. His eyes grazed past us, and I noticed Khaldon had turned to face the window.

Tiffany continued her story. "They took me and my friends. We were shopping at the mall, and these guys came up and asked if we wanted to party. They had some booze in their car. We figured we were in a public place, so what could go wrong? Right?"

"Ya know, Tiffany, I've come to learn almost everything can and will go awry in public." I teased her with a half-hearted smile reflecting on my own attack at a public theme park.

She cracked me a half-smile perhaps agreeing with my sentiments. "So we went. It was stupid. We got drunk, and the next thing I knew, I woke up in this crazy place where people were strung up in racks being fed all different kinds of food. They kept shoving oranges down my throat until I thought I was going to puke citrus juice. They refused to give me anything else."

A thick knot formed in my throat and I checked Khaldon for any reaction. It seemed she was describing a blood orchard, but Khaldon said those were voluntary. He winced at her words. I wondered if the same question crossed his mind.

"It's okay now, Tiffany. You're safe here with us. Then what happened? Is that where you met my sister, Dakota?"

Briggs' family turned their heads toward us. I gave them a small wave with my fingers. "Hi. I'm Cheyenne, a friend of Briggs. This is Torchy, Khaldon, Harris, and Tiffany."

The woman nodded at me and returned her attention to Briggs. The man's eyes were locked onto Khaldon's.

Okay, not much for conversation, are they?

The older man broke the stare-down with Khaldon and abruptly turned back to attend to his son.

Tiffany took another sip from the water cup, and she laughed out loud as though she remembered a funny joke. "You should have seen it. We started taking bets as to how many of those freaks your sister could eat. For a while, they had her in a caged area by herself. Those creepy black-eyed kids kept trying to draw blood from her. But every time anyone got close—she ate them. I think we got up to five before they started getting smart about how to handle her. Can I call my parents now? I really want to go home. Is there any Coca-Cola here?"

I blinked at the way she changed topics, barely able to keep up with her random thoughts. "Yes. Yes, of course. Let's just get a few more cups of water in you, and some food. Then we'll call them, okay?" I tried to give her a genuine, kind smile. One that could convey the message that we cared about her and wanted her to get home.

How were we going to prepare this girl for civilized life without the authorities throwing her into a loony hospital? No one would believe her story. Would Khaldon need to wipe her mind like he did with the human absturger teams?

She nodded and handed Harris another sip from the cup.

I sagged into my seat thinking about what the dhampirs had done to my baby sister. What they were doing to countless other women all over the world. At that very moment, I felt impotent to help any of them.

Tiffany continued her story. "After three days of those bastards shoving oranges down my neck, they started taking my blood. Every time I jerked away, they would Taser me into submission. I finally had enough and let them take the blood. I didn't care anymore. If I cooperated, it wasn't as painful. They took two pints and then pumped me full of liquids and oranges again."

Guilt swelled through my guts as I realized how much I loved the orange bloodwines. How would I ever be able to stomach that luscious infusion knowing I could be consuming blood that wasn't volunteered? Were all the bloodwines illegal? No, they couldn't be. There had to be legitimate orchards set up for vampires. At least I hoped so.

Tiffany used her hand to stretch out her neck by pulling down on her head in the opposite direction. "Over and over, week after week we had the same routine. It was a dream come true when they started feeding me salted chocolates. Then I realized it was going to be the same thing. They didn't give me anything else but those damn candies. I never want to look at that stuff again as long as I live. We were being fed food and then they were draining our blood. Nobody understood it, but every week more and more people and creatures were showing up at this place. It was totally surreal. Then, about three weeks ago, they marched some of us over to the other part of the island. It was me, two other girls who didn't speak any English, and a guy. Your sister too. Where is she, anyway?"

"Wait? What? There are more of you on that island?" Khaldon sat up on his bed.

She nodded with a puzzled expression, almost as though she were shocked to learn that we didn't know there were more prisoners there.

This was truly unexpected news.

"Do you mind me asking how long you were there? At that facility, I mean." Khaldon continued.

Harris squinted with swollen eye lids at Tiffany as she handed him another sip.

"I honestly don't know how long. It was our summer vacation before starting my first year at university. What day is it, anyway? I'm sure my parents are going nuts looking for me."

My gaze met Khaldon's and Torchy's. Harris gently reached for Tiffany's hand with his bloated, puffy fingers and turned his body to look at her. His voice slurred from the way the muscles had contorted around his mouth. "Tiffany, I'm sorry to tell you that it was New Year's last week. This must be hard for you. Can you tell us if there was anyone else in that cave with you?"

She covered her cheeks with her palms. "January?" She fell vacant again, her voice reduced back to a mere whisper. "Yeah, there was another girl, but they were forcing blood from your sister on us." Tiffany's voice cracked. "She turned into the same kind of winged thing your sister is. It was like they were cloning her or something. Look, even my hair is turning red like hers too. They took the other girl away. I'm pretty sure I was next. They kept feeding me jars of the blood to drink. It was the only liquid they would give me. At first, I threw it all up. But then it began to be what I needed. I know that sounds really gross, huh?" Her eyes pleaded with me as if I could grant her forgiveness.

This has got to truly be what nightmares are made of.

"Are you going back for the others?" Tiffany's question jolted me out of my morbid memories. "There're more people and creatures on the other side of the island. You can't see the building because it's covered in vines."

"Tiffany, are you saying there are a lot more survivors on that same island?" Torchy asked.

She nodded. "Didn't you know? Those creepy natives have all kinds of weird people in there. Monsters, even. Hell, I never knew there were real things like trolls, elves, and dragons. I know you think I'm crazy, but I'm not lying."

"You saw people who weren't human looking?" Harris asked. "Maybe like huge dogs?"

"Uh huh." Tiffany pulled up the sleeve of her ragged shirt and showed us the festering, infected bite marks on her arm. "The worst part about it was the freakish dog-elk-zombie-creatures. The other prisoners called them the Wendigos or something, and they walked on their hind legs and had hideous long arms that dragged on the ground. There was nothing inside their rib cages; they were possessed like zombies."

She held out her arm for the doctor and winced as he applied the peroxide. "The creepy-assed black-eyed kids who would order the

Wendigos to bite us if we didn't do what they wanted. I'll never look at a little girl in piggy tails the same ever again in my life. They're evil." Tiffany pulled down her sleeve. "I almost preferred the Taser to the wolves, but those freaky kids were the worst. It was like they were sucking everything out of me and all I could feel was fear. My head always ached after they left me, so I did whatever I could do to avoid them."

Harris winced at the sight of the Wendigo bite marks.

"Black-eyed kids?" I asked.

"Aye, I've heard of such creatures in folktales," Torchy said. "Claim to roam the countryside, and if you're unlucky t'see them, they'll shroud you with doom and fill yer guts with fear."

Dr. Rattanakosin looked over the tops of his glasses at Tiffany and pulled out the necessary tools for stitching her up.

Tiffany continued, "It's true, I never felt well after those creepy little kids were around me. But I could've sworn I saw something that looked like a Bigfoot once, but it had huge fangs. Scary as hell, but they had it in chains. Then a couple weeks ago, they moved us over to those disgusting caves."

My eyes darted at Khaldon and Torchy. Harris met our sentiment. It seemed as though we all had the exact same thought. How in the hell were we going to rescue those people without getting ourselves captured, killed, or eaten in the process? We had to save them. But the bigger question was: *Why were they there in the first place?*

"Tiffany, can you tell us about how many people were there? Ten, fifty, a hundred?" Khaldon asked.

"I dunno." She shrugged. "Twenty or thirty, maybe. They brought new people or things in all hours of the day, but when they left, you never saw them come back again." Tiffany's voice trailed off and quieted as she took another drink of water through a straw while staring at the floor.

Harris put his arm around Tiffany as her body shook. I noticed a quiet tear drip onto the lid of her cup. I winced at the reality of what she had revealed to us.

"What are we going to do? We can't just leave them there," I said. "There's a crazy weird, experimental blood farm turning other creatures into more blood demons like my sister?"

I was met with no words. Only blank expressions from everyone in the room, including the doctors, nurses, and even Briggs' family. Possibly, it seemed they were considering the same questions as well.

Briggs tried to roll over and gasped out in pain. My attention turned toward his bed. I watched as his sister held his hand and it looked as though they were mind-messaging one another. Maybe he was too weak to speak out loud.

I noticed Khaldon and the older man were staring at each other again. *What the hell is going on?*

Chapter 7

Phuket Hospital - Thailand

The La Rivière Family

K alina La Rivière searched the room for the energy presence of her brother among a group of strangers. She slowly walked past each bed searching for the face of her younger brother. She stopped at the foot of a man she did not recognize, but his scent was familiar. Warm, spiced tobacco with a hint of vanilla. His signature blend. Was her brother wearing the mask of another man?

Blaize gestured for her to come. He took the hand of his sister as soon as her tentative fingers reached him. He looked up at his father, Draconis, and a sour taste stained his lips. It had been five years since he'd last spoken to his sister, and much longer with his father. Blaize's body shook, his teeth biting down on his bottom lip as he suffered through the pain.

He mind-messaged them both with such lackluster, they could barely decipher his words.

Kalina, Father—do not address me as Blaize in front of these people. They only know me as Tony Briggs. This is a different identity I wear around them.

Kalina nodded and spoke back to him with her mind. *I will honor your request. What can I do for you, my brother? You have been injured in a mortal form?*

Blaize's back arched and then convulsed back into a cradling position. *Yes. Someone put a hit out on me. Somebody set a trap for us. They used weapons to try and kill us all.*

Blaize's father pressed his lips tightly together. *Well, what do you expect from dzee line of thug work you've created?* He tilted his chin down at his son and frowned.

Kalina waved a hand at her father in dismissal. *Someone put a hit on you? Where have you been?*

Draconis held up a handkerchief to his nose to quiet the qualm of disinfectant and decomposing flesh. *Son, what have you been doing? What do you mean there was a trap? Who did this to you?*

Briggs messaged again. *We went to an island, North Sentinel—east of the Andamans. The Rakshasa were holding my girlfriend prisoner there.*

Amicula Darkrose, the niece to the Vampyre Queen Civetateo, stole my Dakota. His mind message voice broke into a sob even though his face merely showed a single tear falling down his cheek. *I went to rescue her, and they ... and they blew her up.*

Both Kalina and Draconis returned concerned furrowed brows toward Blaize. Kalina slicked back her baby brother's hair.

Draconis turned to his daughter and sent a private mind-message chat only to her. *Did you know about this? Why wasn't I told? How in the hell did your brother get caught up in this mess? How in the world was he dating one of the O'Cuinn sisters?*

Kalina responded to her father in the private chat message between them. *How the hell am I supposed to know? Last I heard, just before Thanksgiving, Blaize was in New Orleans putting the screws to some ghoulies who were stealing dead bodies out of the morgue. That's nowhere near where Ludovic had the breeding den in Orlando.*

Draconis laid a gentle hand on his son's head. *Blaize, are you saying this is the work of Vampyre? Who is this Dakota? Why didn't you ask for my help? I could have provided you with the protection needed, and you never would have endangered you or your friends.*

Briggs looked up at his father. Color drained from his face with each thought. *It's not like I left on the best of terms, but I've been sliced open with a dragon scythe. The blade has drained my adrenaline and I cannot shift. I fear this wound will kill me in this mortal form. And I need to live. I need to find the bastard who stole my Dakota and kill him with his own blade!*

Draconis restlessly bunched the handkerchief in a wad and then released it again. Kalina turned to look at the group of people in the room and made eye contact with a woman and a couple of men. A woman with wavy, black hair greeted them.

"Hi, I'm Cheyenne O'Cuinn, a friend of Briggs." Cheyenne gestured toward the others in the room. "This is Torchy, Khaldon, Harris, and Tiffany."

Both Draconis and Kalina stiffened and instantly recognized Cheyenne as Dakota's older sister. They nodded in a curtly fashion. Draconis' attention was drawn to the man sitting beside her. Khaldon Seters. They stared at one another with an intense, heated radiation. Khaldon did not break eye contact.

Blaize cried out as he tried to adjust his position. Draconis turned his attention back to his son without acknowledging anyone else in the room.

Draconis spoke out loud. "No need to worry, my son. I 'ave spoken with Dr. Rattanokosin and we both feel dzee best course of action is dzee transfer of adrenaline. We'll take you 'ome to recover and you can tell us everything dzen. You need to rest now."

Across the room, Kalina and Draconis could hear a young girl talk. "There wasn't anyone else in the cave with us, but as they took that other girl away, I heard talking about them doing blood experiments on people. Something about making them into an army, but I could never hear what kind of army or what they were for."

Draconis tried to maintain a modicum of calm and spoke again on the private mind-messaging channel with his daughter. *You need to kill the girl—Tiffany. She knows too much. She will blow dzee cover on dze blood trials. She will expose who kidnapped 'er and reveal dzee entire operation. You must kill dzis girl tonight. Cheyenne is well aware of the breeder dens. We cannot afford for anything more to go wrong.*

Kalina answered him back. *But, Baba-ji, kill the girl? She is still useful. I can arrange to have her extrication this evening. Her transformation is not far off. We can take her and not waste any more time for the queen.*

Draconis glared at her for arguing his request. *If you don't kill her, she will recognize you from dzee blood orchard and your brother will learn dzee truth.*

Tiffany asked another question. Both Draconis and Kalina turned toward one another to listen covertly to the answer. "Are you going back for the others?"

Draconis stepped away from his son's bed and pulled his daughter to the side. He mind-messaged her privately once again. *I will leave and make dzee arrangements for Blaize's recovery. You need to kill Tiffany tonight! We can 'arrest more 'umans another day."*

Draconis re-approached his son and gingerly touched his head, speaking in a kind, fatherly tone. *"Je suis désolé de ce qui vous est arrivé. Je vais trouver le démon qui vous a fait du mal. Je dois préparer un endroit sûr pour vous de récupérer. Je t'aime, mon fils.* (I'm sorry this has happened to you. I will find the fiend who has hurt you. I must prepare a safe place for you to recover. I love you, my son.)" He bent and kissed his son's forehead.

Blaize's pale and sickly face turned to look up at his father. His heart was thankful, but his mind dreaded the payback he would have to render for his father's assistance if the transfer of adrenaline was a success. He watched as his father lovingly hugged his daughter goodbye. It was then he noticed his father staring toward Khaldon.

Draconis intently studied Khaldon as though he couldn't decide whether he wanted to speak to the man or not. Khaldon shook his head, and Draconis nodded and then walked away.

Chapter 8

Phuket Hospital - Thailand

Cheyenne O'Cuinn

"What's going on between you and Briggs' father?" I whispered to Khaldon. "Do you know him from somewhere?"

Khaldon pressed his lips together tight and pulled me close to his face. I noticed he placed my body between himself and Briggs. "Let's just say I now understand why Briggs is so connected. If Draconis is his father, then—"

The EKG machine strapped onto Briggs' chest alarmed and a missed beat.

Dr. Rattanakosin said, "He isn't long for this world."

Without another thought, Torchy ripped off his shirt and lay on the bed next to Briggs. I held my arms tightly around myself, acknowledging the sacrifice Torchy was making for a man, a fellow dragon, whom he barely knew. I prayed no one else died tonight because of this failed rescue mission.

Khaldon reached for my hand, and warmth caressed my nerves.

"Mr. Gravenor, we're ready to take the adrenaline now," Dr. Rattanakosin said. "This won't hurt much, but if you tense up your abdomen muscles, it will burn as though you are being branded. Hold as still as you can. Try to relax."

"Easier said than done, knowing that yer gettin' ready to jam that needle into me gullet."

The doctor smiled down at Torchy and acknowledged the sentiment.

"I understand. I'll tell you exactly what I'm doing the entire time. I'm going to press just below your liver to gain access into your energy vortex."

Briggs reached out toward Torchy and touched his arm. His eyes weeped thankfulness with a glint of a prayer.

Torchy gave him a wry half-smile. "I sure as hell pray my essence doesn't make you go crazy."

"*Oui.* Can't get any crazier than I already am, my man." Briggs gave Torchy a gentle fist bump and then turned his head. He took a deep breath and tried to relax. "*Bonne santé*, Doc."

Dr. Rattanakosin picked up a needle the size of Alaska.

Briggs' eyes opened wide and he swallowed hard. He looked at Torchy once again, and whispered a *merci* to Torchy as the needle inserted deep into his belly.

I prayed both of them would be all right.

Torchy stayed stoic as a rock and didn't flinch. He held his breath as we watched a golden, almost white, fluid being sucked into the needle's syringe. The nurse prepared the gash on Briggs' abdomen and exposed the dismal brown, sickly light dying within him.

Dr. Rattanakosin changed the needle head on the syringe and moved over to Briggs. He inserted the golden adrenaline deep into the abdomen of the man who had tried, in vain, to rescue my sister.

I strained my neck to observe the procedure as Briggs gasped out loud and passed out.

His EKG blipped and flat-lined. The room fell silent like in the suspended moments before a wine glass shatters into a million shards against a marble floor.

I held my breath to listen closer. Not another heartbeat returned.

I cried out, "No! Please, no. Hang on, Briggs!"

Kalina ran to her brother with tears streaming. She whispered into his ear in a language I'd never heard before. She wiped the tears from her face, looked me dead in the eyes and then centered herself. She pulled her hands together in front of her face and then over her heart, chanting her incantation.

Kalina held her hands over Briggs' bleeding wound and spoke aloud. The tattoos on her arms moved like they'd come alive. She continued to chant in her native tongue. I couldn't understand any of it except for one word.

Was she calling on the blood goddess of birth and death, Kali, for help?

This can't be good.

Kalina's chanting escalated into a harsh, full-throated bleating as an indigo geometric shape emerged from Kalina's hands and formed a container vessel. I watched as she seemingly sucked the death out of Briggs and contained it.

Most everyone gave her space, moving several feet away, but I wanted to know what she was doing. The golden light from within Briggs amplified and shot out in a spectrum of healing light from inside his abdomen.

The EKG monitor fluttered back to life.

A stable, rhythmic beat pulsed green in steady pings, echoing his heart rate.

The flesh within his belly pinked up again.

For the first time throughout the tense procedure, I grew conscious of my breathing once again. Had I been holding my breath the entire time?

Dr. Rattanakosin said, "Okay, I think that will be good for the first dose."

"First dose?" Khaldon asked. "How many will he need? Is that going to happen every time?"

The doctor responded, "Oh no. Now that we have his heart started once again, thanks to his half-sister, we can proceed without any further snarls."

Khaldon and I looked at one another, both seemingly to have the same questions run through our minds.

Half-sister? Snarls?

I placed my fists on my hips. "You think Briggs losing his heartbeat was a "snarl" to your procedure?"

Dr. Rattanakosin adjusted his glasses and tugged down on his white doctor's coat. "Yes, it was a deviation from standard textbook procedures, but it will most likely take a series of at least three of these adrenaline donations to jump-start his energy vortex."

I stared at the little beads of sweat forming at his hairline. "You've never done this before have you? Textbook procedures?" My cheeks reddened as heat plumed up out of my shirt. A nurse stood by with a syringe and stared hard at me, almost waiting for an excuse to put me back down into a drug-induced haze.

Khaldon touched me lightly on the shoulder. I knew I needed to stand down or I might get strapped to a bed again. I would be of no use to anyone then.

"How long will this take?" Harris stood up, his lips still swollen from the wolfsbane reaction. "How will this affect Torchy?"

Dr. Rattanakosin cleared his throat, seemingly tired of all the questions. "The first couple of shots are needed just for Mr. Briggs to heal his human form. The third one will help him with the strength he'll need to transform into a dragon once again. He can then complete the healing and be fine in due time, but neither one of them will be more than a shadow of their former selves for a while." The doctor shot me a sideways glance. "If everything goes well and there are no more complications, we can expect to see significant improvements for Mr. Briggs within a few hours."

Kalina now seemed quite tired herself and took a stance behind Tiffany's chair. Tiffany tensed up as Kalina sat behind her. Even though I was thankful Kalina most likely just saved Briggs' life, I was still unsure of what she was or how she was able to conjure up the juju. Nobody lightly called down the goddess Kali like that.

Kalina. Kali. Could she be a descendant?

I walked over and stood close to Torchy's head. "Won't Torchy be able to shift into dragon form and heal himself just like Briggs? Why does it take so long for him to recover?"

Torchy reached for my hand. "It's all right, lassie. I'll be at home with Sheridan and the bairns soon. I willna have a need to shift for a long time. It takes years to build dragon adrenaline, ya ken? What I'm giving Briggs will only be the seed of what he'll need to rebuild in his own system. Neither of us willna be flying for a few weeks. I'm afraid it's going to be airplanes for a while."

Dr. Rattanakosin prepared a new syringe and drew another dose of the golden adrenaline from Torchy, then injected it into Briggs.

Torchy's face grew weary and his mouth relaxed. Even though I was worried, I managed to conjure a confident smile. I stroked my fingers through his coppery spikes. "You're not alone Torch. We're here with you. Nothing is going to keep us away, you hear me?"

He smiled a weakened half-smile. "Oh, aye." He fell off to what seemed to be a peaceful sleep.

The nurse shooed me out of the way so she could insert an IV into his arm. She said, "We don't know how long he'll be out, but we'll need to keep fluids in him."

I nodded and stepped farther out of the way. Khaldon leaned on the side of Briggs' bed and reached for a chair to sit. Both dragons were out cold. We watched as Dr. Rattanakosin took one last dosage from Torchy and gave it to Briggs. Finally, despite our injuries, it seemed we were all going to live.

I decided to take a moment to sit and relax, to finally catch my breath, maybe even find a cool shower and some clean clothes, when Tiffany cried out.

I stared at several purplish colors swimming inside of Tiffany's IV bottle and tube line. In an instant, the color swirls escaped down the tube, through the needle, and squirmed into her arm.

Tiffany cried out again and slapped her forearm. "Ouch! It hurts! Get it out of me!" She pulled the IV needle out of her arm.

As fast as she stood up, she lost her balance and fell over on top of me. I tried to help her stand, but within seconds, Tiffany bubbled purple mucus from her mouth and nose. She held her hands up to her throat to indicate she couldn't breathe.

"Doctor, she's choking!" Harris grabbed her from my arms. He tried to perform what looked like the Heimlich maneuver on her. He squeezed his hands so tight around her waist that his own IV and blood line were wrenched from his arms. His hands burst open from his swollen injuries, squirting yellow pus and goo.

Tiffany gasped for breath while she slid out of his arms and down to the floor. She opened her mouth mimicking a fish pulled out of the water desperately trying to breathe, her eyes wildly vacant as she thrashed at her neck, struggling to take in oxygen.

She's drowning!

"I saw something purple flow into her arm from the IV. What was it?" I cried out to everyone.

Additional hospital personnel ran into our emergency area, picked Tiffany up, and took her to the bed beside Torchy.

Kalina stood back over by Briggs' bed and observed with perceived nonchalance about the whole situation. She picked at her fingernails.

Khaldon stood back with me as we watched the hospital staff suck the suffocating mess out of Tiffany's throat and nasal passages.

Nothing was working.

Dr. Rattanakosin ordered, "Get me a trach kit, stat!"

Within moments, Tiffany was breathing through a tube in her throat while they continued to draw out the purplish gray ooze.

The doctor murmured, "What the—"

I retched into my mouth as the slimy mucus thickened and puddled out of her—not only from her nostrils—but her ears and eyes as well. Her skull warped and contorted like a baby were struggling to get out. Within moments, Tiffany's eyes dissolved and her head imploded in on itself. No amount of oxygen through the trach tube was going to save her life.

In an instant, she was dead.

Chapter 9

"You killed her!" Helpless to keep my hand from shaking, I pointed toward Kalina. "There was a purple snake or something in Tiffany's IV tube. You poisoned her—I know you murdered her! You took that poison out of Briggs and gave it to Tiffany."

Kalina stared at me as if I had just spat on her mother.

Khaldon touched my shoulder and turned me to look at him. His lips were hard. His forehead creased and eyes narrowed. "Blimey, Cheyenne, I understand you're upset, but you can't accuse her like that. There's no telling what parasite Tiffany may have picked up in that place."

My mouth gaped open. "But I saw the purple stuff floating around in her IV bag. It was the same geometric pattern we saw Kalina pull out of Briggs."

The nurse pulled a fresh sheet out from the metal cabinet and draped it over Tiffany's body. Dr. Rattanakosin instructed an orderly to move the corpse to the morgue.

I raised my voice. "What are you doing? You're destroying evidence." I stopped the bed from leaving the room. "This is a crime scene now! You haven't even taken any pictures."

Everyone in the room gawked at me, making me feel as though I were the one who had committed the crime.

I pointed at Tiffany's disintegrating body. "I know what I saw. She was fine until Kalina stood behind her. I'm so not buying this. What gives?" My finger changed direction and pointed accusatorily at Kalina. "Who the hell are you, and why did you kill that innocent girl?"

Briggs' sister stood taller and straightened her blouse. "I am Kalina. A direct descendant of Kali. You would be wise not to cross me, vampyre." Her East Indian accent gave her threat a particular appeal, but her words were poison. "It is true. I used her to save my brother."

Everyone in the room stared at Kalina, echoing my shock.

"You had no right to kill her." I moved forward to bitch slap the smug grin off her face, but Khaldon jerked my arm back.

Trespassing deep into my personal comfort zone, Kalina coolly took a step forward and stood directly in front of me. Toe to toe. "I saved my brother's life."

Khaldon's hands held me steady.

She tilted her chin up and loomed over me. "Kali had every right. She must have a life to save a life. Tiffany was the most insignificant being here, and Kali chose her. You should thank me for sparing your life, vampyre." Kalina popped the letter "p" in vampyre as a disgusted sneer dripped from her lips.

A million ways to slam this skank to the floor flew through my mind, but I wasn't stupid either. I'd heard about how gods and goddesses were never to be called upon unless you offered a sacrifice. Horrible things could happen to you if you didn't. One would not ask for Kali to cleanse your home after you bought it. To Kali, a home cleansing meant sending a tornado and razing it to the ground.

I bit my lip to stave off any further outbreaks and eased my arm down. Khaldon stood close beside me.

Kalina cocked an eyebrow at me as if to say, "I win," and she turned to sit by her brother's side.

I walked away disgusted and leaned against the window frame. I couldn't handle the self-righteous attitude. "We need to call the police. She confessed to her murder. Everyone in this room heard it."

Dr. Rattanakosin addressed us. "Stand down, everyone. The proper authorities have been notified. It will all be handled within the standard supernatural protocols."

I returned a cocky eyebrow to Miss Holier-Than-Thou, and she didn't even flinch.

Harris sat down next to Tiffany's body and pounded the bed next to her. "I promised her I would help her parents. She was going to be okay, right?" Harris shook with his words. "She went through hell. She deserved better than this." Genuine tears ran down his cheeks. "All those people do. We can't let those jerks kidnap and kill innocent kids like that! We've got to locate this blood-orchard torture factory and put a stop to it, right?"

My stomach lurched at the possibility of going back to that island. "Wait. Why do *we* have to do this? Isn't there some kind of supernatural governing body or police we can call? Why do we have to risk our own lives again? Can't we report this place?"

"Absolutely. We need to expose it, we must tell the International Council," Harris said. He stood up, a little wobbly on his legs. "I don't know who or what's ultimately profiting from it, but we can't allow this inhumanity to continue."

"We were tipped off this was going on," Khaldon said. "Remember the evil sect of werewolves who were trafficking humans inside *ExsanguiNation*?"

"Wait a *gawddamn* minute. Are you saying that *my* people are doing this? To work for vampires?" Harris hissed the word as though it was a vile, nasty taste in his mouth. I'd never seen him this upset before.

"Harris, you even said yourself there were bad wolves moving through Florida." I touched his arm. "He's right, H. We talked about what was happening in the game on various sims. Remember when—"

"I know, dammit." He cut me off sharply and shook his head.

"Hey, I don't mean it was you or your pack." I placed my hand on his shoulder and gently squeezed. "But it's conceivable there could be supes working together for blood profit."

His face creased causing leaks to spill out from the bloated sacks. "You're right. I'm just ... just kinda on pins and needles right now." He slumped his shoulders.

I plucked several tissues from the table and blotted the drips before they ran into his eyes. "Stop doing that—you'll make your swelling worse. Sit back so I can clean you up."

Harris sat further back in his chair and looked up toward the ceiling avoiding my gaze. "I know you didn't mean it that way, Chey. We should check the game's database to learn if there's any kind of reference to this blood orchard."

Khaldon said, "We might be able to find out who's running it. I'm sure we can track the orders if they've been purchasing through the game platform."

Kalina shot a curious glance toward Khaldon.

A nurse approached with a tray of brownish looking slugs. "Okay, Mr. Archer, we finally located the leeches that thrive on the wolfsbane. Let's try to bring down that swelling off your face."

"Leeches?" I raised my hand to my mouth, miserably failing to hide my revulsion. "Seriously? What is this, the 1700s? What's next? Bloodletting?"

"We don't use the word bloodletting any longer, Cheyenne." Khaldon sat down at the head of Torchy's bed. "It's called exsanguinating."

I started to question him further, but an orderly poked his head into our room. "There's an emergency phone call for a Cheyenne O'Cuinn. Anybody here by that name?"

I pointed at Khaldon, gesturing to Kalina. "Please don't take your eyes off her."

Kalina rolled her eyes as though she were a bored, eighth grade bully.

I stepped out of our hospital room and was directed to an ancient phone at the nurses' station. The cord must have stretched over a hundred feet as it twisted and turned its circular curly-Qs into a tangled mess.

In the corner, the TV droned on with the political wars escalating between North Korea and China. China was ready to advance forces on the small country because its military leaders had threatened to test an EMP not too far from the coastline.

Children played with wooden blocks while row upon row of patients wore surgical masks to keep from catching other contagious ailments in this place. One child in particular was obviously not human since he had gills on the side of his neck. One side much more green and swollen than the other. He had a terrible cough and his mother's face grew more concerned by the minute.

I heard the phone ring and make the connection. "Hello, this is Cheyenne O'Cuinn."

"Cheyenne! Oh, thank the heavens I've found you." My father's panicked voice burst over the line.

"Daddy? Is everything all right? How—how did you know I was here? Why didn't you call my cell phone?"

"Calls are goin' straight to yer voicemail. Never mind that. Yer sister is being taken to the hospital. She's in severe pain. She's been haverin' on in the worst way not long after you left. When are you coming home? Are you able to leave now?"

I took a deep breath and bit back the bitter words I needed to say. I opted for a small fib to buy us time. "We can probably fly home pretty quick, Daddy. Is she in labor? Are the babies okay?"

"I'm not sure. Yer mum never had this kind of pain when she birthed you three. I've got the screaming abdabs from all this, luv."

"We'll be there as fast as we can. Are you at Orlando Hospital?"

"Right."

"Have you called Dr. Meyer? He's Sheridan's OB-GYN specialist. His number is programmed into her phone. If we don't make it back in time, he'll know exactly what to do with the babies and how best to take care of Sheridan."

"Right."

"Just breathe, Daddy. Tell Sheridan I love her. We'll be there as soon as we can."

"Have you heard anything about Dakota?"

Of course ... the question I dreaded the most.

Pressing a thumb into my right eye socket, up under the eyebrow, I tried to stave off the never-ending headache.

My fingers reached for a stray piece of paper to crumble. Licking my lips, I hesitated. I considered faking a lost telephone line connection. I pulled my hand back.

I can't lie to my dad.

Do I tell my father how I watched my baby sister blow up into a million silver shrapnel pieces to kill me?

"Yeah, Daddy ... about that."

"Cheyenne, call me back on my mobile if you can. The paramedics are here. I need to go tend to yer sister. Come home as soon as you can." And with that he had hung up the phone.

"Okay. *Gráim thú.* Love you." I spoke to the handset as I replaced it onto its cradle hanging on the yellowing wall.

An out-of-place song filled the waiting room speakers. It was only then I realized the Muzak version of "Closer" by Nine Inch Nails had been playing the whole time I was on the phone. Even more surreal was to watch people of all ages tapping their feet to the beat.

Returning to our room, I found Harris laid out on a bed with doctors and nurses surrounding him.

"No. No! *No!* What's going on?" I ran to his bedside. If he was lying in a puddle of purple goo, I would kill Kalina with my bare hands.

Khaldon's fists were white as marble as he held onto the side of the bed rails.

His eyes met mine. "It's all right, Cheyenne." Khaldon spun on his heels and stopped me. "Well, not all right. He's having an allergic reaction to the wolfsbane antidote."

I dashed over as Dr. Rattanakosin injected an EpiPen into him. Harris' face was as bloated as the Stay Puft Marshmallow Man.

"Obviously, your seventeenth-century leeches didn't help. Is he going into anaphylactic shock?" I watched, helpless as his tongue swelled and his skin took on a pallor of ashen gray. "Is there a different remedy we can give him?"

"We don't have any other medicines here. The leeches are helping remove the swelling from his face. They have nothing to do with the allergy treatment." Dr. Rattanakosin said. "We need to put him on a ventilator, or we're going to have to perform another tracheotomy."

"A ventilator? Won't you have to induce a coma?" I asked, stepping closer to Harris' head. "Hang in there, buddy. Just relax." He clutched onto the oxygen mask as strong as the leeches clutched onto his skin. "Breathe as deep as you can. We're here, and everything will be just peaches soon. You hearing me?"

His golden eyes tried to open wide while he held on to me. His irises were ringed in black as he appeared to be turning into his werewolf form. "Harris, don't, buddy. Stay in control. You're gonna be a lot harder to fix if you wolf out on us." I grinned at him. "Don't make me take you to the vet."

"How b-big does Mr. Archer get when he morphs?" Dr. Rattanakosin's lip quivered in a nervous twitch.

"Well, the last I saw—he was maybe eleven feet long from nose to tail."

"Nurse, bring me propofol. We're going to need it." The doctor stepped toward the metal cabinet and took out padded restraints. He handed two of them to Khaldon. "Quick. Help me hold him. If he shifts, all our safety will be compromised. He'll especially be a danger to himself."

Blowing out a series of short breaths to gain control, I tried to relax when my eyes caught Khaldon's. Glacier prickles ran up my spine and tap-danced at the base of my neck. I turned to find Kalina staring at me. I challenged her. "This better not be any more of your shite, Kalina. Are you responsible for this?"

She shrugged as if our new emergency was intensely annoying to her. "I had nothing to do with it." She waved the back of her hand toward Harris. "But perhaps Kali should have chosen him instead."

I lunged at her, willing to choke the ever livin' hell out of her.

Khaldon held onto me while I jabbed a finger at her face. "One day, Kalina. One day, it'll be me and you."

She tilted her head accepting the challenge. "I look forward to it."

"I will put you both in restraints and call security if you two can't control yourselves." Dr. Rattanakosin gestured to the heavy belts he held.

Giving Kalina one last warning look, I focused my energy back onto Harris again. I bent down close to his ear and whispered. "I love you, bro. We're going to help you relax and sleep okay?" I slipped my hand into his. "I'm with you. Everything's gonna be all right when you wake up. Hang in there. You'll beat this."

Harris squeezed me back and nodded as best he could.

I watched them tie him down, remembering how helpless I felt when I awoke blind and bound. I didn't wish that on anyone. Well, maybe Kalina.

I've got to stay with him and let him know he's safe. What am I going to do about Sheridan?

Another nurse hustled in and laid a tray with a white bottle next to Torchy's bedside. She checked his IV lines and ran his vitals. She recorded the findings on her tablet and then left again.

We watched as the hospital staff intubated Harris for the respirator. Inducing his coma couldn't have come at a better time. His hands elongated, sprouted fur, and long, black claws extended below where his fingernails normally were. The ventilator manually inflated his lungs and hummed with a *whoosh-whoosh* sound. His life support machine showed he was stable, and his face looked as peaceful as a puppy after a long day of tug-o-war.

"He needs special treatment for several more days," the doctor said, standing back from the table. "He is not in any position to be discharged. We are sending him to the specialists at the poison control center in Bangkok."

I rubbed my temples. This was too much. "Khaldon, I don't know what to do. Daddy just called me, and he said they're taking Sheridan to the emergency room. She may be going into premature labor."

"Bloody hell, could this day get any worse?" Khaldon pulled on fistfuls of his hair close to his scalp.

I blew out puffed cheeks. "We need to stay here for Harris, but we've got to be there for Sheridan."

As though on cue, Torchy sat up in a screaming fit. He clutched his stomach and threw up in the trashcan next to the bed. "Fire, me gut's on fire."

"What do you need, Torch? Water, ice, dry ice?"

Khaldon gave me side-glance while a smirk turned up the corner of his lips. "He needs an antacid. Albeit a boat load of antacid."

"Is that supposed to be a joke or something?" I asked.

"I was waiting for that." Dr. Rattanakosin opened the white bottle on the tray next to Torchy and measured a milky substance into a glass. "Here, help me get him sat up."

Khaldon and I helped Torchy to sit. He was wobbly but stabilizing. He held his shaking hands out for the glass.

"Here, drink this. It will help keep the fire squelches down. It won't douse the flames completely, but it will help control them."

Torchy gulped the chalky liquid while it ran out the sides of the glass and down his cheeks. He held the glass out. "More," he gasped. "I need more."

"That's enough for now. Give it a few minutes to work. Once you gave up your adrenaline, your system didn't have as much to burn. Now, we must treat your stomach ulcers and other maladies until you can chemically modify your system and build up your stores again."

"Wait. You knew about this, and you didn't tell him?" I clenched my fists on my hips again totally getting tired of how much Dr. Rattanakosin didn't communicate to us.

"If I had told you, would it have made any difference? Were you going to just let your friend die?" The doctor studied me through with his ancient Coke bottle glasses. His eyes questioned me as if I were a tiny bug under his microscope lens.

"No. Of course not. But we could've found another donor. Like his father." I stared at Kalina and her eyes met my glare. "Or sister."

Khaldon slapped Torchy's back. "Mate, Sheridan is going into labor."

Torchy's face changed from utter pain to surprised worry in an instant. "Wait? Is she all right?" Torchy tried to get up off the bed but nearly fell to his knees. "The bairns? They're two weeks early. We've got to get back to the States."

"Whoa, there, big fella." Khaldon held on to Torchy's arm and helped him back up. "I guess I'm a wee bit weaker than I thought." Torchy gained his balance and sat straighter. "Ya, wanker, you're not leavin' me here if Sheridan's in trouble. We'll need to fly home." He wiped his face with a warm, wet towel the nurse provided him.

"But we can't leave with Harris like this." I pointed at Kalina. "What if Miss Life-For-a-Life over there decides Tiffany wasn't enough, and she wants to take him out too? I don't trust her."

Khaldon grinned from ear to ear, and he snapped his fingers up beside his head. "We don't have to leave him alone. I have trusted allies close by. They'll come in and watch over him. Harris will be as safe with them here, maybe even safer."

I studied Khaldon from the corner of my eyes as I stepped closer to Harris. "What do you mean?"

Khaldon turned and swiped open his phone. Moments later, he spoke in a language I couldn't recognize. It wasn't exactly Farsi, but it wasn't Spanish either. Hell, for all I knew it could have been his native Egyptian or Latin.

Harris' breathing was steady, his hands in loose fists. Even though he was unconscious, I tried to reassure him on some level that he wasn't alone.

Khaldon swiped off the phone. "Dog's Bollocks! Vhalencia, Ichi, Devdan, and Chuck will be here in a few hours. You can count on them to take care of Harris. They'll watch out after Briggs as well."

"We don't need anyone else looking out after my brother." Kalina took a defensive posture above his body as though she were a momma eagle guarding her nest. "I'm here, and no one will do anything to him."

"Could you be any more melodramatic?" I asked.

Kalina straightened and went back to inspecting her fingernails.

I pulled on Khaldon's sleeve. "Who are these people, and why would you trust them to take care of my family?"

"It's quite simple really. Vhalencia is my progeny. She is family too."

Chapter 10

Cheyenne O'Cuinn

The noonday sun beat down on me with the force of a lead pipe while the tang of hot asphalt and greasy street vendor food produced a heavy cloying sensation in my mouth. My stomach grumbled with an ache for more blood. Live blood. Not that pasteurized, in-a-plastic-bag type of blood. I needed the real deal—or Cheetos. I couldn't tell anymore.

The hunger surging through my veins ran deeper. It was getting to the point where I was desperate enough to drain a human, a dog, or even a rat. Any minute, I was going to start looking for places to stash bodies.

My filthy clothes clung to me with the remnants of my little sister, blood, and sweat. I dared a sniff under my arms and was rewarded with my own foul, pungent odor.

I was in dire need of a shower.

Paramedics drove up with the ambulance to transport Harris to the poison control center. Looking skyward, desperately hoping for inspiration, I silently waited for that inner voice to give me a hint that my decision was the right one.

I should leave with Harris, but dammit, I have to get back to Sheridan.

Khaldon walked up to me with four people I'd never seen before.

It took me off guard to be meeting his closest friends while I looked, felt, and smelled pathetic. But it's inevitable, right? No one ever sees you dressed up in your best. But be damned if you run to the 7-11 for gas, a bottle of Coke, and some powdered donuts with your hair thrown up in pony tail and pre-period breakouts all over your face. Of course you're wearing the pajama bottoms you didn't bother to change out of either. You'll run into three people you haven't seen since high school.

Khaldon held his hand at the small of a woman's back. "Cheyenne, I would like to introduce you to Vhalencia De La Fuente. The slyest fox of a thief you'll ever have the pleasure of meeting." Khaldon presented me with a stunningly beautiful Spanish woman on his arm.

Shell-shocked, I gawked at her and secretly coveted the leather thigh-high boots that seemed to accentuate every curve of her muscular legs. She had to be the most attractive lady I'd ever seen, with feathery black hair and seductive brown eyes. Her mouth was alluring, even to me.

Seriously? She is his progeny? So that is who he must have been contacting when he showed Ludovic how to mind-message Dakota.

Khaldon continued his introductions of the three intimidating men standing beside him. "This is Ichi Murasaki—our master healer of Eastern medicine. Devdan Sarat—a clerical mage with a deadly prayer. And Chlodochar Lothar, our alchemist of the group, but everyone calls him Chuck. He's quite handy with a chainsaw, too."

He gestured to all of them with a broad spread of his hands. "These crazy peeps are my family. I am honored to finally introduce you. My crew—this is m'lady—Cheyenne O'Cuinn."

They resembled an ancient wall of unified purpose, as though they'd been a team, a made-for-each-other family, for a millennium. For all I knew, they had. I envisioned a battlefield tapestry hanging somewhere or an oil painting of this troupe after a night of debauchery and human exploit.

Standing in front of me, they revealed silly grins on their faces possibly hiding an ancient mystical secret. It seemed they knew quite a bit more about me since I apparently knew nothing about them.

Not sure whether to curtsy, nod, or shake their hands, I swallowed and tried to plaster a genuine smile despite the fact I was still covered in goo and reeked to high heaven. Plus, I would be turning Harris over to their care in a few minutes.

"It's a pleasure meeting you. I wish I could say I've heard more of you, but I don't believe an opportune time has come up." I perked an eyebrow in Khaldon's direction.

Vhalencia peeked up at Khaldon and winked. I imprisoned the green monster crawling out of my heart and managed to keep him at bay. She stepped forward and hugged me tightly around the shoulders and then held my face close to hers as she studied me.

She turned her head toward Khaldon without letting go. In a thick Spanish accent, she greeted me. "Oh, Señor Khaldon, she is simply captivating. Wherever did you find her? She is so … American."

Devdan snapped off a picture from a camera hung around his neck, and Vhalencia pinched my cheeks like I was a Christmas puppy.

I smiled, stepped back, and broke the embrace, managing to square my shoulders and speak the best Irish I could muster. "I was born in Kerry, Ireland, and bloody proud of it."

"Of course you were, my dear." She patted my shoulder and then discreetly wiped her hand on her hip-huggin' jeans. Vhalencia pulled a Kleenex out of her bag and glanced at Khaldon and then back at me. "Now don't you worry about a dhing. We are here to take care of your brother, Harris, isn't it?"

I tried to correct her, but she didn't allow a single word.

"No worries, my sweet. We'll have him under 24/7 security guard. He'll never be alone." She peeked back over her shoulder and giggled. "You're practically family."

She handed me an overnight bag. "Here, I brought you a change of clothing, some personal toiletries, some makeup…." She rumbled through the bag and pulled out a small crystal vial with a hose-and-bulb spray pump. She spritzed the toilet water into the air. "Some perfume...." She held her fingers under her nose, but she smiled and danced her eyes, all while breathing in the crisp, clean scent of lavender. "And a little gift from all of us. We are so endeared to finally meet you." She cupped my cheek and pursed her pouty lips. She turned to stare at Khaldon and placed her hands on her hips as though this topic had been a bone of contention. "Unfortunately, we are meeting under such trying circumstances. *Tsk tsk tsk*. I'm sure next time our visit will be much nicer. I hope you'll come to the villa soon."

Not sure what to say, I opened my mouth to thank her, but she seemed to be done with me and moved on to the next shiny thing.

"Where's my Torchy? I simply must see him before we leave." Vhalencia gracefully pirouetted and scanned the area for him.

Can you say "squirrel?"

"Thank you, but you didn't have to. I just haven't had a chance to—"

Vhalencia looked back at me pressed and her index finger to my lips, flashing me a sweet wicked grin.

"It was nothing. When Señor Seters asked me to bring you a few dhings, we couldn't resist."

Her smile was so contagious; it actually made my whole body feel better. I couldn't quite put my finger on the reason, but if I had to describe Vhalencia, I would venture to say she reminded me of my sister Dakota. Or at least the way she used to be. Immaculate, manicured, beautiful, and not a hair out of place. Always giving me little presents and wanting me to fix myself up. I wanted to like her, but now knowing she was also a master thief, I knew there was no way I would ever completely trust her.

Chuck picked me up and tossed me into the air a couple times like I was a rag doll. The bile in my stomach threatened to come up. He was huge and his arms were as big around as my thigh.

Ichi said, "You make her toss cookies. Put her down." Ichi reached up and eased me down from Chuck's grasp.

Chuck then handed me a bottle of pomegranate bloodwine, and my stomach fell in love with him.

I hope this stuff isn't from an illegal blood orchard.

"Oh, thank you. You're a saint."

"*Ja*, I've been called vorse," Chuck winked.

"Chainsaw, huh?"

He shrugged. "It gets the job done." His eyes grew wild as though he were begging for some of that action Khaldon had spoken of before.

"Yeah, that's a little frightening." I patted his chest. It was as solid as an oak door.

Why weren't these guys with us on that island?

From a distance, I heard Torchy call out, "I'm here, Vhal."

An orderly pushed him in a wheelchair out toward us.

Vhalencia darted her eyes back at me and winked, "Enjoy the goodies.

I'll see you soon, my dear. Ta ta!"

Ichi handed me a little gold paper sack. "You take these twice day. It will heal damage no object has touched." He handed me the bag with both hands. I accepted his gift in kind, and then he held a hand over his heart.

Was he offering me Chinese herbs for depression?

Ichi was straight out of a kung-fu movie. He could have been a brother to Master Pai Mei from *Kill Bill*. His brilliantly white top knot hair was held up with a wooden chopstick. I'm sure the ornamental stick had seen more action than sushi. He stroked his white beard down to a point on his chest. His outfit was complete with the little black bootie shoes kung fu fighters wore. I wasn't about to piss off this guy.

"Thank you. Do I take them on a full stomach?"

Ichi bowed toward me, and I returned the gesture remembering to look him in the eyes.

For the briefest of moments, he smiled, and then as soon as it arrived, it fled once again.

"Bù, you drink first thing in morning and then in twelve hour. No soon, no later."

"Okay, got it. I will take them until they're gone." I bowed again and Devden snapped another photo.

I turned my attention to him. "Oh, please don't. I'm a total wreck. I'm a grand-prize winner for one of *The Walking Dead* premieres. All I need is to lose a shoe, and I'd be complete."

Devden laughed in a quick *ha-ha-ha*. He wore a white turban and a knee-length dress shirt of sorts. The leather boots were made of a laced-up suede and flat-footed soles. He also toted a formidable blade at his side.

"Is that a scimitar?" I reached to touch the hilt but then thought better of it. "Do you carry an exclusive license for that thing?"

Devden laughed out loud once again. "*Babuji*, you never told me she would keep me in stitches."

Khaldon slapped him on the back. "Oh yes. Stick with her, and you'll never know what bodily harm she may do to you." He blew me a kiss.

I scowled at him.

Devden pulled the scimitar out of the leather catch he wore around his waist and held out the intimidating blade. "I finished this myself."

I gawked at the mastery of the craftsmanship and gently handed it back to him. This guy was definitely not someone to mess with. I shook my head in disbelief. "Wow, I don't have words for how beautiful this is. I hope one day to watch you work."

From what I could tell, Devden blushed at my words and gave me a small bow, accepting my compliment. "I sometimes will hold expeditions at Torchy's Super Market locations. Perhaps you'll see me there one day."

My eyes shone with delight. "Yes, I would truly enjoy that very much."

"Vait ein minute. I pounded the heavy metals, Devdan." Chuck stood straighter and taller than before.

Dude was an oak and looked like he could break one in half.

"It took both of us together to make that blade. Devdan does the fine finishing details." A look of immense pride came over both of the men as Chuck continued. "Ve are ein good team."

I turned to Khaldon. "Why weren't these guys with us on that island?"

Khaldon's eyes grew as wide as an Anime character as if the thought never occurred to him. He opened his mouth to answer but I hushed him.

"Hold that thought," I said.

The paramedics wheeled Harris out, and I ran over before they could load him into the ambulance. I reached for his hand, hoping he might have gained enough consciousness for me to explain the circumstances.

No luck.

I knew he couldn't squeeze back, but I wanted him to know he was not alone and he was going to be all right soon. At least I prayed he would.

I glanced up at the laughter and commotion from Torchy. It was good to see his spirits up. He apparently knew these people and seemed more at peace than I had ever seen him. I trusted his judgment, so I presumed they were legit. Vhalencia bent over and kissed him soundly on the mouth.

Interesting ... maybe too good. They sure are a friendly bunch.

Khaldon placed his hand in the small of my back. "Are you all right, m'sweet?" He gazed down at Harris and also touched his shoulder as well. It was though he completed a circuit of love between us.

I halfway nodded and tilted my head in a shake, not clear on how I felt or what to say. Dazed, numb, and starving, I wanted nothing more than to hit *control-Z* on this whole ordeal and return to pre-SHTF—shit hit the fan—days. Bygone was the time when everyone was alive, no one was undead, no one was a demon, vampire, werewolf, or a dragon. My so-called life was normal.

Khaldon leaned in and squeezed my hand. I looked down at Harris and worried the fabric of the sheet between my fingers. Even though I didn't know them, Khaldon had called in close friends, family members, to watch Harris for me. I would have to trust, something I wasn't especially adept at.

"It's going to be fine. I'm sure we'll be able to talk to him by tomorrow. Ichi and Chuck will be with him constantly, and you can text them anytime you want, all right?" Khaldon's calm reassurance helped to reduce the tension that had been building in my gut.

With Harris still harnessed to the bed, Ichi, Chuck, and the paramedic bumped elbows to noses more than once. He tried to make the fellas exit the ambulance, but their stoic faces told everyone they weren't leaving.

Somewhat placated that things would be all right for Harris, Chuck nodded to me. His silent gesture purchased me a moment to exhale a held breath of discomfort.

Torchy called out, "They're releasing you too, mate?"

I popped my head up and noticed Kalina hurriedly pushing Briggs in a wheelchair away from the entrance and toward a red pickup truck.

I gave Harris' toe one last squeeze. "Please guys, take care of him for me. I wish I had more time to get to know you." I handed Chuck an envelope. "Could you give this to him when he wakes up?"

Ichi Murasaki bent forward in a *namaste* type hand gesture. Chuck took hold of the envelope and stuffed it in his breast jacket pocket. In a strong German accent said, "*Ja*, it vould be my honor to deliver zis message to him vhen he avakes." Chuck then blew me a kiss.

These guys are friendly, I'll give them that.

"Thank you." I released the bed rail and instinctively kissed the tips of my fingers, blowing kisses back to the men. I prayed for the Goddess to shower healing and protection over them all.

I ran after Briggs.

"What the hell are you doing?" I caught up to Kalina and pulled on her upper arm to stop her from moving. "Where are you going with him?" I squinted at the sunlight bouncing off the concrete pavement. "How are you even able to leave here of your own free will, or are you bailing before the cops get here?"

My grasp held firm. She had well-defined muscles under her shirt. A tattoo of a dragon slithered out from under her sleeve and snaked around my wrist. Heated red marks formed around my fingers where the purple dragon curled and dug in. Its claws and teeth were about to draw blood.

"What the...." I wrenched my hand away as Kalina jerked her bicep out of my grasp.

The dragon receded and whooshed away with the wind.

Her eyes spoke volumes of warning.

Khaldon rolled up, pushing Torchy in the wheelchair with Vhalencia and Devden beside him.

I turned to them. "Shouldn't Kalina be going to jail for Tiffany's murder or manslaughter or accidental on-purpose homicide or something?"

She opened her mouth to speak, but Briggs held out his hand to quiet her.

"Now, Chey Chey—the proper authorities 'ave been notified about dzis unfortunate incident with dze girl. But dzese things 'appen with 'umans, no? They're quite fragile to dze likes of us. I will be eternally grateful to the young lady, and I've ensured Tiffany's family receives closure and recompense."

I opened my mouth to protest, but Khaldon explained further. "It happens. Remember when you killed those innocents when you first changed? You didn't go to jail, did you? In fact, you were simply doing what came naturally. Humans are not the top of the food chain on this planet, and this is simply an incidental event. This death is justifiable in our culture because Kalina used the human power source to save Briggs' life. No crime was committed here. The real crime would have been to allow a dragon to perish."

Kalina dazzled a brilliant smile as the righteous indignation of the moment crashed over me like a cooler full of ice water. I understood it, and Khaldon was right.

I blinked at him. Hating his logic and my actions.

I had killed those kids and heaven knows who else, and I didn't land any trouble. It never even occurred to me that I would. Lord Stovall had sent out an absturger team for cleanup. Other than dealing with the guilt of my human emotions, I never thought about their deaths again.

Knowing I had properly been put in my place, I couldn't accuse Kalina of wrongdoing if I too had exacted the same crime against humanity.

But it wasn't a crime, it was survival. And Briggs needed to survive.

My eyes asked for agreement from Vhalencia and Torchy, but they had equally sad expressions on their faces and nodded their heads in agreement.

"I guess this is something I'll have to get used to." I rubbed my forehead and winced in the sunlight. I wished for a pair of sunglasses to hide my embarrassment.

"So help me understand," I scratched my head. "One person or two persons can easily go under the radar as missing and/or dead and it doesn't bother anyone, but illegal blood orchards and kidnapping people, that's a crime? Where is the line drawn in the sand? Who makes these decisions?"

Vhalencia stepped forward and brushed my arm. I marveled at her lyrical Spanish accent. "My dear, sweet one. De Queen Civetateo, of course. Stealing humans against their wills is not acceptable. But it certainly wouldn't be the first time in history it's happened. Each species has dheir own queen, and it is up to dhem if an actual crime has been committed. If one has, normally dhat person is subject to the dhrone for a period of time to conduct the royal bidding, but it's better dhan dying, don't you dhink?"

Devden spoke with a thick, East Indian accent. "Think of it this way. If it weren't for supernatural beings on this planet, the human race would have destroyed itself centuries ago. We have helped mankind survive many times over. Who do you think stopped the inquisitions and the wars? Humans are idiots, and they're on their way to blowing up the planet again. It won't be long until there is another intervention. Queen Civetateo has seen to that."

Briggs rubbed his hands together. "It's all right, *ma chére*. Don't you worry yourself about dzis untidy business, *oui*? My father notified the Draconian Council in this district. It's all 'andled. You need to go 'ome to Sheridan. I'm going to Tibet to be with family for a while."

I followed his eyes as he gazed up at the truck. "Truthfully, Chey Chey ... I need time to process dzis stuff with Dakota. I'm going to see if I can dig up any dirt about who owns dzat island." Wincing, he took as deep a breath as his incision would allow and tried to sit up straighter in his chair. He bent his face toward his lap, and before he brought up his head, his hand had wiped away tears he wanted no one to see but me.

"Hey, you take it easy, and don't worry about anything, okay?" I attempted to keep the energy positive for him and found that practiced smile Amicula always used on me. "But you let me know if you need anything if you want to get out of Tibet."

I stood up and glared over at Miss Mother Hen, shielding my eyes from the sun reflecting off Briggs' wheelchair. I was pretty sure she was angling the handle to blind me. Secretly, I worried if Kalina wasn't something of an Annie Wilkes character from *Misery*. Visions of Kalina cutting off his legs to keep her brother captive filled my thoughts while I challenged her deep brown eyes. I gave Briggs a wry half-smile as Devden helped load him into the truck.

"Thank you. I'm sorry you had to go through all this. Don't worry about any of the hospital expenses. The company has it covered. Not sure we can claim it on workman's comp, though. We'll have to file it under hazardous duty pay. Can you imagine the insurance audit we would get?"

My voice failed me as thoughts of Dakota pooled into my eyes.

He tried to give me a deep belly laugh, but the pain was too much. He cupped my chin up in his hand. "Dzere is a massive 'ole in my 'eart I fear may never be filled. 'Ell, I don't even get dze pleasure of eating Ludovic after all dzis—and I had the perfect recipe!" He hugged me with the gentleness of a kitten as I touched his face. We both smiled. I was sure I heard Kalina growl low into the back of her throat while she slammed closed her driver's side door.

Khaldon shook Briggs' hand and said, "I'll see you again soon, my friend. Oh, I almost forgot your souvenir. Here's the dragon scythe. Thought you might want this. I am anxious to learn more about this magical blade. There's an interesting marking here on the bottom of the hilt. I took a rubbing of it to see if I can trace it back to its origins."

Briggs examined the scythe blade. "Looks Norse to me. Torchy, do you recognize this rune?"

Briggs passed the scythe to Torchy.

"Aye, I do. This blacksmith had a sense of humor, he did. This rune is called Kauma, which means ulcer. Surely gave yin one of those, didn't it?"

Briggs grimaced and nodded. His eyes revealed creased edges of worry into his brow.

Torchy handed Devden the scythe. "What do you think of this?"

Devden studied the rune engraved in the blade. "The meaning usually involves mortality and pain to whoever is unlucky enough to receive its gifts. Whoever commissioned to magically enhance this blade knew their Norse history and where to strike a dragon."

Everyone stood quiet and stared at the odd knife.

Torchy handed it back to Briggs. "You keep it. I dinnae want that bad juju hangin' around."

Briggs accepted the knife and scraped a splotch of dried blood off the hilt. The monogrammed letters DLR emerged. He creased his brow and then placed the blade on the seat between him and Kalina.

Devdan collapsed the wheelchair and loaded it into the bed of the pickup truck.

Through the rolled down window, Briggs reached out and took hold of Torchy's forearm. "I cannot thank you enough for helping me. I am forever indebted to you and to your selfless kindness."

Torchy saluted him. "*Aye*, if any of my old memories pop up, just squash them, will ya? I dinnae need any jokes of when I was a wee one and learning to fly." Torchy flattened his lips and shook his head, possibly recalling a long forgotten memory. "Weren't a proud sight. That's all I can say."

Briggs tried to laugh once again, but held his abdomen and grinned. "Indeed, I too remember those days. I am forever indebted to your soul, my brother."

"It has been a delight meeting you, mademoiselle. Sir. I hope to see you again one day." Briggs addressed Devden and Vhalencia.

Devden nodded his head and waved.

"Señor Briggs, it was a pleasure." Vhalencia warmed the bitter cold of separation between us all.

"If I don't hear from you in a month—I'm coming after you." I glanced over at Kalina, letting her know my comment was directed more toward her than it was to him. "I'll keep you abreast on what kind of memorial services we'll hold for Dakota. I have no idea when or where. Hell, I'm scared to death just to tell the rest of the family."

He summoned up a wry smile for me and nodded. "I do not envy you that moment, Chey Chey."

He then sent me a mind message in my head. *I will always be able to contact you, Cheyenne. We have an established link. Thank you for everything. Contact me if you need anything.*

I snapped my eyes up to his. He winked at me with his blue opalescent orbs. I'd forgotten the communication bond link we'd shared when he was in dragon form. I felt a ton better knowing he was also going to be all right.

A remake of Pat Benatar's song, "Heartbreaker" by Heaven Below screamed out of the speakers as Kalina revved up the engine and raced out of the parking lot. The ambulance Harris was in had also pulled out to take him to the poison center.

I wrapped my arms around my chest, my heart aching.

Will I ever see them again?

Chapter 11

Orlando Hospital ~ Florida

Cheyenne O'Cuinn

The doors to the elevator couldn't close fast enough. I swore I could have run the emergency stairs faster than the lift moved. Finally, the chime rang and granted us passage to the maternity ward on the eighth floor. I bolted to the nurses' station while Khaldon pushed Torchy in a wheelchair.

"Sheridan O'Cuinn. What room?" I didn't even wait for an answer—I stared at the patients' board behind the computers and found her name assigned to room 813. I ran down the hallway, the nurse hot on my heels.

"Miss, miss! I'm sorry, but you'll have to prepare. You can't just go in there—she's in isolation."

I stopped on the balls of my feet just outside her door. It wasn't an ordinary room. It had an observation window with glass partitions and hanging curtains.

I peered through the glass. "What's going on? What do I need to do?"

"Is that you, Cheyenne?"

Refocusing my attention on the nurse, I blinked. "Ruthie Anne?"

I recognized her as the grandmotherly nurse who had taken care of me. I was in this very hospital, recovering from my rogue vampire attack a few months ago, and Ruthie Anne was the best nurse on staff. I simply loved her. She'd taken amazing care of me, and I knew she would be excellent with Sheridan.

Ruthie Anne lowered her voice to a whisper. "Are you Sheridan's sister?"

I hugged her, and it wasn't just a pat, pat, pat hug. It was a full-bodied bear hug. "Yes, it's wonderful to see you again. Are you her nurse, too?"

"I'll tell the OB-GYN nurse that we're prepping you." She hugged me back and put her hand under my chin. "My, how well you've come back from the dead. I just can't believe it."

If she only knew.

"What do I need to be prepped for?" I scanned through the glass wall to try and find Sheridan.

Khaldon and Torchy caught up to us. "Cheyenne, listen—this might not be easy for you to accept. Most likely what's happening is she's in massive labor pains because the babies are ready, but her body isn't. She may have to have a Cesarean-section."

I slowed my thoughts and considered what Khaldon said. I massaged my temples trying to evade that sick headache nagging in the back of my eyes.

A C-section! I'm glad we got here when we did.

Ruthie Anne asked, "Are either of you two gentlemen the father?"

I looked up at Khaldon. He ran a stressed hand through his hair. "I am, but I don't think it's appropriate I'm in there with you, Cheyenne."

I nodded in agreement but was saddened by the circumstances. This was too surreal—as if we were in the Middle Ages, where men didn't go into the birthing rooms. They stayed outside in waiting lounge areas and passed out cigars of congratulations while the women did all the labor-intensive work.

But that wasn't the case with this odd, cantilevering family.

Khaldon and Sheridan had been vicious victims of kidnapping, rape, and insemination. Neither of them had ever even met until it was discovered they were going to be parents.

My first instinct was to keep him out, but I thought it better to ask Sheridan what she wanted to do. "I'm not sure either one of you should be in there. Torchy, I know you love her, but I'll ask her what she wants to do, okay? I'm sure Daddy could use a break anyway."

Torchy slapped Khaldon on the back. "No worries, we'll go out and find ourselves a few Cuban Montecristo cigars and keep Kiernan company." He grinned at me. "We can wait—it's what is best for Sheridan. That's what's important."

We all knew Torchy was joking at the seemingly sexist decision we'd made, but I was less nervous knowing that my sister wasn't going to have to show off her girly bits.

I turned to Ruthie Anne, "Okay—what do I need to do?"

Ruthie Anne curled her index finger at me. "C'mon, I have just the thing for you—but you better hurry. She's not long now."

Within ten minutes, I emerged sanitized and suited up in scrubs, finally able to see her. Sheridan lay quietly in a warm Jacuzzi bath with an oxygen cannula in her nose while perusing a parenting magazine.

"Well, you don't look any worse for wear." Knowing I had made it in time, my heart warmed at her healthy maternal glow.

Sheridan looked up from her reading and smiled her classic cheesy grin at me. She was a sight for sore eyes. She seemed peaceful enough, but then she pulled back the shower curtain to reveal her swollen behemoth belly.

The mirror over the tub reflected black and purple bruises, which covered her entire abdomen. The coloring of her skin looked like someone had beaten her with a ball bat and sliced her with rusty razors. She had a patchwork quilt of bloody paper cuts. I fell to my knees and cradled her in my arms. "Oh my God, Sheridan. This is ... are you ... oh, my *gawd!* Are you all right?"

She mimicked a drunk, and her words slurred a bit. "Ima okay. They gave me somethin' a little while ago to help with the pain. I think the babaes are finally sleepin' again. But most of the time, the twins think my uterus is their personal jungle gym." She pulled on the transparent tube strapped over her ears. "I have to wear the oxygen, though. I guess it's cramped in there."

"Are there still just the two of them?"

Sheridan nodded. "Dr. Meyer is preparing me for a Cesarean. Says the babaes are ready to come out, but my body hasn't released any hormones to begin the birthing process."

I looked at Ruthie Anne for more explanation.

Ruthie Anne blotted Sheridan's head with a cool cloth and then held a straw for to drink small sips from a water cup. "She's spot on. We've been giving her the Pitocin typically used to bring on labor, but her cervix hasn't responded. We've been trying to keep her as comfortable as possible between sessions."

"Between sessions?" I scrunched up my face wondering just what the hell that meant.

"Here, come feel them move." Her face was that of an angel. Sheridan reached for a cup from under the water and then poured a cup of warm water over her belly. She ran her hand along the top of it. She seemed completely at peace with the fact these two kiddos were close to puncturing through her abdominal wall.

It was almost ... creepy.

I rubbed over her distended tummy. The movement inside her belly was like a cat scrambling to attack my foot under a blanket. My thoughts wandered as to what kind of beasty could sense where my hand was, and one that had fast enough reflexes to catch it.

Our eyes glistened as we smiled at one another. The unknowingness of the whole situation reminded me of the first night we went to Halloween Scream Nights. We were so scared to attend but so thrilled with anticipation we could simply burst. I suppose in her case now ... that's exactly what she was going to do.

"Oh, Sher—having children around the house is gonna rock. Can you believe it? Two unbelievable babies to take care of?" Pulling my hand out of the water, I reached for a towel. I wanted to help comfort her any way I could. "Did you bring a hair brush?"

"Yes, over in my ditty bag." Sheridan pointed across the room to the sink.

I loved it when we were younger, and we would spend hours braiding each other's hair. I picked around through her overnight case and found a half-eaten roll of Life Savers. I popped the lemon one into my mouth and offered her the next flavor.

"Mmm ... green, my favorite." She grinned as she slipped the sweet hard candy into her mouth when Ruthie Anne wasn't looking.

Her smile was a masterpiece to my eyes. What I wouldn't give to have a painting of how incredibly beautiful she looked amid the pain she'd been experiencing. I only wished I didn't have to ruin her visage with my tainted paint brush stained with Dakota's blood.

Rubbing her belly, Sheridan laughed, "Remember when we got grounded for a week 'cause I cut your bangs?"

I chuckled at the memory. "Right? Mom was ready to tan all our hides." A smile grew from ear-to-ear and genuinely warmed my heart. "Or the time we dyed Dakota's hair green on St. Patrick's Day with the food coloring we'd used in the cookies." I regretted my words as soon as they left my mouth. Hiding my face behind Sheridan's head, I didn't want her to catch sight of my eyes in the mirror as they welled up from the memory.

"Won't it be wonderful? One day we'll have wee little ones running around." Sheridan's eyes danced with future memories. "Me, you, Dakota. So many cousins. We'll have huge family reunions."

A miniature foot pushed up high against the inside of Sheridan's abdomen. My stomach lurched as it continued to push, stretching her skin. One inch ... and then two inches.

Sheridan hollered in guttural pain.

Her voice growing louder as the foot pushed higher and higher.

The nurse grabbed a towel and pushed against the wannabe escape artist.

Three inches. Sheridan's skin looked like it might split wide open.

Intense visions of *Alien* crossed my mind.

Were these kids going to eat their way out of her belly?

With the gentle counter pressure, the baby's foot finally subsided and disappeared back somewhere below the fleshy surface.

Sheridan's skin cracked, opening a wound seeping droplets of blood from the scabbed-over abrasions.

Sheridan held my hand as I kneeled in shock.

"Is—is that what's been happening to you? Is that why you look like you've been beaten with a tire iron and raked over with razor blades?"

She nodded. "Yes, they push to make room and it's been causing these contusions and ruptures." She heaved in a deep breath and pushed a little foot down from under her rib cage. She looked around. "Have you seen Daddy?"

"I saw him while I was changing into scrubs. Torchy and Khaldon are with him and grabbing a quick bite."

Her eyes brightened. "They're here too? Dakota—is she with you?"

I hedged.

Seriously not ready for this question, I thought of a way to stall.

I ran her red silken strands between my fingers. "Your hair is freaking gorgeous. I should try those prenatals you're taking."

"Thanks, but they make my toenails grow like crazy. Do you have any idea how hard it is to cut them when your belly is as big as this? It's feckin' impossible."

I couldn't contain my laughter with images of Sheridan rolling around on the bathroom floor trying to trim the nails.

Giggling, I said, "Umm ... this may sound a little weird, but do you want either Khaldon or Torchy in here with you during the delivery?"

She outwardly stared at nothing and blinked while I looked at her reflection in the mirror over the bathtub. I could tell the drugs were working, and I had successfully dodged the Dakota bullet for a few more minutes.

"Well ... uh—hmm? I really like Torchy and all, but ... we haven't ... ya know." She blushed with an expression on her face as if to say she didn't want her business laundered in front of Ruthie Anne. "So I don't ... wanna be *au naturel*."

"No worries. I totally get it." I waved my hand away in mock dismissal.

"Khaldon should be here for the birth of his kids, but it's not like we were ever dating or anything. He's your fella, not mine. Not that he isn't hot an' all that but—"

Ruthie Anne knitted her brows together. I could tell she was pretty confused by our conversation, but I wasn't about to explain what happened.

"No worries, sweetie. There's a waiting area right outside. I can hold up the babies for them. Would that be okay?"

A remarkable expression of relief crossed her face as Sheridan sighed. She didn't need any additional discomfort after everything she'd been through.

"I'll go tell the gentlemen to stay put then." Ruthie Anne gestured to the waiting room.

"Cheyenne—you haven't answered my question? Did you find out anything about Dakota?" She looked at me sideways as a hand slid across the top of her abdomen all the way to the bottom.

"That shite is spooky as hell, Sher."

She grabbed my arm and water splashed to the floor. In my head, I could hear her big sister voice without her saying a word. *You're not getting away from me that fast, li'l sis.*

"Cheyenne—please tell me. Where's Dakota? Is Ludovic with you? What do we need to do to make sure the babies are safe? I don't even know how to feed them."

I scanned the room to find the closest exit.

Can I go through with this?

I bit a fingernail as my stomach roiled in angst.

"Stop doing that. Mom always said biting your nails would give you worms."

Determined to stay strong, I picked up the hairbrush again. "Sheridan, I think we should wait after our precious babies are born to talk about this. Dr. Meyer will be back here any moment. They're prepping in the other room."

She hadn't released her hold on me and she dug in her nails. She stared me straight in the eyes.

I just couldn't do it. The words weren't coming. I needed to be strong for her. Sheridan didn't need to hear that her baby sister was dead.

"Cheyenne Madeline O'Cuinn. You tell me what's going on!"

My eyes pooled as my lips quivered. I pulled away from her grasp and sat on the outside edge of the tub. I laid the brush down and picked up the cup she had been using to pour the warm water over her belly. I filled it and watched a single drop of blood fall from my cheek and splash into the bath.

"There was an accident." I started.

"Ludovic isn't coming, is he?" she urged with increasing concern to her voice.

I shook my head. "Neither is Dakota. I don't want to go into details right now, Sher—but—"

I was cut off with Sheridan arching her back, up and over the edge of the tub. Her eyes bulged out of her face as her jaw locked and clenched tight.

Ruthie Anne ran, and I screamed bloody horror.

Chapter 12

"Help! Doctor, Nurse!" I ran toward the window separating the two rooms and banged on the glass to gain their attention. I hurried back to Sheridan just as she struggled to stand. I grabbed her as she fell hard against the side of the tub, grasping the safety rail on the wall. I could have sworn I heard ribs crack.

"Here, let me help you." I shoved my shoulder under her and reached around her body.

Sheridan's face flushed beet red. Her body tensed up in muscular cramps. She cradled her belly in her arms.

"You need to breathe. Don't hold in the pain. You're going to bust if you do that. Breathe with me."

Sheridan let out a huge exhale and then panted in quick, short breaths. "It hurts ... too much. They're ... killing ...me!"

"Let's get you over to the bed." One step at a time, I eased her over to the bed. Her breaths coming a little easier.

The bed had been lowered, allowing her to crawl up onto it. Her abdomen sagged under her delicate frame as though she were giving birth to an elephant instead of two infants.

Hands, feet, and a face pushed out against her sides. I could have sworn I heard the rib micro-fractures from the internal pressure. At this point, I wasn't sure if the demon possessed dhampirs weren't eating their way out of her belly.

Witnessing the writing faces push through her skin, I reminded my own self to breathe.

Sheridan rocked back and forth on her hands and knees.

Dr. Meyer shot through the door with two additional nurses. "What's developed?"

"They're digging their way out of her!" I cried.

Ruthie Anne placed an oxygen mask over Sheridan's mouth and we encouraged her to take deep breaths. Sheridan favored her aching side and gasped for more oxygen.

Ruthie Anne grimaced. "I'm afraid she might have punctured a lung. I need to inform Dr. Meyer."

We helped Sheridan get into the position for the epidural pain block needed for the surgery.

"You'll be feeling much better soon, Ms. O'Cuinn." Ruthie Anne rubbed her shoulders and tried to give her a kind smile. I was pretty sure Ruthie Anne hadn't seen the likes of anything like this before either.

I shook my head in confusion and rubbed my own belly out a sheer sympathy pains. "How will they be able to do this procedure with the babies moving so hard? Do they calm down?"

Sheridan gasped for breath. "It ... it comes in waves. They'll calm down in a minute ... or two."

They handed my sister a funky shaped pillow and had her lean forward. I stood in front of her face and helped her to focus on me. I peeked over her shoulder as they inserted a huge-assed needle into her spine. I winced at the sight but stayed stoic to help keep her calm.

Who was I fooling? To help keep me calm too. She was the one who was important here, not me. Within minutes, the tension in her muscles relaxed, and she was breathing easier. I relaxed finally feeling as though this situation were under control.

Suddenly she screamed out, "My legs! I can't feel my legs!"

She grabbed onto my shoulders to steady herself as she fell sideways. The nurses helped her to lie down into the birthing position.

"It's okay. The medicine is working. Remember, Dr. Meyer and the anesthesiologist said this would happen." Ruthie Anne rubbed Sheridan's shoulders and spoke in such a kind, grandmotherly tone. "Shh, now. You won't feel anything from your chest down, okay? So just relax, everything is going all right." Ruthie Anne tried to smile. "We'll be holding those little ... darlings soon."

You could tell she was trying to be as polite as possible. Did any of us really know what was going to come out of Sheridan's uterus? What if they were demon babies like in *Rosemary's Baby*?

I watched as a tiny fist pushed up three inches or more out of her stomach. The mottled yellow and deep purple skin around the little hand started to crack and bleed as this was somehow a favorite pushing spot. I plucked a nearby towel from the counter and applied gentle counter-pressure against the protruding hand.

The alien creature retreated.

"Everything okay?" Sheridan probed. Her eyes were bleary-looking.

Ruthie Anne's eyes were as big as mine. "I take it you didn't feel that?"

"Feel what?"

"Okay—good. It's almost time. They're gonna move you into the surgery room. Hold on, Sher. They're almost here." I stroked her face and smiled as best I could to calm her and myself.

Unholy hell this is an emotional roller coaster. Stay strong for her. You can collapse later; right now, this is all about Sheridan.

Faster than I was ready for it, Dr. Meyer and the surgical staff had moved Sheridan into an operating room. They dressed me in a hair net and shoe booties so I could keep her company since all the uber-scary surgical stuff was going on behind the curtain.

They had Sheridan's arms strapped down with IVs to the arm boards and she could barely move from being so weak.

She scrunched up her face as though trying to remove a fly from her cheek. "My face is itchy, Chey, can you scratch my nose?"

"Miss O'Cuinn that is a side effect from the pain blocker medicine. I promise the itchies will go away soon." The chief operating nurse hung two IV bags and plugged them into her line.

She sighed in relief as I scratched the phantom itches.

Sheridan took a deep breath. And then another. And then another. She tried to sit up. "I ... I c-can't breathe. Hard ... t-to breathe."

The anesthesiologist called out. "Dr. Meyer, her pressure is dropping. I need to load her to maintain enough system blood pressure."

I didn't like the sound of that. We didn't need any more complications.

They adjusted various things about her and turned up her oxygen. She resumed breathing easier once again.

Sheridan's eyes laser focused on me. I could feel and smell her fear. She was genuinely frightened for her life, and I was too.

She tightened her grip on my hand as I looked into her blue eyes. "I love you, Sher. I know I'm not always the best sister in the world, but I've always loved you, and I promise I'll be here for you and the babies."

Dr. Meyer called out. "All right, Miss O'Cuinn—you're going to feel some tugging and pulling, but you won't feel any pain, okay? Are you good? We're ready to bring them into the world if you are."

She smiled a nervous half-grin as a single tear escaped. "I'm so scared, Chey. I don't think I can do this."

"You are the strongest woman I know. You will do this and I will be right here beside you. Pinkie swear!" I kissed her hand and another tear slowly descended down her cheek.

A glorious sweet, gentle cry rang out in the room. It was the most joyous sound I'd ever heard. I imagined it to be the sigh of an angel.

Sheridan's eyes cascaded over with tears. She opened and closed her hands, "I want to hold them. Please, let me see."

"We're getting *her* cleaned up. I'm bringing your little girl right over!" Ruthie Anne handed the infant daughter to Sheridan, but she was too weak to hold her. I held the delicate bundle so she could gaze into her daughter's beautiful dark blue eyes. She had a full head of raven black hair. Her features were an enchanted melding of Sheridan and Khaldon. They might not have planned this, but they sure did make adorable babies.

"What's her name?" I asked.

"Teagan Aisling—after Mom."

I lost my words as my breath hitched in my chest. Another cry rang out in the room.

This one had a real set of pipes.

The piercing wail startled Teagan in my arms as she also cried once again. Sheridan stroked Teagan's little cheek, and she calmed down immediately. Teagan mouthed her fingers.

"She must be hungry. Are you planning to breastfeed them?" I asked.

Sheridan nodded as best she could. Her eyes had glazed over. I wondered if she could see Teagan at all.

I dared a peek over the separation sheet, only to see Sheridan's insides in a bloody mess everywhere. Dr. Meyer's hand had disappeared deep inside her. If I hadn't known any better, I would have thought she wasn't going to live through this. I swallowed hard.

Thank goodness Vhalencia had brought Khaldon and me enough blood to consume on the plane. Otherwise with all of Sheridan's blood everywhere, I wasn't so sure if I could squelch the rapid desire to feed off my sister.

"This big guy sure has a healthy set of lungs on him." The nurse came over to show Sheridan her new son. Compared to Teagan, he was monstrous. He must have been over ten pounds. Teagan was such a delicate little flower, his antithesis.

"Do you have a name for your son?" the nurse questioned Sheridan.

"Khai Kiernan." She barely muttered through whispered lips.

I smiled realizing she used Khaldon's middle and our father's first names. They would be honored to learn she had named her son after them.

"Sher, you feeling okay?" I stroked her hair, and it looked as though she were falling asleep.

Smiling down at Teagan, I noticed something wasn't quite right. She was turning a little blue. Trying to remain calm, I looked for Ruthie Anne.

"I'll be right back, Sheridan." I stood up and took the baby over to the nurse. I whispered, "Something's wrong; Teagan's not pink anymore."

The staff immediately whisked Teagan away from me and left for the baby unit in the next room. I grasped the counter to hold myself up. Dread filled my heart as I felt my knees give way from under me.

I learned the surgical team had given Sheridan more relaxant to complete the final procedure, and I prayed Teagan would recover.

This is all normal.

I nervously sang Bob Marley's "Every Little Thing's Gonna Be Alright" between my teeth to calm my nerves. Who was I kidding when every human in the room stunk with worry and death? I had to trust them. I had to believe the Mother Goddess wouldn't abandon us right now. I had to believe Sheridan and Teagan would make it through. It was hard to trust when all other signs pointed in the opposite direction.

None of us had ever been around babies much, other than Dakota. Another shot of pain punched me in the gut with memories of holding Dakota when Mom came home from the hospital.

Another cry rang out and Khai filled the delivery room with healthy wails again. Swaddling him tight in a warm blanket, another nurse handed him to me.

I sat over by Sheridan once again. "Mommy, would you like to meet this young man you call Khai?"

Her eyes were completely out of focus, but she turned her head toward me and lifted a finger to touch his nose.

Her hand fell across her face with a thud.

Alarms blared out.

"She's crashing," the anesthesiologist called out.

"What's happening?" My voice demanded an answer and Khai cried out.

Sheridan's face fell completely slack, and her head drooped to one shoulder. Her mouth hung open as spittle ran out the corner.

Dr. Meyer stated, "She's losing a lot of blood. We need to stabilize her." He paused a moment and looked down at his shoe booties. "There's a chance, Cheyenne, we might lose her. She's frail and the twins may have taxed her more than she could handle."

"No! Get in there and fix her, dammit," I demanded. "Fix both of them!"

Dr. Meyer inhaled a deep breath and nodded. He immediately left me in a whirlwind of scrubs and medical terminology while machines screamed out more alarms informing the staff and scaring the hell out of me.

My body shook while holding Khai, and I watched as the doctors and nurses surrounded Teagan and Sheridan. Their faces stressed and creased with worry.

I can't lose both my sisters!

Ruthie Anne walked me to the adjacent room with the window next to the nursery. She sat me down and brought me a cup of water.

"Take a couple minutes now, deary. I know this isn't easy. Hang in there; you've got a healthy young man to parade right now." She handed me a crisp, fresh towel to wipe my face.

How can I possibly show off Khai knowing we could lose Sheridan and Teagan any minute?

I patted my eyes and tried to paint a proud auntie smile on my face before walking in to see my father, Khaldon, and Torchy.

Gaining some composure, I held Khai up to the window for everyone to see.

Baby Khai was simply radiant. His eyes were bright and wide awake. He marveled at everything and actively reached out and grabbed hold of my fingers.

Strong, handsome with a full set of raven black locks, like Teagan's. He looked like a miniature Egyptian god. An exact replica of his father, Khaldon.

Khaldon's eyes were affixed, possibly looking at the most amazing creature in the world. It occurred to me that I didn't know if Khaldon had ever sired any other children.

My father beamed with pride at seeing the young chap, and I could tell he was finally relieved to have a boy in the family. "Too much estrogen in this house for me," he always used to say when we were younger. "I'm going fishing."

It was hard to decipher what Torchy was thinking through the glass. He stood back a bit, allowing Khaldon and Daddy to have the best views. I wondered if he thought this kind of responsibility might be too much for him, but his energy expressed a radiant warmth of love.

Ruthie Anne emerged from the baby care center and asked to take Khai so she could footprint him. She then ushered me out of the room and to an area where Dr. Meyer would meet the family.

Over two hours later, Dr. Meyer joined us in the private waiting room and suggested we sit down. His face was weary, tired, and I sensed a terrible dread exuding from his pores.

I sat beside Khaldon and he reached for my hand. I held his fingers tight, fearing the coming words.

My father took a seat in a standalone chair next to us while Torchy stood stoic behind Dr. Meyer. The energy in the room kinked the knots in my stomach even tighter, as I desperately needed to know they were all right.

Dr. Meyer sat on a bench couch across from us. He swallowed hard and then looked me in the eyes. "We've had some complications." We all stood. Dr. Meyers held up his palms and asked us to sit again. "However, Sheridan is finally stable. She's lost a lot of blood. We're going to have to find an alternate way to help feed the baby."

"Oh, thank the Goddess!" I let out an exhale and sat on the edge of my seat, eager to learn all the details. "We can do that. Does the blood need to be wholly human or will our vampyric blood satisfy? Oh wait, will our blood do something odd to them?"

"That is a decision you'll need to address among yourselves. Whichever your choice, it could influence his development."

I looked at Khaldon; his face didn't seem to reveal any answers either. *Ludovic would have known what to do.*

"In the meantime, it's probably best to have him on the human sustenance that he needs. Sheridan has expressed she wants to breastfeed, but she won't be able to create that kind of nourishment for the dhampir until she's recovered."

Dr. Meyer looked at the floor and came up with a breath, stalling or bracing himself for an attack. "However, the infant girl … she … she did not make it. She had a faulty heart valve which we saw on the ultrasound this morning. We operated immediately, but her defective heart could not maintain an electrical rhythm."

My hands held my face in shocked horror. "What? You mean … Teagan didn't—"

My father inquired, "Teagan?" His face crumpled from the sound of mom's middle name. He scooted to the edge of his chair and held his head on his fists.

Khaldon whispered, "A daughter?"

"The boy is very healthy and does not seem to show any signs of the same heart defect. I'm very sorry for your family's loss," Dr. Meyer stated with saddened brows. His own face on the verge of crumpling in grief.

"But I was holding her!" I exploded. "She looked at us with the bluest of eyes. She was alive!" I stood up convinced I didn't hear right.

"You have us mixed up with some other patient. She has black hair!" My voice cracked with sobs. "She has blue eyes! Her name is Teagan!"

Dr. Meyer stood up, as did the rest of us. His eyes welled with emotion. He took my hands and enclosed them in his. "I'm sorry, Cheyenne. I know this is terribly difficult. This kind of news is always tragically bittersweet." He steadied himself. "Fortunately, mom and son are doing well, and you'll be able to see them in a little while. But we'll need to make arrangements for her daughter."

Torchy had moved closer to Dr. Meyer. The tendons in his neck protruded. His rigid muscles clenched his jaw tight. It looked like he was doing everything he could to keep from shifting and eating the doctor.

Khaldon's chin trembled as he pulled me in close to him. His own breath hitching in his chest.

I squinted in denial and suddenly became intensely sick to my stomach. "Dr. Meyer, does Sheridan know?"

He cleared his throat. "She's still unconscious." He stalled and shifted his weight to the other foot. "This is going to be very difficult when she awakes and wants to see her daughter. I strongly encourage you to be here for her when she wakes up."

A fog of sludgy silence filled the room. I fell into a vortex of mind-numbing grief.

This isn't happening! Oh dear, God! No! I'm begging you ... No!

Kind, gentle hands lay upon my back as I sobbed uncontrollably.

Torchy whispered an Irish prayer in Gaelic. My father joined in, and by the time the prayer was over we all were whispering the words between heaving sobs.

May the road rise to meet you.
May the wind be always at your back.
May the sun shine warm upon your face.
May the rains fall soft upon your fields and until we meet again, little Teagan.
May the Lord hold you in the palm of His hand.

I reached out for my family to anchor me in this reality. We hung our heads in desperate prayers, heaving chests, and vanquished hearts.

What did we ever do to deserve this?

Chapter 13

Tears are the Silent Language of Grief.
~ Voltaire

Cheyenne O'Cuinn

It was the fourth worst night of my life. The first being the night we learned our mother was murdered. The second when I was left for dead by a rogue vampire. The third when Dakota was killed in front of me, and then—last night.

It was the worst.

We had a tormented, painful evening explaining to Sheridan what had happened with Teagan. She screamed, demanding for us to leave, insisting we were lying to her, and accusing us of stealing her daughter.

Frantically, Sheridan's wild eyes searched for Teagan from room-to-room. She banged on patients' doors, convinced someone was hiding her. There was one baby who had a very similar cry to Teagan's, and Sheridan demanded to see the child. She accused the other mother of cutting the baby's hair and dying it blond. She wanted to contact the FBI.

If I were honest with myself, I can't say I would have acted any differently if the same situation had happened to me.

Dr. Meyer administered a sedative to help calm her down, but Sheridan's inconsolable wailing continued to echo through the halls. I was afraid she would rupture her staples clamoring to be let into the nursery. The hospital staff called security and moved Sheridan to a room much further away from the rest of the maternity patients.

On Dr. Meyer's orders, the nursing staff administered a second sedative to help Sheridan find comfort, but the only thing that would quiet her was holding Khai in her arms. Finally, while I stroked her hair, and Torchy holding her beside him, she fell into a disquieted sleep as the drug took effect. She jerked while sleeping, and I could tell she was still searching for Teagan even beyond the veil.

I prayed Morpheus could bring her the peace none of us had been able to provide. My heart ached for women who had still-born babies and had to leave the hospitals with empty baby baskets.

It was real horror. The kind you prayed never happened to you or your family.

The hospital staff asked that we leave for a while and find solace and rest for ourselves. I regretted leaving Sheridan alone. It didn't feel like the right thing to do, but there was nothing any of us could do but love and support her.

By mid-morning the next day, Daddy, Khaldon, Torchy, and I returned to the maternity ward hoping to help ease the suffering of the prior events. Unfortunately, I knew Sheridan's heartache and pain were only halfway done.

I had to be the one to deliver the final blow.

I watched as Sheridan cradled and rocked baby Khai in an instinctive motherly fashion. She seemed to be receptive to my presence, despite last night's events. I wondered if she even remembered what had happened. There was a part of me that hoped she didn't.

"Ya know, Sheridan—I've heard of breastfeeding advocates, but I can tell you, I've never met a bloodletting advocate."

Sheridan waved goodbye to the ladies who stopped by to help her with Khai's new feeding schedule. "I wasn't really sure what to expect either, Chey. It's not like I would find an article in *Time Magazine* about how to blood-feed your dhampir child."

"You have a valid point." I tried to paint on the kindest smile I could muster.

Sheridan seemed much calmer than the night before, almost as if a sense of peace had come over her. Captivated by the antics of her new son, she continued the conversation. That was a good sign.

"At least Dr. Meyer helped me learn how to feed him naturally. I didn't want to try to drain blood from a shunt and then bottle-feed."

I asked the question I'd been thinking for weeks. "How in the world is your body going to keep up? Won't you like shrivel up or something?"

"I thought so too, but I'm not the first human to have a dhampir child." She actually smiled at my silly question and tweaked Khai's nose. "Dr. Meyer instructed me to drink three times as much water and electrolytes than I did before. Plus he prescribed these specialty vitamins to avoid anemia." She shrugged as though she were feeding a normal, human baby. That fact that Khai needed blood to help sustain his system didn't seem to be any issue at all. "Dr. Meyer also said this bloodletting part won't last too long before Khai can accept donated whole blood."

This was definitely something I'd never considered. "Do they make whole blood baby formula?" I put away my magazine and stood. "Can Torchy line that up from his suppliers through The Super Market?"

"I'm not sure." Her face lit up with a soft smile. "If anyone would know, he's the guy."

I watched as she shifted Khai from her breast to the crook of her arm and then held her wrist out to his mouth. Instinctively, his little fangs dropped and pierced her skin. Khai drank her blood as happily as he did her milk. Sheridan already looked like a pro-mom.

I winced. "Does that hurt? It's not like the baby can enthrall you to take away the pain." Watching my nephew drink his mother's blood made even me squeamish. Baby blood suckers just sounded creepy as hell. I supposed I could get used to it if she could.

"It's a little uncomfortable." She shrugged again. "But his saliva helps to close the wound. So after you're over the whole *he's drinking my blood thing*, it's not so weird. This is what he needs, and I am his mother." She looked at me with a *what the hell else am I supposed to do* face.

"You're gonna be a great mom, Sher. I just know it."

Tracing his chubby little cheeks while he ate, a silent tear from her dripped onto Khai's hand.

I stood and then squatted down beside them, hugging them tight. We fell into a calming, rhythmic sway in time with our heartbeats.

The silence comforted my aching loss for a few stolen moments, but the weight was as vast as a bottomless, black ocean.

Sheridan exuded sorrow in plumes of soured scent around her. Our hearts were breaking at the loss of Teagan. I would have bet if she didn't have Khai to hold and care for, she could have easily chosen to leave this physical plane to join her daughter.

There were just never any words to heal the loss of a child.

My heart died another silent death knowing that I now needed to tell the family about Dakota.

How can I do this? Breathe ... find the right words.

Wanting to find a way to perk her up as much as possible, I stood and poured a cup of cold water from the pitcher on the rolling cart. "Hey, although you had alien man diggin' his way to China from your insides less than twelve hours ago, you're looking real good. How're you feeling? Is there anything I can get for you? Do you want me to brush your hair or rub your back?"

She gave me a half-hearted smile, but she was trying to keep it together. "I have quite a bit of pain in my right shoulder, but Ruthie Anne says that's normal from the anesthesia wearing off from the epidural." She rolled her right shoulder back to loosen up the muscle as though she'd been programming for hours.

I recognized that pain from way too many all-night gaming sessions and date nights with Khaldon online. "Maybe Torchy can help it feel better." I gave her shoulder blade a rub and her muscle was harder than an anvil.

She leaned forward, away from my hands, wincing. "I need morphine and an industrial size heating pad. Here—can you hold Khai for a couple minutes?"

"Sure. Is it okay to bring the guys in now? They've been dying to see you and the baby."

Idiot!

I cringed at my stupid, insensitive words. I grimaced and stared at Khai, realizing those were the worst words I could have chosen at a time like this.

Sheridan shot me a sideways smirk while she handed me the baby. "Yeah, gimme a minute."

"I'm sorry, Sher. I'm a jerk." My eyes pleaded forgiveness.

"I know, but I still love ya." She touched my arm and pulled me in for a hug. After a long moment and Khai's squirmy body wanting attention, Sheridan reached for her walker and scooted to the bathroom.

My gaze stared into Khai's immense brown eyes. "So, you little monster—couldn't wait to get some fresh air? Too cramped for quarters?" I patted him on the back until a substantial air bubble burped out of him. He might be half-vampire, but he was half-human too.

I hadn't held a baby since Dakota was born. I was just a wee tyke myself. My heart ached more with memories of my sister as they flashed through my mind like old, yellowed pages of a photo album.

Sheridan stepped out of the bathroom and I adjusted her hospital bed into a sitting position. She shuffled gingerly, being careful not to strain her incision. She reached for Khai as though he grounded her to this life. I handed him to her, and his smile captivated us. She tickled his toes and he blew bubbles. Seemed odd that a tiny newborn could be smiling already.

It must be gas.

"I'll be back in a minute."

Torchy, Khaldon, and Daddy had been in the adjoining waiting room. I motioned for them to come on. "Hey, guys, can you bring in a couple of extra chairs?"

It was a joyous moment of family love even though it was under such unusual circumstances. We took pictures of everyone holding Khai. Khaldon was especially smitten with him. A sound sleeper, Khai slept through all the *oohs and aahs* and even snored a little. It seemed a bit strange for a newborn to exhibit attributes of an older child already. But dhampir children would grow just as fast after they were born. By seven, they were fully grown humans, and that is how the queen had built her dhampir army. Sheridan and Khaldon were victims of that plan, and we knew we needed to watch over Khai, and to keep Amicula's paws off him.

Torchy rubbed Sheridan's back, and it looked as though she might fall asleep any moment. He must have a much gentler touch, or maybe he has the ability to send heat through his hands. She was relaxed, and I could sense a tender and genuine love forming between them. Khaldon even winked at me when he too noticed the bond building between them.

I took a deep breath and knew the time had finally come. I couldn't delay the inevitable any longer. I stood up and walked toward the window and drummed a nervous tempo with my fingers on the marble pane.

"What's the matter, Cheyenne? Come back over and sit with us. Are you all right?" Sheridan asked.

How would Lady Caz handle this situation?

My gaming avatar, Lady Cazenove, who always ate fear as though it were a bag of Cheetos, never stalled or delayed in what she needed to do. She was direct, confident, and never second guessed herself. She always protected her online guild members inside the game and beat off any baddie with her katana.

But this time, it was only me and I was scared as hell.

Would they blame me? Hate me for failing them?

Now, having to share the news of Dakota with my family, after losing Teagan, was more than I could do. But I had to. It was my place to do it.

I shot a glance at both Khaldon and Torchy for confirmation. Was the moment right?

They each gave me a head nod.

I can do this.

I skulked over to Sheridan and squatted down in front of her. In a whisper I asked, "I was—was wondering if you needed help in making the arrangements for Teagan."

I watched the fleeting moment of happiness drain from Sheridan's face as her smile turned to a flat expression in a single heartbeat.

"I honestly haven't wanted to think about it." Her voice cracked again. "I'm afraid I was rather obscene and vulgar to the nurses on the last shift. I threw my water pitcher at them. I just … just couldn't handle it."

Unwanted tears threatened to fall, but I had to be strong for her and for our father.

I grabbed the tissue box from the rolling bed cart, snatched a few Kleenexes, and dabbed my eyes. I handed her the box. She reluctantly accepted it and held the box in her lap, all while watching my face for telltale signs.

"I have something I need to tell both of you." The tone of my voice resigned. My eyes shifted from my father to Sheridan.

Torchy stood up and offered to take Khai from Sheridan's arms. She handed him the sleeping babe and plumes of nervous questioning radiated from her pores.

I stared at them both and bit my lip hard enough to taste blood. "Look, umm … I want to help however you need me to, okay? I'm here for you in any capacity you need. Please know that."

Sheridan blew her nose and wiped her face. Both she and Daddy stared back at me with questioning eyes. I scooted a chair closer to both of them and reached for their hands. They each reluctantly took hold of a hand and I pulled them in close, inhaling a deep breath of prayer for the right words.

Both Torchy and Khaldon had moved in and flanked either side of me. I hoped it was their non-verbal show of support for delivery of this horrific news.

She nodded her head. "Of course, I know—"

I cut her off.

It was now or never.

I sat straight up and looked down into the depth of their eyes. "I have to tell you something, and truthfully, there's *never* going to be a good time to talk about it."

They sat there waiting for me to speak.

My mouth wouldn't open and my voice was lost until I blurted it out. "We found Dakota."

Sheridan stole a breath and held it. Her face already contorting. My father also held his breath, but his bottom lip hinted at a tremble. I could clearly see he wasn't doing much better than my sister.

"They set a trap for us. We don't know who, but they set a trap to stop anyone who tried to rescue Dakota. But we think we were specifically targeted."

I swallowed a thick mass of grief as my words finally spilled out of my mouth. "The trap … the trap set off a bomb. We … we … *oh, God* … we lost Dakota and Ludovic." Uncontrollable tears flowed over my cheeks. "They almost killed us. We've been recuperating in a Phuket Hospital." I wiped my face, smearing the bloody tears and took out another tissue. "We barely escaped with our own lives."

They blinked in what seemed like shocked denial.

Squeezing my father's hand, it felt numb as there was no resistance. I looked him deep into his eyes and whispered. "She's gone, Daddy. I tried to save her, but Dakota is gone." My horror overcame me as I couldn't control my grief any longer.

The words I'd been dreading were finally spoken and coming out in sobs.

Sheridan wailed out with the same grieving pain of loss we'd heard the night before, and my father stayed frozen for what seemed like eons. Our hands clasped tight around one another, and we each held on for dear life while our bodies shook with another family loss.

ॐ

Khaldon left the room and brought back a fresh water pitcher with cups of ice. He handed each one of us a drink. After an hour or more of explaining exactly what had happened on the island, the crying abated a bit and morphed into numb shock. Khaldon and Torchy further explained how the weapons were targeted to attack our exact supernatural weaknesses and how we almost lost Briggs.

I reached out to Torchy. "If it weren't for him donating his dragon adrenaline, we would have lost Briggs too. Torchy saved his life! He saved all our lives getting us off that island."

Sheridan stretched her hand him to and gave a soft, quivering smile.

Torchy explained the story from his point of view, and I learned so much more about what happened because I had been blinded the entire time.

My body, raw with exposed nerves, was overcome with pure emotional, mental, and physical exhaustion. I needed to sleep for a month— straight.

Khaldon poured himself another cup of water and sat down close to my dad. "Harris is doing much better. He's not out of the woods yet, but if he responds well to the new wolfsbane treatment, he should be allowed to come home soon. I have family over there with him, so he's not alone."

I rubbed my temples trying to abate the headache from last night. "I didn't want to tell you, especially not after this." I gestured to Khai.

Sheridan's tears were a never-ending waterfall of anguish. She exuded a spectrum of emotional scents from anger to disbelief, to flat out nothingness.

She shook with her words. "I don't believe it. First mom was killed, Teagan is taken from me, and now Dakota." She looked at me, her red, puffy eyes pleading why. "Do you think they did something to Teagan's DNA to reject her because she was female? Do they only want boys in their dhampir army?" Sheridan hugged herself and lowered her voice to a whisper. She looked to see if the door was closed. "Would they steal Khai away from us?"

"She's got a helluva question. I dinnae think we have thought about that." Torchy moved in closer. " That nutter will nay lay a hand on the bairn."

"I can't handle it anymore. I'm done." Sheridan stood up from the bed, holding her belly. "If someone else has one more wretched thing to say to me, you might as well lock me up in a padded cell, cause I'm going cuckoo!"

Khai made a funny face with the word "cuckoo."

I leaned in and hugged her. "I know. Let's just get you home, okay?"

"No, that's not okay either! I'm afraid to go home. I just can't face seeing the nursery set up for both of them." Sheridan pointed at Khai in Torchy's arms. "Half pink, half blue. I just can't do it. And now ... this?"

I nodded in respect to her feelings. I hadn't looked at it from that point of view. "Don't worry—you can come to my place, and we'll take care of the rest, all right?"

"No, that's not all right either. Thanks for the offer, though." Her voice quieted down to a melancholy drone. "Seeing Dakota's room ... Chey, I just can't."

"You are welcome to stay with me, lass." Torchy's invitation lit up his face. He had walked over to the other side of the bed with Khai and reached down to touch Sheridan's shoulder. She took his hand and cradled it in her neck. "I'm happy to be there for ye. You dinnae have to do anything that makes you uncomfortable."

Sheridan looked up at him, possibly considering his offer.

"Yer li'l Stormaggedon loves my pups, Ash and Soot. Aye, I have plenty of rooms. If ye prefer, we can even set you up in your own adjacent condo. We can do whatever ye want for as long as ye want."

A small smile breached her mouth. No matter how much she was hurting, I knew she couldn't bear to insult him.

"I've been looking forward to baking you my famous tottie scones fer breakfast. But it's whenever yer ready, lass." Torchy bent down and kissed the top of her head and then Khai's.

Our father finally spoke, but his stutter was in full force. "I ... I w-want the funeral service and m-memorial to be n-n-next to your mother, in M-ma-montana." His voice faltered under extreme duress.

Losing his wife, his youngest daughter, and now his granddaughter was more than any one man should ever have to endure. Daddy placed his elbows on his knees and cradled his head in his hands. He shielded his face as the earth-shattering sobs finally came.

All I could do was join him.

The room grew silent once again as another wave of grief and reality hit.

Neither Dakota nor Teagan was coming home.

Sheridan sniffed, wiped her face, and quietly nodded. "Yes. I love that idea, Daddy. Both our daughters will be safe with Mother."

It was a perfect and beautiful solution.

"Okay, I'll contact Uncle Charlie and Aunt Maisie and let them know what's going on—as much as I can anyway." I stood up and breathed in, knowing the worst was over. "I don't think they'll quite understand the specialty needs we'll require. Leave all that to Torchy and me, okay?"

Both Sheridan and Daddy imperceptibly nodded.

Shock still encompassed the room as Khai's squirmy wails pierced the silence. Babies waited for no schedule, no matter what was happening around them.

Chapter 14

The Penthouse ~ Orlando, Florida

Three Weeks Later

Cheyenne O'Cuinn

I had invited Sheridan and Torchy over with baby Khai, and we now relaxed out on the veranda overlooking Lake Lola. I hadn't seen them for a couple weeks as they were trying to find a rhythm with their new living arrangement, a newborn dhampir baby, and the live-in nanny.

Briggs, Harris, and Khaldon had come over, and I had a buffet of pizza boxes set out for our evening meal. We congregated in the outdoor kitchen area and everyone found a seat, a bar stool, or a countertop to sit on.

It was nice being back home, safe and quiet, but I'd realized that no matter how hard I tried to maintain normalcy or return to old routines, nothing would ever be the same. Especially every time I walked past Dakota's room. I had even gone to the lengths of closing her door and avoiding that side of the house at all costs, but it didn't seem to matter. The *clack, clack, clack* of her high heels and the *whirring* of her blow dryer were sounds I would never hear again.

Orlando temperatures in February could fluctuate in between the twenties to the nineties, so it was always a crapshoot for planning events outside. But tonight the weather gods graced us with a balmy seventy-four degrees and the winds were fairly mild, so it was nice to entertain on the patio. The setting sun blazed streaks of pinks and orange across the sky until they melted into the velvety indigos of the stars. I reflected back to the last time I appreciated the sunset and remembered that was the final night I'd seen Dakota.

Would I ever look at a sunset again and not think of her?

Harris reached into the wine fridge and pulled out a Coke with the *Werewolf* personalization label I'd purchased from The Super Market. He leaned against the center pergola beam and then cracked open the bottle's seal. My own Coke's label read *Witch's Brew* as I had already drank everything labeled *Vampire* and *Mummy*.

"Harris, I'm so glad you're home and looking well. The way your body was bloated from the toxins, I was afraid you'd be in Bangkok a lot longer."

My heart soared seeing him alive and vibrant with renewed vitality. Much better than his condition the last time I'd seen him. "When I got your text that you were on the way home, I cried, I was so happy." I seized him in a huge heart-to-heart hug, and it helped to heal some of the guilt I'd experienced leaving him in Phuket.

Harris drank down almost half the bottle of Coke and then belched an exuberant carbonated burp. "From what Chuck and Ichi tell me, I was given a series of antidote for the wolfsbane poisoning. They called in a Lycan specialist and they gave me some kind of tranquilizer meds that kept me awake. Kinda an oxymoron, right?" He nudged me in the ribs. I called him a real moron and nudged him back.

"Anyways..." he bugged his eyes at me. "The semi-wolfing out allowed the Were transformation *just* enough to kick the metabolism and consume the toxins. The treatment worked without me endangering myself or anyone else."

"Dzat's fantastic news. I wish dzey could've done dzat with me." Briggs patted his belly and stroked the scar where the dragon scythe blade had marked him for life.

"Right? That would've been sweet, but they might not have been too sure about letting you drag out in the ER." Harris swigged the remainder of his Coke.

Briggs huffed with a small smile, agreeing with an appreciative sound in the back of his throat.

"Dr. Rattanakosin also said if I hadn't responded to the treatment that the wolfsbane could have sterilized me."

I grimaced at the thought because I knew how much he wanted to have a pack of his own one day. My words tiptoed around the intimately personal topic. "So—did they test you to make sure all was well in that department?"

"Oh, hell yeah. I made damn sure my junk still worked." Harris gently patted his nether regions. "Boys are doing just fine, thank you."

"TMI, Harris. TMI." I about dropped my new bottle of 1738 Rémy Martin Cognac. "I can honestly say I've never thought about your "boys" before, but I'm glad to hear things are all right in the plumbing department."

"Chey, I'll have to tell you about this machine they used on me. Damned freaking awesome. They should make those things open to sell to the public. If we could replicate the design, we'd make millions."

"Harris, I don't want to know." I removed the Cognac from the cylindrical packaging tube and cracked the seal. The aroma instantly invigorated my taste buds, making them dance with anticipation.

"We could call it the iSuck and market it right alongside of your iBrate."

I about spit the fangs out of my head. "Dude, don't make me drop this bottle." I laughed so hard I couldn't hold the brandy up any longer.

Opening the cabinet doors to the bar, I pulled out six brandy tumblers and set them on the quartzite counter. I added a few granite rock ice cubes for whoever wanted their drink chilled. "I'm glad it worked out to where you and Briggs could travel together. That's a long flight and having someone to talk to really helps pass the time."

"You should have seen it, Chey. Briggs and I stomped everyone's asses playing trivia on the plane. Too bad we weren't playing for money. It would have paid for our drinks."

Briggs chuckled, and he also looked much better than when I saw him last in Phuket. His color was returning, but there was a definite change in his personality. Guarded, not his usual draconian confident and boisterous self. "*Oui—dz*ere was dzis one fella who 'ad a serious competition complex and every time 'e lost, 'e ordered another drink. By dze fifth game, 'e was passed out." Briggs inhaled the butterscotchy aroma and slid a glass to his hand in anticipation.

I poured the first round for everyone. I added a couple of the granite ice cubes and swirled it around in my tumbler admiring the oaky scents with just a hint of dark chocolate.

Opening the lids on the pizza boxes, I inspected the Italian yumminess hidden within. I snagged a couple pieces and some garlic bread for myself and a small slice for Beano.

Harris reached for a plate on the bar and opened the second pizza box. "It was great to meet Khaldon's friends too, they're pretty bad-assed guys. Vhalencia was easy on the eyes too, if you know what I mean." He jabbed me with his elbow and danced his eyebrows. "Loads of war stories. Some of the crazy shit they told about Khaldon were hilarious. There was this one time, in Australia—"

"Blimey, Harris, not that one. Seriously, that's enough." Khaldon interrupted. "We're definitely not going there." He ran a nervous hand through his hair and rubbed the back of his neck. "I'll teach those guys. Some things aren't meant to be repeated."

"Dude, but that kangaroo laid you out flat. You can't write that kind of fiction. I laughed for hours over that one."

Khaldon shook his head and inspected the Italian offerings in the to-go boxes. "I bet they didn't tell you the part where Ichi had to bandage up Chuck's arse because he battled the Gila monster and lost. He couldn't sit and was laid up for a couple days from that bout."

"Yeah, they all told on themselves reminiscing over the years and the stupidity you guys got messed up in. You should write those stories down. I bet they'd be best sellers if you did." Harris laughed and reached into the greasy cardboard boxes and snatched up five slices of the meat lovers supreme. "But despite the good times with them, I was anxious to come home and run with my pack. I couldn't wait to tell them what happened and most of them didn't believe me until I showed them my wolfsbane shivs and a selfie I took after waking up."

"What cha wearing there, Harris? *Aye*, is that what I think it is?" Torchy spied Harris' back end, and that's when I realized he wasn't wearing pants.

"It's called an Utilikilt. It was a *see-ya-later* gift from the guys. I'll admit I wasn't too sure about it, but I read about it in a magazine, and they're worn all over Europe. After you get used to the breeziness of it, I have to admit, I rather like it. Every time I wear it, it's like a chick magnet."

"Is it true what they say about what men wear under their kilts?" I asked him and began to lift up the backside of the fabric.

He snapped it out of my hands. "That's a trade secret, ma'am. And one I'm not gonna divulge."

Torchy winked at him and gave him an accepting nod. "Good fer the bollocks, mate."

"Well—I like it." It wasn't very ladylike, but I spoke with a piece of garlic bread in my mouth. "Looks like it gives you lots of room to move around in. As far as I'm concerned, it takes a real man to wear something like that. So go for it." I finished off my last bite of pizza with a swallow of soda. "I'm surprised you're here too, Tony. I figured you'd have stayed in Tibet a lot longer than you did. The wound from the dragon scythe healed up without any complications? What brought you home so soon?"

Briggs merely shook his head while it seemed he also marveled at the werewolf's appetite. He loaded a calzone onto his plate with a side of marinara. It was wonderful to hear his smooth French accent again. "Let's just say you can't choose your family. After about a week, I was ready to come 'ome and get away from my sister with all 'er *'oodoo*. Kalina means well, but she drives me *cinglé,* preaching to me on 'ow I should be running my own business for more profit. Dzat's all she dzinks about is money. *Mon père* wants me to take over 'is international interests, but I prefer to keep dzings stateside. If I'd stayed any longer, I dzink I would 'ave killed one of dzem, especially my papa."

Khaldon eyed Briggs and then shifted his eyes to me and shrugged. He swirled the ice cube in his brandy and didn't say anything.

He never did finish telling me what he knew about Briggs' father.

Everyone completed serving up their plates, and we ate in the quiet peace of the night. I addressed my guests for an informal business meeting. "So now that we're all together, stuffed our faces, and feeling a little safe for the moment, I wanted to talk about a few things that have been bothering me. Right, wrong, or indifferent. We've took action and made some decisions."

Harris leaned against the door frame leading back into the butler pantry, he wrenched the plastic wrap from around a stack of red solo plastic cups. "Oh man, is this gonna take all night? Briggs and I were hoping to throw down in the *Star Battle* SIM for a while before he flies out for New Orleans in the morning, and I wanted to show him this cool cups game using our guns."

Baby Khai squirmed in Sheridan's arms and Torchy held out his hands to hold the little guy. She looked up at the man who wore the red dragon, and her smile reached her eyes. Overall, she seemed happy. I could tell there was still something lost, an innocence maybe, but through all the challenges, it was easy to see they were indeed falling in love.

I stole my eyes away from them as my own heart ached because of the increased distance Khaldon and I had experienced since returning home. Recently, there'd been days when we didn't call, talk, text, or even chat online. In many ways, I think I was associating my sadness over Dakota with seeing him and I just didn't want to deal with it. Somewhere in the back of my mind, I thought denying it would make her death go away if I kept myself busy with other things. And thinking about Khaldon was not one of them.

But I was learning that line of thinking was wrong too. Staying AWOL from everyone was safe, but it wasn't solving anything.

I threw my crumpled up napkin at Harris. "There'll be plenty of time for playing in the battle SIMs." I hopped down from sitting on the counter and walked out on the patio, closer to the wall's edge. "So anyway, thanks for coming over tonight. I've thought long and hard about a few things and Sheridan and I have taken action. We wanted to share them with you. I'll understand if you don't support them, and you're not obligated to join in what we did."

Faces stared back at me with varying degrees of puzzlement and encouragement. Sheridan nodded, fueling me forward.

"The first thing is, since we've learned about these illegal blood orchards, we considered taking down the whole *ExsanguiNation* platform so we could stop the sales."

"Are you freakin' kidding?" Harris pulled up a chair, turned it backward, and straddled it. "Have you gone mad?"

"What? Chey Chey, you can't do dzat." Briggs objected with open arms. "Why would you consider such a dzing?"

"Don't you feel that's a trifle rash? Have you even thought this through?" Khaldon chimed in with the chorus of objections.

I stared at all of them almost regretting my words, but my nails bit into my palm while I tried to control the heat pluming up my neck. Admittedly, I was tired of these guys telling me what I could and couldn't do anymore, but I did value their opinions.

I took another sip of my drink and purposefully swallowed. I pointed at Harris. Opening my eyes wide, I said, "As a matter of fact, Mr. Archer, I can. There are some things I still have control over. This is still my brainchild, and I can blow the whole damn thing up if I want." I tapped my toe on the slate tile in time with my finger against the side of my glass. "But that's not my aim."

The guys stared at me as though trying to figure me out. I hated acting like a bitch, but I also loathed being run over by other people's opinions even more. Ever since the failed attempt on North Sentinel, my patience for advice was next to nil.

I walked a little closer to everyone and leaned against a solar-generated, wrought iron lamp post. "After we had looked into what Tiffany had told us about North Sentinel, we knew there had to be more facilities like it. We figured if there's no buying platform, then there'd be no way supply can fuel the trade."

"Don't you think that's a bit naïve in your thinking, Cheyenne?" Khaldon stood against one of the pergola pillars with his arms folded across his chest. It was as if he were daring me to pick a fight with him. "If people want to purchase the bloodwine, legal or not, they'll find a way."

"I'm not finished, and I have put a considerable amount of time and energy into the research we're going to share with you." Forcing down my irritation, I inhaled a calming breath and counted to five. With a carefully controlled tone to my voice, I continued. "Instead of turning off the game, we're using it for gathering intelligence. Already, we have a list of trails to where potential illegal blood orchards are located by their eCommerce transactions."

Briggs held his chin in his hand, seeming to pensively think about the idea. "So you went all NSA with *ExsanguiNation,* 'uh? What about gamer privacy rights?" He tipped his glass at me with a half-warning, half-threatening tone in his voice. "If anyone learns what you're doing, dzen you'll 'ave a lot more dzan some silly vampire queen on your ass."

Torchy bounced Khai to quiet his fussiness. It would be feeding time soon. "Aye, but what about the privacy rights of the Supes and the people who've been involuntarily held against their will to fill the bloodwine orders? Knowing what I do now, I dinnae want to sell that kind of shite in my Super Market stores. I want to know if the product is certifiable volunteered, ya kin?"

Sheridan spoke up. "You're correct, Briggs. I'm sure the queen will eventually get word, so we'll need to find a way to gather intel without anyone knowing who is doing it."

Khaldon *hrmphed* and sarcastically added, "Ya think?"

I pulled my mouth over to the side and began to give him what for, but I pushed down the emotion and ignored his obvious irritation. I grinned a fake smile and felt the feelers of angst crawling out of my gut.

I wish I had more of those herbal pills Ichi had given me. I needed to relax.

Beano sniffed and nudged my hand searching for more tasty morsels. "I'm sure there're thousands of legitimate merchants and consumers such as Torchy and myself. I'm not worried about people like us."

Walking back to the counter, I gathered up a small bite of sausage for Beano. The final sip of Cognac drained from my glass and I grabbed for the bottle. "I wrote a program for the checkout pages, sniffing out the purchaser's IP address. This code identifies and tracks the seller's shipping activity."

I opened the crystal decanter and Sheridan held the bottle down, thwarting my efforts for a refill. She knew what brandy did to me. My *don't test me eyes* spoke volumes, and she released the decanter. I poured myself another glass and turned to face everyone again.

"Briggs, I figured this kind of intel work might be right up your black market alley, ya know? We can hire some Ghoulie thugs to 'collect' more information on who's buying and who's selling the latest bloodwine. Find out what's the word on the street." I finger quoted "collect", accentuating my double-entendre meaning.

Briggs toasted his glass with a wry smile. Normally, he had powerful, opalescent eyes which spewed confidence, but for some reason, I sensed a bit of hesitancy and a deeper layer of darkness or remorse that wasn't present before.

Sheridan shook her head, possibly shaking off bad memories, and she took Khai from Torchy and held him in her arms. She played with his little toes and vocalized in mommy-baby talk. "The second thing we did is programmed PADME to find the geo-locations where a lot of women have gone missing. Oh yes we did." Khai squealed with a laugh and her whole face lit up with a motherly love. She then looked up at us and spoke normal again. "Queen Civetateo is still kidnapping women like me and Dakota for her dhampir breeding regime. We need to expose these places and rescue those women. We must contact the authorities to tear them down. If *we* don't do something, who will?"

"This is just bloody pish ridiculous! Are you listening to yourselves? Just what sodden authorities are you planning to report to?" Khaldon placed his glass on the table beside him with a loud *clang*, and I thought for sure it would explode under his force. His voice raised in volume along with hand gestures. "These are the queen's private facilities." He pulled on his hair as though he were trying to communicate his frustration further. "You aren't thinking straight. We're powerless against the queen and her generals. Do you honestly think anyone under her, any lord and lady, are going to defy her wishes of building this dhampir army?" His hands vibrated showing his frustration. "I can almost guarantee you Civetateo is using the commerce from these blood orchards to finance her new troops."

"She doesn't need to know who tips off the cops." I held my hands on my hips and defended my point of view. "We just have to provide the information on where they're located."

Khaldon slammed his hand down on the table again. The liquid from his glass sloshed and spilled, puddling in a pool of emotion that matched my own. "Don't you get it? There are no bloody coppers to report to. You're being ridiculously naïve and just begging for a death wish if you keep going down this path. There's no way to keep you safe."

The calm breathing I'd been using to control my emotions escaped me. The edge of control I'd been maintaining was gone and I spilled my own drink gesticulating my reactions to his inhuman words.

"Naïve? Naïve?!" The tone of my voice grew incredulous. "You have the fucking nerve to call *me* naïve when I've found a solution? At least I'm trying to do something instead of rolling over dead and taking for granted we can't do anything."

Unexpected words loaded with pent-up energy exploded before I could stop them. "Keep me safe? Seriously? If I recall, all three of you had very specific words."

"'Everything will go as planned,' you said." My hand gestured toward Briggs.

"'Nothin's gonna hurt us tonight,' you said." I looked at Harris and he winced with every angry word I punctuated.

My hands shook and gulped another shot of cognac.

"'Our plan is solid,' you said." I stabbed my fingers into Khaldon's chest, spewing my words. "How dare you call *me* naïve when I was the one who said we weren't prepared. Dakota is dead because we needed more help and you all refused to listen." My hands gestured in the air as I encircled the room. "I told every one of you on that beach I didn't think we had enough support, but you convinced me to believe otherwise."

Khaldon didn't say a word, but his laser-focused eyes met my own. Seething, my inner vampire came out as my fangs slowly descended. "Dakota is dead! Ludovic is dead, and we barely made it out alive because I *was* naïve. I trusted all of you to protect us."

I stared Khaldon down with a heated agenda. His own fangs had dropped at the energy attack. "And you—you had a team of experienced fighters at your disposal. Vhalencia, Devden, Chuck, and Ichi. Why didn't you ask for their help before we landed on that hellhole in the first place?" My vision tunneled in on me as the depth of my words hit inside my solar plexus chakra. "I asked you this on the day you introduced me to them and you never answered me. Why didn't you tell me about your progeny?"

Khaldon's lips pulled tight to the side of his mouth and he broke the stare-down. He walked out to the edge of the patio where I'd stood earlier, and quietly drank his Cognac.

He kept his back to me, not responding to my accusations or questions.

"Fine, turn your back on me." I cried out to everyone because I just couldn't hold it in any longer.

I walked around the room and stumbled over a bar stool.

I lowered my voice back down to a dull roar. "Look, guys, I can't stand feeling this way, but these awful questions keep haunting me. What if Ludovic hadn't used that gawd damned key, setting off the bomb? What if we had cut her away from all the chains first? What if we had inspected her for wires? Could we have kept it from exploding? Could we have saved her?"

The patio fell silent. Even the seagulls had lowered their voices and listened to my rantings. I stole glances at others, and everyone looked at their feet or stared into the depths of their glasses. Beano rubbed his head inside my hand and leaned against me. I inhaled cleansing breaths—in and out—for a long, slow minute. I had more bitter, evil, and terribly unkind words I wanted to spew at every single one of them, but my conscience argued with me as to how to handle the situation. There was nothing I could say or do to erase the sting, the pain of what I just said. I was angry at myself and everyone else. We all were to blame for her death. There was no ocean vast enough to hold the guilt I swam in every day.

The silence in the room was deafening. When Briggs and Harris did meet my eyes, their faces told me volumes of what they were feeling too.

Without a word, Torchy stood and poured another Cognac for himself. He lifted the decanter, asking the room if any of us wanted a refill. I ran into a chair and then stuck my glass out to him as did everyone else, except Khaldon. He remained at the edge of the patio as far away from me as he could get.

The amber liquid tinkled the ice against the side of my glass. I downed the refill and held out the cup again. Torchy raised a single eyebrow and then gave me a slight nod of his head and refilled it.

Sheridan reached for my other hand and pulled it in under her chin and squeezed. She took my finger and ran it down Khai's sweet nose. Looking at me with her blue eyes, she tried to give me a small smile. But I knew deep inside that she too was blaming me, thinking I didn't do enough to help Dakota. I knew that she knew how much I had failed her.

Briggs sat down heavily in a chaise lounge with an exasperated sigh. "I'm so immensely sorry, Chey Chey. *Oui*, you are right. I 'ad no idea the Rakshasa were so well informed and 'ad been prepared for our arrival. Dzey were supposed to be simple natives. I've lost my precious Dakota because I failed 'er. I'm so angry Ludovic was such a lousy communicator dzat 'e couldn't tell us more. I even miss dzat stupid bastard. I can never get my Dakota back and I may never regain your trust. I 'ave failed all of you."

It wasn't until I heard the level of guilt in his defeated voice that I realized just how much my words had stung him to the core. I shouldn't have been so unkind, so ungrateful. He'd lost the woman he loved. That has to be a special form of self-loathing. Knowing you tried your best, or didn't try your best, and failed? He had to have been beating himself up more than I ever could.

"If only I had—we could have—I knew I should have checked that cell for traps." Harris hung his face in his hands and his shoulders shook. "But it looked so primitive it never occurred to me that anything electrical was down there." His muffled words were a little hard to understand as he spoke to the floor. "I could've saved her if only I'd taken the time to investigate, scan, and secure the room before I left to find Tiffany. It's all my fault. I didn't clean the room like I should have."

I had no idea they were blaming themselves for what happened.

They risked everything to help us. I'm such a jerk to be so angry.

I needed to sprout ears and be condemned to say "eee aaw" the rest of my life because of what an ass I'd been.

Sheridan handed the baby to Torchy, and he took over bottle duty. Her kindness helped ease the tension in the room. She put her hand on my shoulder, and with a squeeze, forced me to sit down on the bar stool. I looked up at her, and she gave me those big sister *don't test me eyes* right back at me.

The tone of Sheridan's voice was full of empathy and had a soothing lilt that wasn't condescending, but instead provided healing to my ragged nerves. "I know this is hard for each one of us. We're all grieving in our own ways and trying to understand what happened." She reminded me of our mother with her gentle kindness. "The *what ifs* are killing me too. If we're going to survive this, then we have to keep moving and we need to do it together because we are all feeling the same thing. Dakota would not have wanted us to fight over how she died or how we failed, but she would want us to kill the motherfuckers who did this to her."

Listening to my sister curse in the voice of a whisper gave it a deadly appeal. She walked out toward Khaldon and touched him on the back of the shoulders embracing him with both hands. She urged him to turn around. After a moment, with her kind insistence, he reluctantly came back to the group. His hand hid a bloody handkerchief and his eyes were crimson with emotion.

As she led him back, Khaldon sat down on the opposite side of the room not meeting my eyes. How could I look at him now for all the things I'd said out loud?

Sheridan addressed all of us. "I've been studying about it, and the stages of grief are interminably terrible. Every single one of us is going through those steps, but at different times and in very different ways. You've heard that old expression 'dying from a broken heart'? People really die from this kind of pain every day. Whether we grieve together, with a support group, or alone, we have to stop blaming ourselves and each other for everything that's happened."

She picked up her own glass of brandy, sipped it, and studied me directly. "Truthfully, I'm surprised we haven't already had this conversation or blown up at each other before now. I know my own emotions are so crazy, I've felt it's just been easier to stay away from everyone. Some minutes I'm fine, and then others, I'm a complete basket case. Just ask Torchy."

Torchy edged a small laugh to his voice. "Aye, those words will ensure me nothing but trouble. It's best I tend the wee bairn for safety." He winked at her and a rush of blush bloomed across her cheeks.

Sheridan gave him a sweet smile and continued to explain her own emotions in a way that honored my feelings. "I can't tell you how ashamed I feel about myself. I've blamed every creature on this planet for what has happened."

She refilled her glass and explained things I never knew about her. "The day I learned our mother was murdered was the day my life ended. Mom and I were closer than peanut butter and jelly, and she made me promise to always take care of you and Dakota. I prayed one day I would honor her with a beautiful daughter. I have failed her on both promises and I'm filled with so much guilt. Why did Teagan have to die? How did I fail her as a mother? Why didn't my body make her a healthy one? Did I not eat the right kinds of foods? Did that one cup of coffee do it? Why didn't the doctors tell me earlier about her heart defect? Couldn't we have fixed it in utero?"

Her voice cracked with emotion as a tear escaped her eyes. She wiped it away as quickly as it emerged and pounded her fist on the table. "But more than anything, I'm so angry I could spit. If Ludovic had been alive, would he have known how to help her? Teagan might be alive now if he hadn't been killed. Did he set all if us up for failure? Was he trying to kill all of you? Why did Amicula do this to me in the first place?" She stopped and stared at us for a moment. "The questions are never-ending. And you're right, Chey. They're driving me mad."

Sheridan turned to face Torchy and caressed Khai's sleeping little cheek. "But what I've learned and have been enduring, despite all those stupid questions that won't release me, is I must take care of this amazing little fella and simply try to remember how to breathe. One moment at a time. We must go on."

She cradled her arms around her ribcage as if the hug could help provide the comfort she needed. "There are times when my chest is cracking in half, the pain is so fucking bad. It's all I can do to gasp for air." A quiet moment filled the room. She covered her face with her hands, and with a whisper she said, "I just want it all to go away." She looked up with glistening eyes. "I pray for the day this all gets better. But blaming and being angry with one another doesn't help. It leaves me exhausted. If I breathe and move forward into the next moment, I can try to stay focused. If I choose to remain a victim and cower behind the deaths of my mother, my sister, and my daughter, then I might as well join them. I am no good to anyone if I cannot do something positive to avenge them."

Crimson tears flowed over my cheeks as the realization of just how much Sheridan had lost hit me. Among us all, she had lost the most. And here she was selflessly healing and helping the rest of us.

Sheridan walked over to Briggs and put her hand on his cheek. "I know you're hurting, I honor that. When you're ready, let's put our pain to work and find these awful people." His eyes met hers and he tried to smile, but his lip quivered and he lowered his gaze again.

"Think about it. You know how awful you're hurting, but imagine for just a moment, all the human mums and dads, sisters, brothers, husbands, and wives of these persons who are missing? They have to be living in a wicked-nasty kind of hell. They'll never know if their family member will ever be found or their body recovered. They've vanished without a trace." Sheridan scanned the room. "These people live in a perpetual state of unknowing. I can't imagine that kind of horror, and it's got to hurt worse than anything we've already experienced."

Briggs nodded and inhaled a slow, deep breath. His shoulders shook while he stared at the floor. Plumes of dis-ease filled the room, coming from every one of us.

"We owe it to these suffering people to try. We owe it to Dakota to give meaning to her death." Sheridan moved on to Harris, and she lifted his chin. His eyes were thick and red with emotion. She placed both her hands on his head and stroked her fingers through his sandy brown curls. "All we can do is find a way to channel everything that's tearing us down and find the strength to fight what caused it to begin with. Please stop killing yourself with what you could have done. It won't bring her back."

Harris lifted his head again and looked her straight in the eyes. With her thumb, she wiped away his tears. "If we don't do something proactive and find a way to take down these places, then Dakota died in vain. Our grief means nothing. The only way we can honor her now is to rescue those poor souls and reunite them with their families."

Sheridan stood tall and returned to her former CEO self. The tone of her voice was firm, determined and full of resolve. "And we're going to use *ExsanguiNation* to do it."

Chapter 15

The sun blazed its final crowning flags of color while the moon crested over the edge of the balcony revealing its mysterious crescent. I noticed several bats fly past the patio, and Beano took an interest in trying to catch them.

Had a a shift in consciousness occurred within me? I knew I needed to get out of this funk and make something happen. We needed to move on. To heal, and my anger wasn't going to make it happen.

"Sheridan is right." I swiveled in my seat and put my elbows on the bar behind me. "If we don't channel this ridiculous hate and blame for something productive, then the bad guys win. Amicula and the queen will have destroyed us mentally and emotionally, instead of physically. We can't give up. We can't just roll over and accept this hand of fate the Norns have handed us. We need to write our own destinies and do what's right. I'm sorry—I've been a jerk."

Sheridan continued her agenda with a gentle kindness. Single-handedly, she was successfully diffusing the scritchy energy and helping everyone relax. "Let's just think out loud here for a few minutes. Khaldon has a solid point, he really does. If we can't tip off any local paranormal authorities without risking our own hides, then can we give anonymous tips to the human FBI? That might be a way to get the women out of the breeding dens at least." She picked off the anchovies and bit into the cheesy goodness of her pizza slice. "Isn't there a Supernatural police department? Some of my favorite urban fantasy book characters are cops, detectives, and bounty hunters for paranormal worlds. We've got to have a form of protective force we can call on for help, right?"

Torchy raised his glass acknowledging my question. "Yes, there is an International Interspecies Council, but they rely on each group to take care of their own kind first. In other words, we have the Draconian Council for dragons, and the vampyre has the Queen's Council."

"But that's just it, what if those councils are corrupt? Who holds them in contempt?" I asked.

Harris shrugged. "We've not really experienced that before. Everyone keeps to themselves, and they let the area packs handle the situations."

"Okay, for months now, you guys have told me about the old wars between the vamps and werewolves." I pointed toward my home office down the hall. "You even spoke about the war on our Friday team meeting, remember? Who settles those disagreements? Are you telling me no one helps keep the peace?"

They looked at me, and then they glanced at one another and then back at me as though they were keeping a secret or were at an utter loss to answer my question. Everyone was so hard to read with the overwhelming scents of emotions in the air. Or maybe it was the stench of werewolf musk clouding my thoughts.

"Usually, it's the local lord and lady and pack masters. Squabbles are settled." Khaldon responded, finding a way back into the conversation after my attacks.

I offered him an embarrassed smile. I needed to say what I did, but I didn't mean to hurt anyone, especially him.

"Okay, so we dinnae have any answers for now." Torchy tried to follow suit and give Sheridan the moral support she was rallying for earlier. "We'll cross that battlefield when we get there. Let's focus on what we can change today."

"Torch is right. This is a bigger problem than we can solve right now. We need to explore options and find a solution soon."

"Agreed—three hundred percent. I'll see what I can figure out and I'll talk privately to Lord Stovall about what options might be available to us. We'll find a way, Chey." He reached out and gently took my hand. "I'm not sure this is the right time, but I need to leave for a while to go get the *M'lady* from the Andamans."

"What? You're leaving again? So soon?" I stammered and looked down at my feet knowing he probably needed to be away from all the chaos too. It wasn't as though he were my husband. Most boyfriends would have flown the coop by now. If I were honest with myself, I'm not sure I would have stuck around if the situation had been reversed.

Khaldon ticked his head out toward the edge of the patio. "Can I talk to you alone for a few minutes?"

We picked up our drinks, and he hoisted a leather satchel from the floor up over his shoulder. He lifted the bag and placed it onto the chaise lounge grouping where we sat. Khaldon reached into the bag and pulled out an old book. "I'm sorry, Cheyenne. I don't want to leave, but we both have a lot to work through. I think it would be best to just to have a time-out and we both sit in our own corners for a few weeks. We're going through some bloody dark shite and it's best we allow ourselves some time to heal the emotional wounds. It'll all work out soon enough.You have my word. But while I'm gone, I wanted to give you my copy of *The Canons.*"

I nodded, and with a heavy sigh, offered him up a smile that said, *You're right; we need a time-out,* and accepted the book. It was long overdue for me to spend quality progress in it. It was a well leather-worn, dog-eared, water-stained tome. It must have been ancient.

"Reach out to me if you have any questions, and I'm sure you'll have plenty. As far as I am aware, Lord Stovall is still local on his yacht, *The Resurrection,* so he can help you too."

I gave him a half-hearted smile and tried to avoid giving him the guilt-ridden puppy dog eyes.

He reached out to me and pulled me in close. His touch seemed foreign, but I relaxed and lowered my guard. I wanted his touch to feel safe again, even if it was for just a moment.

"I love you, Cheyenne. It'll take a bit of time to get the *M'Lady* back to port in Dubai. I'll be gone for a few weeks, possibly over a month. You should be here to complete your research." He tried to give me a quirky thin-lipped grin.

I nodded my head and halfway appreciated the reprieve. "I'm sorry too; it's not fair that I'm dumping all my anger and grief out onto you. I'm such a toad."

"Well I don't know about that, my sweet lass. But you're right. I should *have* called in Vhal and the guys. I honestly didn't think it was going to be that big of a deal, and I was wrong. I'm not sure if I'll ever forgive myself because of it. It's quite possibly the worst mistake I've made in my life." He kissed my forehead and the touch of his lips radiated a clear message. "I can fully understand why you're angry with me as I hold myself to the same account." He kissed my hands and pointedly waited for my reaction.

I didn't respond. Sometimes words weren't needed and spoke the message loud and clear. I gave him a flat smile and squeezed his fingers.

He kissed them again and held them close to his chest. "You need time reading, testing, learning who you are. You'll find balance. I have faith you'll awaken your inner vampire on your terms. I need time to analyze a few things in my own life. I've grown too complacent over the past few decades, and I need to reconnect to my own inner vampire as well."

"You mean, you don't feel complete? Like something's not right inside you?"

"Exactly that, Cheyenne. I can't quite put my finger on the sodden thing either. I'm hoping this time on the ship will help me rediscover a few things about myself as well."

He reached into the satchel again and pulled out the oilcloth I'd seen in the hospital. "I tried hanging this in my house, but it doesn't glow anymore. I wanted to see if this orb still reacted to you."

I stared at him in surprise and had forgotten about the damn thing. Inching my hand toward it, I cupped it with my palm. Immediately, the orb hummed and turned a neon green once again. I stared up at Khaldon. The verdant light glowed with such intensity, it shined off his bronzed skin.

"Why did you bring it here? I don't want it." My heart raced once again. It disturbed feelings of overwhelming anxiousness deep inside me.

"But here's the rub. I think it wants you." His eyes stared so deep into mine that I almost fell over from the dizzying spell.

"I can't find anything about it in any lore or legend, nor how it would have been on that island to begin with." He opened the orb from the confines from the rest of the cloth and held it up closer to our faces. "There's nothing written about it or where it came from."

I swallowed hard and immediately covered it with my hands. "Don't! Please, put it away. I don't want anyone knowing we have it." I shoved it back in the bag. "We can look at this later?" I turned to look at the rest of the gang and they weren't paying any attention to us. "In private?"

"Fair enough. I think we both could use a little *private* time." He pulled me in close to him intoxicating me further with his frankincense.

My heart ached knowing it would be an extended period until I saw him again. We needed to reconnect before he left. "Will you come to Dakota and Teagan's memorial in Montana? Sheridan is having the marble statue commissioned and it will take about six to eight weeks to complete. So we're thinking about sometime in late March or April."

"Of course I'll be there." He took my hand and placed it over his heart. "You'll always be right here, Cheyenne. That will never change."

His eyes lit up. "I almost forgot. There's something else before I go, but I'll understand if you don't want them. Just a trinket really." He let go of my hand and reached down into his satchel once again. He held a small box and placed it into my palm.

I sucked in a breath, not sure of what to think. He'd never given me anything in a jewelry box before in our real lives. As a digital avatar character, he had given Lady Cazenove many things but this was the first time in this reality. I opened the little black velvet container, revealing two ruby teardrops surrounded by white diamonds. I stole a quick glance at him from under my curls. "Umm—just a trinket, huh?"

"Well, I was going to get you the matching bracelet, but I know how much you curse them when you code, so it's only the earrings."

I fully looked up at him and smiled, accidentally hiccupping a brandy burp in his face. "I love them."

"That's m'lady!" He slid my arms up around his neck, and I wanted to hide my embarrassment into his shoulder. My nerves were edgy and raw. My emotions were all over the place. Listening to the quiet rhythms of his heart beating, I knew the decisions we'd made were the right ones and one day everything would work out.

At least, that's what I wanted to tell myself.

After experiencing how much we had lost over the past few weeks, it was time to recoup and I was determined to do everything it took to learn more about who I was and make peace with it. At this point in my life, I had no idea how I would do it, but I knew I had four distinct goals to meet:

To read *The Vampyric Canons* and embrace my inner vampire dynamics.

Identify the locations of the illegal blood orchards and breeding dens.

Search and destroy whoever was behind Dakota's death.

Identify my rogue vampire attacker and annihilate him.

Somehow, on a transcendental level, I knew all of those goals were connected. In time, the answers would come, but for now I needed to seek balance and ask the right questions. I needed to train and hone my new skills. It was time to prepare. Time to heal. But most of all, it was time for me to discover who I truly was.

When the day comes, I will be ready to seize my own destiny and no longer fall prey to it.

Chapter 16

Wolf Creek, Montana

Late March

Aisling O'Cuinn

Aisling O'Cuinn, the mother of three of the most vivacious daughters on the planet, stood stoic and silent as she observed the cemetery crew erect the marble memorial on the family plot where she was supposedly buried. A crisp Montana morning sky promised a brilliant sun-filled service on the day of Dakota and Teagan's memorial.

Mother Nature blessed the event with six inches of angelic, new snow blanketing the land in an etheric peace. Reflecting the radiant crimson, orange, and pink hues in the morning sky, the pine trees seemed to bow in respect as lumbering icicles hung from their branches. The red-breasted robins, along with the black and white magpies, sang their morning greetings. A great gray owl softly whooed her lamented lullaby as she drifted to sleep after her nightly hunt.

Spring threatened, as it always did in March, to tease with warmer days and then pummel again with below freezing temperatures at night. The mountain residents of Wolf Creek, Montana, were greatly adept at living in this frigid weather, knowing they couldn't plant their gardens safely until the second week of June.

The Rocky Mountain terrain guaranteed a blizzard the last week of April. Inevitably, they would receive a light dusting of snow the week before planting. Any day in between was fair game from zero to fifty degrees, especially on the Flying F Ranch just north of Wolf Creek, with its vast acres of open terrain.

Aisling silently shape-shifted into a tree nymph, staying out of sight among the evergreen pines. Sheridan had commissioned a winged angel with Dakota's face, holding an infant in her arms. The angelic, marble statue simply stole her breath away. The child reached up and touched the lips of her weeping aunt. Stunning, the memorial told their tragic stories. The longer Aisling looked at the statue, it somehow left her with a sense of hope that her daughter and granddaughter were safe and happy together.

One by one, the mourners arrived to stand at the gravesite and pay tribute to the family. Aisling spied through her branches while her cousin,

Maisie MacCarthy, and her family drove up alongside the other vehicles in time for the service. Upon seeing the memorial, Abbey MacCarthy, Charles and Maisie's daughter, wept at the foot of the statue of her beloved cousin.

At a remote and concealed distance, Aisling had watched the family over the past six weeks. She was careful to maintain a cloaked presence as to not tip them off she was nearby. She had been dead to them for nearly nine years now, ever since the Vampyre Queen Civetateo had called in her blood oath to the throne. To reveal herself would mean instant death to her entire family.

Aisling's thoughts followed each person standing in the reception line of the service. Each one of her family members showed their despair in myriad ways.

Kiernan. Her beloved husband. How she missed him and ached to reveal herself to him. He had involved himself in taking care of his new grandson, hauling hay and feed for the cattle on the Flying F Ranch, and had found out he liked to blow glass in the hot shop. He spent his quiet nights in the blissful mind-meld of Aisling's embrace. She knew he would wake dreaming of her, but not quite remembering if the encounter was real. He once told her, when she allowed him a lucid moment, that he had learned to keep his mouth shut about her since no one believed him. He knew they would force him to see doctors, spend weeks at the loony bin, and make him take more drugs to alleviate the hallucinations. She kept her distance, allowing him more time to heal between her feedings.

Sheridan's newfound dragon boyfriend, Torchy Gravenor, was someone Aisling would need to learn more about. He seemed to be an astute businessman and an attentive caretaker to both Sheridan and Khai. As a mother, she wondered if Sheridan was handling the dragon aspect of the relationship in stride. Dragons always were a passionate species. Especially Scottish dragons. Aisling thought about it and wondered if perhaps she could send an anonymous book about the peculiarities of dragons.

Aisling approved of Cheyenne's boyfriend. She liked Khaldon Seters and had heard of his lineage many times before from Queen Civetateo. The queen desired Khaldon to father an elite line of assassins for the throne, but he had turned down her offer. That defiance endeared Khaldon to her liking even more.

The boy Cheyenne room-mated with in college also stood in the family memorial service line. Harris Archer could have been the son she never had. He was like a brother to the girls, and she made an extra effort to watch over him and communicate with the Werewolves for his protection.

There was another man with her family, Tony Briggs. She had not known of this man, but his energy and thoughts surrounded Dakota. Aisling learned his draconian clan had a French heritage.

How did her girls manage to get mixed up with the supernatural community? She and Kiernan tried to keep them away from their birthright and raise them as normal, human girls for as long as they could.

Quite a clan they all were. Aisling absorbed the love among all of them as her family stood in a semi-circle around the marble statue.

Bouquet upon bouquet of fresh flowers were laid at the feet of the angel while people she once knew, and many others she did not know, came out to express their condolences.

A black limo pulled up among the pickup trucks and SUVs. It looked as out of place as a pink hippopotamus in the Montana mountains. A driver opened the back door of the limousine as a pair of high-heeled boots presented themselves to the ground.

Sliding out of the limo, Amicula Darkrose was draped head to toe in solid white, complete with a mourning veil covering her hat and face. Aisling sucked in a breath and almost walked out from the trees to stop her. From her tree nymph disguise, her branches curled, causing her dried leaves to fall from the limbs. Amicula walked past the tree, apparently without noticing Aisling's disguise.

Everyone fell silent as they looked at the outlandish woman approaching the memorial. Encumbered with several bouquets, Amicula first paid tribute to Aisling's gravesite next to the marble statue and laid down a spray of red roses.

No one in the crowd said a word, but they stared intently at the odd stranger.

Sap ran down the bark of Aisling's tree nymph trunk as her tears freely flowed. This was the *last* thing her family needed after having a few weeks of respite and peace. They were finally beginning to heal.

Amicula continued to make a scene of herself as she plucked the blood-red rose petals from their stems and let them go. Amicula stuffed a couple of the flower petals in the tiny hands of the infant child the angel was holding. A gentle breeze caught the petals. They fell in a crimson flow cascading to the base of the statue.

Cheyenne lunged at Amicula, but Khaldon held her back.

"Why are you here? Feeling guilty? Haven't you already done enough?" Cheyenne's tone seethed with hatred.

Family and friends stood dumbfounded in shock at this woman's taunting behavior. Somewhere in the distance, Aisling heard the distinct cocking of a shotgun barrel. Montana folks didn't take too kindly to outsiders, especially rude outsiders.

The temperatures in the air had warmed just enough, allowing the icicles to drip their own tears of sadness, adding another layer mourning. Dried leaves scattered among the gravestones as a hush fell over everyone.

Amicula stood in front of the statue and addressed the mourners in her Brazilian accent. "My friends. Today we gather in tribute for two beautiful daughters we shall never see again." Amicula continued to pluck at the rose petals.

"I wanted to express my deepest condolences to the O'Cuinn family as we have lost two valuable souls on so many levels. Dakota was a precious entity who was helping to bring balance back to a civilization that required her immense gifts. She will be sadly missed. And blessed little Teagan."

Amicula shook her head *tsking* at the loss. "Teagan had so much hope and promise for an eventful new life." Amicula turned to look at the marble statue once again and then glinted her eyes directly into the grove of trees where Aisling stood. "We wouldn't want to do anything to compromise the natural balance of things. Acceptance is needed now so we can brace ourselves for the coming neoteric world."

Khaldon interlaced his hand with Cheyenne's. His eyes cast daggers at Amicula as if he wished her to incinerate on the spot.

Aisling waited to learn if Khaldon would take action and hoped he wouldn't respond to Amicula's goading. She prayed none of them would reveal their true selves in front of the humans, as that would be a punishable supernatural crime. And with Amicula's eyewitness account, she could distort the facts unfavorably, making the situation worse than it was.

Plucking the last few remaining petals from the red roses, Amicula paraded toward Cheyenne and Sheridan and spoke in a hushed voice. With her hard plaster smile, Amicula stared at the sisters. "Her Majesty, Queen Civetateo, wanted me to express her deepest condolences and that we sincerely regret these unfortunate occurrences."

Khaldon squeezed Cheyenne's shoulder and pulled her in closer to his chest.

Cheyenne held fast and tight to Sheridan's hand.

Sheridan hissed her words. "How do you know our location?"

Khaldon added, "Who tipped you off?"

Amicula sneered her lips and dashed her eyes toward Khaldon. She raised her hands to the rest of the onlookers and cloaked her words for any human ears. "Why, I would think it would be obvious, my dear. Doesn't it make sense that once you've become a breeder for her majesty's court, that we'll always know where you are?"

Sheridan gasped and held a hand to her mouth.

Cheyenne countered, "Why can't you just leave us alone? You've got what you wanted, now leave."

"Oh, *contrar*, Miss O'Cuinn. We did not receive any return on our investment with you or your sisters. You may do wise to keep that consideration in the back of your minds."

Khaldon stepped forward. "Bloody hell, Ami. You do *not* belong here."

"Not an issue, my love, as I do not have plans for staying. But do know this: The court has a watchful eye on all of you." Amicula reached and put her fingertips under Khai's chin. "Especially, the wee one here."

Torchy slapped Amicula's hand away. "You'll nae be touchin' the bairn. Best to heed the warnings. Leave us now."

Amicula retracted and took notice of the red claw marks where Torchy struck her. She returned the growling gesture from Cheyenne, Torchy, Khaldon, Harris, and Briggs, and must have taken it as an opportunity for an amicable retreat.

Amicula studied the family with a stern grace. "None to worry. Soon you'll be coming to me. Ta ta, for now." She discarded the thorny stems at

Sheridan's feet.

Sheridan spat on Amicula's shoes. "Never!"

Amicula looked down at her boots and then released the crowd from their enthrall. "Again, the queen sends her condolences." She nodded her head and stared intently at the eyes of each person as she walked by as though she were daring them to lash out.

♏☓ɢ☓

Thunder roiled and rumbled off the mountain walls and barreled through the meadow. Aisling turned her gaze skyward to see from which direction the storm was coming. Left in Amicula's wake, the rose petals whisked in the wind, littering the snow like large drops of blood.

As Amicula left the memorial and walked toward the pine trees, she turned and put her hand on Aisling's trunk. "What a clever disguise you've made for yourself, dear. It's going to be hell getting all that sap out of your hair, don't you think?"

Aisling didn't say a word or acknowledge Amicula's presence.

"I wanted to remind you of the vampyric protocol of your office. If you decide to contact your family, we will have no choice but to destroy *all* of them." She clucked her tongue. "What a pity. Such a waste. You wouldn't want that, now would you? So I'll see you back in the Amazon—soon? I believe Auntie is waiting for your return. You'll want to travel along the energy vortex ley lines since you do not have a dragon companion for transport. I, on the other hand, have a few electronic manufacturers to see before I return. Please tell Auntie I should arrive by the end of the week. Give her my love."

Amicula turned and waltz toward the limousine and left as deftly as she had arrived.

With the unwelcome visitor's threat looming over her, Aisling watched helplessly as Sheridan sat on the rounded seat of the memorial statue and cried from Amicula's words.

Cheyenne searched the horizon. She cupped her ears, listening to something.

Aisling held tight to the tree as the winds blustered, hurling leaves, petals, and broken twigs through the air.

Against the sun-drenched blue sky, two UH60 Black Hawk helicopters flew overhead. Trailing below the Black Hawks barreled a military convoy with five tractor trailers, armed personnel carriers, and a tank draped in snow white camouflage netting. The trucks clamored over the cattle guard and turned onto the unpaved back road to the south side of the Flying F Ranch. Everyone stopped and stared at the unbelievable sight.

"Well that's my cue, folks." Uncle Charlie tried to speak above the *whomp whomp whomp* of the helicopter blades.

The immediacy of the mourning had altered with the reinstatement of the nuclear missiles. Many Montana landowners dealt with this situation, and there was nothing anyone could do about it other than to cooperate or have their land taken away.

It wouldn't be long until more missiles arrived.

Friends and family paid their last respects to the O'Cuinns. Aisling observed her daughters and husband who stood a mere ten feet away. She ached to hold them and give them her love. She watched as her daughter kissed her granddaughter, carved into the marble statue, one more time.

Sheridan placed her hand upon Dakota's cheek immortalized in stone. One last tear of goodbye rolled down Sheridan's face. "I will always love and cherish you both."

The winds picked up again and Sheridan searched the abandoned cemetery for any sign that the souls of her lost family members, including her mother's, could be standing with her now. Aisling tried to disguise herself deeper into the tree, but Sheridan turned and stared directly at her.

Aisling wondered if Sheridan might still have the sight as strong as when she was younger.

Sheridan approached the tree, intently studying it.

Aisling sucked in a breath and desperately searched for a distraction.

Her daughter advanced one step, two steps, and studied the branches and leaves making up Aisling's disguise. Sheridan reached the tree and tried to converge with her mother's energy as she did when she was a young child.

Aisling conjured and called upon the elementals and a hauntingly beautiful child's laugh and raised the winds once more. The winds blew wild as the clouds raced across the darkening sky. The snow fell once again in quarter-sized flakes obscuring Sheridan's vision. She turned her head toward the laughter and chased it behind her tears.

Sheridan dodged the snow from this tree and around that gravestone. She ran after the etheric child-like laughter. "Teagan? Teagan? Baby, is that you?" The young girl's voice sing-songed around every corner as if to say, "Catch me if you can."

Aisling recoiled from needing to distract her daughter is such a way, but she hoped it would provide the confirmation Sheridan's heart most desperately needed. That sign from above she was seeking prayer for.

Breathing a sigh of relief, Aisling turned to make her way toward the energy portal. She needed to discuss the escalation of the US missile movement to the queen. To keep the idiot politicians from blowing up the planet, it would be time to enact the "power plan," sooner rather than later.

Aisling reflected on Amicula's words:

"Acceptance is needed now so we can move forward to brace ourselves for the coming neoteric world."

Brace ourselves, huh?

Aisling had the peculiar feeling Amicula wasn't just talking about vampires anymore.

Chapter 17

Flying F Ranch

Cheyenne O'Cuinn

The guest house at the Flying F Ranch had been our home for the past couple months. Now that our family memorial service had honored and remembered those we lost, I hoped we might fly back to Florida soon. I was ready to rebuild, pick-up from where we were, and handle the packing up of Dakota's room.

After the exequies, we gathered back at the main ranch house for an early afternoon dinner. Aunt Maisie always made sure the table was filled to overflowing with delicacies. She and my Uncle Charlie had been running a vacation dude ranch in Montana for over thirty years, and they loved having guests from all over the world.

No one was idle at the Flying F, not even the guests. If you stayed there, you worked there. It was a fair deal, but I longed to have lazy days where I could lounge around on the couch, in my jammies, instead of shoveling sidewalks and horse barns. It made the summer task of picking beans or shelling peas a desired event. With the world political news escalating into more panic and heightened alerts, I had the feeling those indulgent days of safety and leisure were quickly coming to a close.

We circled the kitchen table trying to understand the morning's events. I was still reeling in shock that we saw a caravan with a missile drive onto the property.

Uncle Charlie kicked off his boots and set them by the hearth to dry. "The Lt. Base Commander at Malmstrom Air Force Base in Great Falls called me yesterday saying there might be some activity in that old missile silo on the south eighty. Last time they were out here, I had to string up an electric fence to keep lookie-loos and war-haters away. I don't want those silos on my land any more than the next guy, but I don't need people getting shot trying to break in."

Harris lifted the lid of the chili pot and breathed in a big whiff of the spicy soup. "I've never seen somethin' like that before. Is the government reactivating nuclear missiles? Didn't they sell off the silos to end-of-the-world lovin' preppers?"

"There's nothing wrong with preppers." I put my hands on my hips and made sure my tone of voice was one that was heard. "They believe in self-sufficiency and not being dependent on anyone for anything. They're smart for planning ahead."

Aunt Maisie smacked Harris' hand from the chili pot and handed him a stack of plates to set the table with instead of snitching before the meal. Harris kissed Aunt Maisie on the cheek and said, "Maybe so, but I saw a show once where this couple turned their silo into a hippie commune." He put the plates on the counter and took out a glass, filling it with water. "They sat around singin' 'Puff the Magic Dragon' or something weird."

Both Torchy and Briggs laughed out loud, and I couldn't resist a little chuckle myself.

Uncle Charlie shrugged and shook his head, seemingly resigned to be able to do anything about the silo activity. "You never know what the air base is doing, and there's nothing you can do to stop them. It's been years since we've seen any activity, but we've always given them a wide berth when they're here. Mason and I are going to run the fence lines this afternoon to make sure the cattle aren't attacked by aliens or anything. Hey—ya never know, this could be the next Area 51." He winked at Aunt Maisie.

I peeked in the oven at the cornbread. "Ya know, Sher, I could set PADME to monitor what's going on in the local area, and she can inform us if there are any changes.

I mind messaged to the non-humans in the room, *"PADME has been quite forthcoming with information about recent abductions not too far from here—over by Swift Dam, a few hours north. We think there is a breeding den close by. Plus, she has found significant information about shipments we think are coming from the North Sentinel Island."*

Khaldon, Briggs, Torchy, and Harris all turned and looked at me at the same time. It was amazing at how cool these guys were with mind-messaging, but able to keep it a secret. Not a human in the room knew what was what. I did catch Aunt Maisie staring at me with a small smile. I winked back at her. I needed to get to know her better as there seemed to be something more to her than she ever let on.

Hmmmm.

Harris interlaced his hands and turned them inside out. "Wicked. Chey, let's hack into the satellite grid and probe for activity on the global missile positioning systems." He cracked his knuckles readying himself for an all-night programming session. "It'll be just like when  we hacked into the Emergency Broadcast System and sent out those zombie apocalypse messages out over the television and radio stations."

"Who is PADME?" Uncle Charlie took off his cowboy hat and hung it on a hook by the door.

"It's a holographic program I created called PADME. My Personal Automated Domicile Management Executive. I can set her to monitor any kind of data activity and have her report it. At home in Orlando, she maintains all the alarm security, phone and Internet access, electronic functions, temperature settings, and pretty much anything I want to give her."

"Holographic?" Aunt Maisie furrowed her brow. "Like a ghost or somethin'?"

Sheridan squeezed our aunt's shoulder giving her a sweet smile. "Don't worry, Auntie, it's not quite like that. Plus, we don't have the projection cameras to illuminate PADME's holographic body program. Think of it like a really smart computer who can remember to do the things you've asked it to without you having to remind it."

Harris slid the plates and bowls across the table. "Even though we don't have her projection cameras, we do have her base server program. I can set her to watch the news, track satellite movements, and scan headlines for any increases in missile movement around here."

"Damn, that's something I gotta see." Mason Jones, the ranch foreman, snitched a roll from the bread basket and popped it into his mouth. He grimaced when he'd seen he'd been caught and must've known what was coming.

Aunt Maisie smacked the back of his hand with her wooden spoon. "Wait n'til supper's ready. Eat, eat, eat ... that's all you boys do around here."

"Well, Maisie, it's all that good cooking. We can't resist ourselves. I don't know about all this PADME stuff, but whatever you kids think you need to do." Uncle Charlie pointed to the where the trucks turned. "What I do know is—we have to clear out old tumbleweeds from around the silo perimeter fence lines. Any of you city slickers wanna join us?"

"Not me." I shook my head but smiled at my uncle, asking forgiveness. "I want to get ready for the Race Across the Sky Dance tonight. Khaldon promised me two weeks ago he'd take me." I winked at Khaldon and widened my eyes at him, daring him to use fence mending as an excuse to get out of dancing.

Even though he had told me he would be here for the memorial service, I half-way didn't believe it would happen. It seemed as though the time apart helped us both immensely. Khaldon seemed just as excited to move forward with our life as I was. They say *absence makes the heart grow fonder.* Whoever "they" are, they were right. I wasn't crazy about testing the theory, but it did give me time to realize just how important he was to me. *And* that I did want him in my daily life ... again.

"Wouldn't miss it for the world, m'lady." He gestured in a waist-deep bow toward me.

Harris seemed all over the idea. "Sure. How many silos do you have? Can I drive the tractor? Does it have cool levers and stuff to make the bucket go up and down? Or those huge prongs to skewer hay bales?"

Uncle Charlie chuckled. "Woah there, cowboy. We've got three silos on the ranch. Two to the south side and one further along the northern perimeter." He glanced from side to side, looking for Maisie. When he thought the coast was clear, he snitched a finger scoop of mashed potatoes.

Aunt Maisie turned the corner and popped him with a dish towel. "Get! All of you, get!"

Everyone laughed while the guys scooted away with their lives from the vicious, champion towel popper.

"*Oui!* Give dze chef 'er kitchen." Backing her up, Briggs stood behind her with a rolling pin in his hands.

She nodded to him indicating their intimidation was successful, and she winked at him.

I bet they become cooking buddies for life.

"Guess I'll start baking again for those poor military folks stuck in those dreary holes." Aunt Maisie pulled out a *For the Love of Baking Cookbook* from her top shelf and instantly held Briggs' attention. "I just can't imagine living and working underground like that day after day and not seeing the sun. Would drive me bonkers."

Uncle Charlie sat at the head of the table and continued where he left off. "When the silos were active before, Maisie would leave baskets of homemade goodies at the gates for shift changes. They couldn't ever really talk to us, but we figured it might be to our advantage to be friendly."

Torchy licked his lips. "Lucky soldiers. I could really go for some of Aunt Maisie's peach cobbler."

"Well, you're just in luck, Mr. Gravenor." Aunt Maisie's voice, as solid as a battle ax and quick as a whip, interjected. "Sheridan, just this morning, pulled out a couple jars of canned peaches to make a cobbler for dinner tonight. I'm sharing my secret recipe with her."

Briggs looked up from a recipe book with interest. "*Oui?* What's dzis about secret recipes? Is it published?"

"Well, then it wouldn't be a secret anymore, now would it, Mr. Briggs?" Aunt Maisie turned her head as though she were holding an award-winning coveted state fair recipe book.

"Perhaps we should consider writing a recipe book together. *Secret Down Home Recipes from the Flying F Ranch*." Briggs gestured in a circle with his hand. "I believe it has a certain *je nais se qua, oui*? Don't you think?"

Uncle Charlie laughed from deep within his belly. "Now this ought to be interesting. Three cooks in the kitchen trying to write a book?"

Mason Jones, the Flying F Ranch foreman, piped in, "Yeah, but think about it this way. They'll have to test out all the recipes on us first." Mason gave the okay, thumbs-up of approval.

Mason had been at the Flying F for as long as I could remember. A few years older than me, he made it his business to be an expert hunter, tracker, and Mr. Know-It-All. Cute guy, with his short-cropped blond mop he hid under his cowboy hat, but he was also was the kind of guy who always had to have the bigger, better, crazier story than you. Never to be outdone, if a guest at the ranch landed a pheasant during bird season, Mason would show up with three. He meant well, but I think his insecurity always meant he had something to prove, or even more so, something to hide. Not sure if anyone ever challenged Mason's catty behavior, but he seemed to be the kind of guy who needed to be taken down a few notches, just for his own good. But on the other hand, if you got lost in the woods or needed to know how to survive in the wilds, he was your man—hands down.

Uncle Charlie had a boisterous laugh that sucked you in and made you feel as comfortable as a downy quilt in front of a fire. He stood about six foot tall, and his signature Bailey brown cowboy hat gave him the appearance of being even taller. He was the real deal. If ever there was a cowboy, he was one of them. He did it all. He was known all over the state for his horsemanship, blacksmithing, and smoking cured meats.

"Can we turn on the stereo, Aunt Maisie?" Sheridan asked as she accepted a stack of bowls to set the table.

"Sure, child. Might be time for the Huckabee Report," she replied.

"I was hoping for a little music this afternoon to keep up the lightened mood." Sheridan countered with a sweet smile. "Let me check what's on the satellite music channels."

Aunt Maisie couldn't have been five feet tall in high heels. Her bright white hair hung in a long braid down her back. Rarely seen without an apron, Aunt Maisie always looked as though she got stuck in the 1940s and never moved past that era. Uncle Charlie towered over her, but they were the cutest couple and loved one another like newlyweds.

There was always a mountain of work to do around the ranch. Aunt Maisie managed the main house and guest houses, but she didn't do it alone. She had a couple of local women help her after boarders left, but when it came to gardening, harvesting, canning, planning meals, cooking and cleaning, she had it down to a science and ran the schedule like clockwork.

Abbey MacCarthy, our cousin, had returned from walking the dogs and plopped on the bar stool at the end of the granite counter. She smiled at Mason. "I don't think I'm gonna take the dogs into town anymore. Everyone looks at me like I was one of those New Yorkers walking twenty dogs." Beano, my Boxer and Stormaggedon, Sheridan's Pomsky led the pack. Torchy's Labs, Ash and Soot, ran after them along with two Australian Shepherds, a Border Collie, and a Malamute Husky. They ran through the house as though it were their own private playground.

I loved our cousin Abbey. She was one of those women who possessed natural beauty and never even knew it. Her sunkissed skin complemented her straight brunette hair, which she usually wore in a ponytail high up on her head. Abbey always managed to look fresh as roses even when she'd been helping to pull a new born calf from a first-year heifer and was covered in afterbirth.

Rajah, my aunt's Siamese cat, jumped onto the counter as the dogs barreled through the room. His tail puffed out as wide as his body. I stroked him and pulled him closer to me, trying to hush his Siamese yammering at the dogs. Boots, the long-haired tuxedo black and white kitty, ran for a bedroom and was most likely to hide under a bed for a couple days.

The house was alive with energy, dogs, cats, good conversations, laughter, and the delicious aromas of comfort food. It was a soothing feeling of respite and shelter. It had been a long time coming, but I could finally breathe again.

"Okay, soup's on. Let's eat." Aunt Maisie called everyone to the table, and no one wasted a minute finding their seats.

Chapter 18

Flying F Ranch – Main House

Khaldon Seters

We had barely sat down when Sheridan ran into the dining room. "Quick, quick—it's terrible! You've got to see this. They're calling it the Mega City Atrocities!"

One by one, we funneled into the living room and watched the horrific pictures of major cities all over the world up in blazes. The news was reporting power substations had been blown up, leaving millions without electricity, water, and communications.

The news ticker scrolled across the bottom of CCNN listing the cities currently cut off or under siege from fire: Beijing, Osaka-Kobe-Kyoto, Chicago, Las Vegas, New York City, London, Buenos Aires, Los Angeles, Moscow, Mumbai, Cairo, Mexico City, Sao Paulo, Manila, Delhi, Seoul, and Jakarta.

We watched clips of film footage from news stations' helicopters of the rioting, looting, and utter panic of the black-outs.

"This is not good. Not good at all," Charlie muttered.

Cheyenne turned to Harris and Briggs and asked, "Don't we have redundant backup servers located in New York, London, and Beijing?" Her fists clenched and relaxed as she paced. I reached out to help calm her down, but I knew how important it was to her, to all of us, to keep *ExsanguiNation* online.

Sheridan cursed under her breath, "Dammit, I bet we're down. We need to log in and learn what grids are offline. Our game could be a news source of the communication to help people if they're able to access generators and wireless Internet."

I watched as Abbey counted on her fingers. "Those cities alone total up to over a hundred million people without power. Do you have any idea what this could snowball into here in the United States?"

Mason pumped his arm in the air. "Oh, hell yeah—I do! We get to blow us up some terrorists!"

Charlie reached for a shotgun behind the kitchen door. "All right— let's keep our heads on straight. First thing we need to do is fuel up every vehicle and a few of the fifty-five gallon barrels."

Kiernan said, "There's no telling just how long it'll take to get those fires under control, especially if any of those substations are located near refineries. Those cities could be without power for a long time."

The anchorwoman broke the chatter among us. "This just in: We're getting reports that Houston, Vancouver, and Phoenix are now without any power. Electrical substations are continuing to explode in metropolitan areas. Citizens are encouraged to lock down and remain calm. Firefighters are evacuating areas of the city where the fires are uncontained. Officials are working to redirect power from neighboring cities."

"Vancouver?" Abbey questioned, her brown eyes large with panic. "That means they might hit Seattle next, or even Billings. We aren't that far from there."

"Blimey, what a balls ache." I rubbed my head and wondered if Vhalencia and my team in Dubai were experiencing the same situation.

Khai squirmed in Sheridan's arms, and she placed him down in his playpen. I watched as my son pushed himself into a sitting position. He reached up his arms to me and I leaned over and picked him up.

Khai is growing just as fast as he did in utero. He's only two months old, but he's taking on the traits of a six-month-old already.

"What happens if we lose power here?" Aunt Maisie's normal calm, serene voice pitched up a couple notches, revealing her anxiety. "What'll we do if we lose our freezers full of meat?"

Charlie eased a hand down on her shoulder. "It's all right, love. Everything will be fine. I'm sure this won't affect us."

Aunt Maisie wasn't believing a word of it. "Charles, I need to inventory the pantries. We should make a run into Sam's tonight and get more bags of flour and sugar. I can't believe this is happening." She untied her apron and reached for a steno notebook and a pen. Briggs was on his phone and right behind her.

Harris had already pulled out his laptop and checked in on the servers for *ExsanguiNation*. "It looks like we have sections 5, 8, 16, 17, 39, 40, 41, 42 ... oh hell, the whole Asian node is completely gone. Even with the redundancies we've set up, most of them route to one of these cities being affected."

Cheyenne blew out puffed cheeks and her eyes tended to widen when she was deep in thought. "Unholy hell. Seems like the only safe place for our backup servers is somewhere the terrorists can't blow them up. What are we going to do?"

"C'mon, Kiernan, we need you to drive another pickup so we can run into the feed store." Mason was already back in the mudroom, pulling on his boots and coat. "We're gonna need to make sure we have enough chick grower, layer mash, salt blocks, and a few other necessities. We've got just enough time to drive into town and buy these supplies before the farm store closes."

Briggs had been on his cell phone and said, "I've pulled some strings and got a flight back to New Orleans in the morning. They said they can drop you off in Orlando before the flight destinations in New York. They have a flight at six-thirty. There're only a few seats left. I've reserved them if we need them."

Torchy had also been on the phone. He ended his conversation and swiped it off. "Aye, I can take you into town. I'm meeting with a supplier to get some emergency needs for the baby."

Sheridan turned her head toward Torchy and smiled as if shocked that he was thinking of them before anyone else.

He sheepishly smiled back at her. "Listen, I need to make a few more calls and check in with my associates. I'm afraid if the shite continues to hit the fan, I dinnae if we're prepared for this level of security. Since people are already going mental, then it makes me wonder..." Torchy mind messaged the rest of his sentence since there were humans in the room, *But will the Supes go nutters, too? If this power outage continues too long, it'll only be a matter of time before things snowball the feck out of control. I've got to add extra security wards with the Witches around the Super Market locations to ensure the safety of their businesses.*

Torchy spoke out loud again, "Harris, are all the grids down or just the ones you listed? Are we able to use the private communication channels?"

"No, we're at sixty percent. It doesn't look as though Orlando has been affected, but the traffic on the grids is maxing out the capacity on the servers." Harris ran a nervous hand through his brown curls. "Cheyenne, we should consider removing the game graphics and implement a text-based only communication until we can reroute more power. Or at the very least, get the redundancies in a place where they aren't going to blow up."

I patted Khai's back while he sucked his fist. Not sure how the team was going to accept my question, but I figured now was as good a time as ever. "Can we use my satellites? The Iridium Network?"

Cheyenne, Sheridan, Briggs, and Harris turned to look at me as though a Cthulhu crawled out of my nose. A long, warm line of drool slid down my back and Khai tried biting into my shoulder.

He's already teething?

Cheyenne seemed to ask the question on everyone's mind. "What do you mean, your satellites?" She tilted her head waiting for me to reveal I was joking. "Do you—own the Iridium Network?" The tone of her voice revealed that she felt her question was ridiculous, yet she kinda sorta believed it could possibly be true.

I've always been a private man and never cared for anyone to have knowledge of my assets and holdings. However, this situation seemed necessary to trust in Cheyenne as much as trusted in Vhalencia.

I inhaled, opened my eyes wide, and smiled while massaging the back of my neck. "I reckon so. Several of my companies launched and maintain the satellites." I shrugged, not sure of how they were going to accept this new information about me. "That's what it was built for. It's primarily used by Internet and cellular networks. If *ExsanguiNation* needs to be secured to help communicate to people, then it would easily become another network to load up into its software. We could probably have the entire grid back online before midnight."

I was a freak show attraction as they stood there, blinking at me. I shifted Khai to my other shoulder waiting for someone to say something. Any time now, I was sure they were going to bust out laughing.

Harris finally broke the drone of the newscaster spouting more cities without power. "Hell, yeah! Let's do this! How come you never told us you own satellites? Seriously, dude?" His voice was alive and non-stop. "What are you? One of those secret, private bankers the conspiracy theorists always say runs the world? Are you one of the Illuminati?"

I placed Khai into his playpen and noogied Harris on the head and said, "C'mon, mate—let me power up my laptop, and I'll assign you the security protocols you'll need to work with Sheridan to set this up."

Sheridan slowly smiled. One I hadn't seen in months. It was breathtaking to see her engaged in life once again.

Sheridan held her hands in the air as if it were an answer to prayer. "This'll be fantastic. We can really make a difference for people who can get power."

"This is perfect, Khaldon." Cheyenne grinned ear-to-ear and hugged me around the neck. "We'll easily set PADME to monitor the news feeds, and she can help us stay informed. We'll know exactly what's going on. We'll program her to extrapolate news communications and then transmit them to us." She pulled on her red curls when she got excited. It was great to feel the energy of everyone in action.

We had a unified purpose ... again.

Cheyenne talked so fast I almost couldn't keep up. "I can set up PADME to send messages to our smartwatches and phones. If we're in a wi-fi area, we can receive her updates as soon as she learns them."

"Yes, that's perfect." Sheridan kissed Khai on the head. "Then we won't have to be chained to the computers for updates. We can also set it up where she automatically sends the updates to *ExsanguiNation* for people who can access the game."

Everyone started talking at once as the room became a buzz of immediate needs.

Sheridan asked Maisie, "Does Uncle Charlie still have that old ham radio somewhere? I remember playing on it when I was little."

Kiernan asked Charlie as they were walking out the door, "Do you have a generator around here? We could set it up to—" The heavy, outer winter door slammed behind them.

"Hold that thought, Sheridan." Aunt Maisie opened the back door and hollered at her husband, "While you're at Sam's, will you get a few more packages of toilet paper? Here's a list of what I need off the top of my head. We need—" Aunt Maisie's voice cut off after the door slammed shut.

"Abbey, would you mind watching Khai for a little while?" Sheridan asked, "I need to morph out of parental unit mode and put on my programming hat."

"Sure. Dad wants me to inventory the bullets, gunpowder, and reloading supplies down in the basement, but I can bring Khai's playpen with me. I've never seen such an alert infant. He's growing like a weed."

Torchy took over the parental unit decisions and asked in a tentative voice, "Reloading supplies?"

"Of course. No self-respecting Montanan would be without ammunition and reloading supplies for when the shit hits the fan." Abbey eyed her index finger and thumb as though it were a pistol. She narrowed her eyes and pretended to shoot at an imaginary target. Her voice was excited and alive as if this were the most exciting news to ever hit Wolf's Creek. "We've been waiting for this for years. I hope there're zombies. Then I can practice my head shots."

Sheridan sucked in her lower lip and rubbed her chin. She and Torchy exchanged worried glances. "Yeah, umm … are you sure I should let you watch Khai? He won't be too much distraction?"

"No worries, Cuz. I babysat all through high school. We'll have a good time."

Sheridan furrowed her brow with what looked like sincere concern.

"I'm sure it'll be all right, Sher." I handed Khai to Abbey, and they made way for the basement.

"Right. Okay, please don't let him put anything in his mouth?" Sheridan kissed Khai's head, but he seemed enamored with Abbey's brunette ponytail.

"C'mon, you cutie patootie. Let's go find out how much gunpowder we have for rifles and pistols." She blew bubbles into his neck, and Khai squealed at her unmerciful air kisses.

☙◗◖❧

"Listen, guys, I know you wanted to go to that Race Across the Sky thing tonight. I'm gonna have to take a rain check." Harris thumbed over his shoulder back toward his laptop. "I need to check in with the local pack, and then Briggs and I are going to move the main server." Harris punched me in the arm. "Dude, thanks again for the access pathways. This looks like it'll be a clean upload."

"No worries, mate." I returned the punch and we both rubbed our arms. "I'm glad we can put it to good use. If not for *ExsanguiNation* and PADME, then why even have it?"

Cheyenne yanked on the back of my shirt. She turned me around and pulled in tight to her chest.

With perked up eyebrows and a pull to her mouth that expressed, *you're in trouble, but I'm not really mad at you,* she hugged the stuffings out of me. "Thank you. That's seriously an amazing save for the system and for people. When this is all over, let's talk how we can officially pay for that type of bandwidth from the satellite."

"I think we can log this down as a humanitarian relief effort and call it donated time."

She narrowed her eyes at me. Knowing Cheyenne, arguing with her wasn't going to work, but I kissed her forehead and hoped she'd be good with the gesture. The O'Cuinn sisters were savvy business women and always wanted to do the right thing.

It seemed as though everyone had a task and was off, busy preparing for the end of the world. Uncle Charlie popped his head back into the house and asked if Cheyenne and I would run into town to fill water tanks to ensure we had enough potable water. The abandoned dinner table was left with uneaten food as everyone scrambled to help ready the needed supplies.

Not knowing how much time any of us had left on this planet, I knew the time had finally come to ask Cheyenne the one question I'd wanted to ask since I first laid eyes on her.

"Ready to hunt?"

Chapter 19

Race Across the Sky Benefit ~ Downtown Helena, Montana
Cheyenne O'Cuinn

"I t's called *L' Art de la Piquant*," Khaldon whispered deliciously in my ear with a lovely cockney accent, a bit different from his normal London formal British.

He wrapped his arm around my shoulder while we headed toward the dance hall. "Quite literally, the French phrase means the 'art of the prick.' I want to teach you how to evoke a sense of empowerment over a human, arouse their senses, stimulate their blood flow, and have them crave your touch."

I gulped at the idea of consciously enslaving another person for my midnight snack and thought it would be wise to pay attention in case I ever needed to hunt on my own.

Can I do it by myself? Will I have the guts?

"What you've seen in movies isn't that far off from what vampires do," Khaldon continued as we strolled toward the Helena Cathedral from the downtown parking area. "But there's much humans don't know about us. Most importantly, how effortlessly vampyre can take what we want without humans ever realizing it."

We stopped outside the building where the line queued up for admission. We had left the ranch to hunt at the "Race Across the Sky" dog sledding benefit, which was Montana's version of the Alaskan Iditarod.

"Cheyenne, I'll admit I can't believe there are people in town at a fundraiser with the electric power going out everywhere."

"Are you kidding? If anything, Montanans will be out in droves because of all the craziness. These folks are ready for the world to end, and they've totally got their shite together. The last place any foreign country wants to invade is Montana, Idaho, Wyoming, or the Dakotas. These people will kick your ass and forget about the names. You'll just be gone. Sure, there'll be people running to clear the grocery store shelves for last-minute items, but most people here are waiting for the zombies to attack."

Khaldon squeezed me in tight. "Daft, if you ask me."

"Let me put it to you this way—a couple years ago, when Harris pranked the TV stations after the public announcements aired, Montana citizens called the police departments asking how many feet did the zombies have to be inside their property lines before they could legally shoot them. Montanans weren't afraid of the deaders—they were ready for them."

I summoned up my best news anchor voice, "The bodies of the dead are rising from their graves and attacking the living. Do not engage or attempt to apprehend these bodies as they are extremely dangerous."

Khaldon rolled his eyes at me as if I were making up the story.

"Check out the videos on You Tube if you don't believe me."

"He published them? If the FCC learns he was the one—"

I put up my hand to stop him. "Are you serious? This is Harris we're talking about. He teaches hackers how to hack."

"Indeed he does. So this dog sled benefit, is this a drunken party fest or a real fundraiser?" Khaldon queried. "I prefer sober people to teach you on how to properly execute the *piquant*."

"There will probably be a few drunktards, but most everyone is here just wants to have a good time and blow off some steam. Who knows what we'll find in there?" My mouth salivated at the possibility.

"Relax, m'lady, this is a rite of passage in every new vampyre's life. We need to celebrate on the eve of your vampyric virginity."

"Vampyric virginity?" I scrunched up my face. "You make this sound like prom night or something." The music blasted as we stood in the corridor waiting to purchase tickets.

Khaldon handed me my drink ticket as we rounded the corner into a wall of microphone feedback reverberating from the stage. I was conscious of his hand guiding me at the small of my back.

"Vampyric virginity sounds cornball, I know. But think of it this way." Once inside, he reached for my hand and encompassed it in his warm palm, intently staring me in the eyes. "When will you ever have this opportunity again? This will be you first conscious hunt without killing anyone. I want your inaugural solicitation to be a memorable event that you'll cherish for an eternity. Plus, I have a surprise for you afterward."

He playfully tapped me on the nose with his index finger. That Cheshire cat grin reappeared, revealing he was definitely up to something.

"Solicitation? You make it sound like I were going to ask my prey for a date." My eyes questioned his choice of words.

"Hunt, solicitation, inquest, steeplechase—call it what you may." He dismissed my question and let go of my hand and wrapped his arms around me, pulling me tight into his belly.

He skewered me with his green eyes, and with just his gaze, he awakened something inside my vampyric DNA that craved—if not demanded—to escape. My insides ached, wondering with expectancy what the rest of his body could do to me.

The live band music made my toes twitch with anticipation. Recent months of immortal activity had robbed me of any sense of fun. I couldn't remember the last time I had let loose and danced with abandon. Even if the most of the world's population was without power, tonight, I didn't care. I needed to forget. I needed the titillation of the hunt, the thrill of choosing my prey. I needed the sexual release this night promised.

Gawd, it's been waaay too long!

I knew this was the moment that would change my life forever. A conscious, pivotal moment that I willingly succumbed to embrace this vampyric lifestyle. I just hoped that with this new change, deep down inside, I would still be me and not that crazed creature who kills for sport.

The thought of a premeditated quest aroused me even further and I knew immediately that something inside me was taking over my normal human emotions—sensations I'd never entertained before—and they made me feel alive in every meaning of the word.

Once inside the dance hall, each person with whom I exchanged eye contact instantly became my potential first meal.

Should I choose a guy? Would Khaldon think I was hot for some other fella? I'm not sure how I would charm a woman. Would that be considered a vampyric faux pas? What if I messed this up?

With each writhing body on the dance floor, the possibilities were endless. I covered my face and tried to shake off the torrent of bad B-movies churning through my head. Would I walk out of this place how Stephen's King *Carrie* walked out of that highschool?

This night could end so badly if I mess this up. How will I ever choose. There's more choices here than a Las Vegas buffet.

"You need to quell your nerves, m'lady. You're giving off such a nervous pheromone cloud, you won't be able to arouse a mouse."

I uncrossed my arms from around my chest, shook out my hands, and inhaled a deep breath as I tried to hide my sheepish naiveté.

He's right ... try to loosen up, relax. I can do this!

All of the sudden I felt as if I was Chevy Chase in the movie *Vacation* getting ready to jump into a pool with Christie Brinkley. I whispered under my breath. "This is crazy, this is crazy!" I unbuttoned the top of my blouse and allowed my fingers to linger in my cleavage, enjoying the full embodiment of my arousal.

Narrowing his eyes to seductive slits, he followed my fingers and stole a peek into my blouse. He lifted one eyebrow as though inquiring if the night had more to reveal after our feast. Khaldon kissed my forehead. The heat from his torso inflamed my thirst, my desire, and my imagination. I fantasized a scene where we bathed in a claw foot cast iron tub of blood after a night of luxurious lovemaking.

"Let's drink up, dance for a while, and scope out tonight's menu, shall we?" Khaldon handed me a fiery sex on the beach cocktail, startling me back to this reality.

Perusing the crowd, my eyes feasted on the delicious appetizers dancing around us. "That's just it, babe. I'm having a real issue with who or what my potentials should be." My hands propped onto my hips and my questions poured out of me. "What if I botch this escapade and we end up in jail for assault? Couldn't we find an elk or something in the mountains?"

He considered me for a moment and then tilted his head, thinking about my questions. His face held a kind, knowing half-smile for me. "You've got a lot to learn, my poppet."

We found a place to rest our drinks, and Khaldon pulled me through the crowd and out onto the dance floor. The band played "Shake Your Groove Thing" by Peaches and Herb. Khaldon clasped my hand and twirled me around without another word. He let go of me and settled into his own rhythm. For an old vampire dude, he sure had the moves. I let the beat urge my feet, finding the pulsating jive.

For the first time in months, I allowed my body to let loose. The pounding of the bass pulsed fire up and down my legs as I shook my groove thang in front of Khaldon. He seized my hips and proceeded to show me how dirty dancing was done right.

It wasn't long until I sensed the growing awareness of how other people watched and mimicked our dancing. Several couples licked their lips as if they wanted to taste us. I couldn't tell if it was an unconscious gesture or one my mind conjured up.

Khaldon energized the floor when he invited another couple to dance within our circle. The couple might have still been in college, or their early twenties. Surprisingly enough, the guy with short-cropped brown hair danced well with an open cup of beer in his hand. Not a drop spilled. His date for the night seemed rather awakened by the invitation of Khaldon's eyes. Her ponytail bobbed while she mimicked his body language, and I followed suit.

Mr. I'm-Not-Spilling-My-Beer guy muscled his way in closer to me. He offered me a sip of his drink. I shook my head no, but I teased him instead by dancing in and out with my shoulders. It wasn't long until I caressed Khaldon's hips behind mine, and I reached back to graze his excitement.

Khaldon evoked a sense of ease with the couple, hell even with me, as though we'd been dancing here for hours, but in all actuality, it had only been twenty minutes or so. After watching Khaldon's suave charisma come to life, I realized that it wasn't until tonight how I understood the dynamic of the dance. But as I watched Khaldon marinate our dinner, I had an *aha* moment and realized dancing was the body's primal invitation of unspoken sexual possibilities.

The band finished rocking out to a classic Prince tune, "1999", and took a thirty-minute sound break. How appropriate to end on an apocalyptic song when the rest of the world was in a panicked frenzy and I was at a heightened state of arousal.

Before Khaldon could say a word, Beer Guy said, "Hey, I've got something outside in the car. You two interested?"

I shot Khaldon a nervous grin.

Khaldon winked at me and then put his arm around Pony Tail. I reached for Beer Guy, and within seconds we were out the side door scuffing through the snow-filled park and out to the cars.

Khaldon stopped us before we arrived at the parking lot and said, "I've got what you two need right over here." Khaldon gave a wink.

Beer Guy shrugged. "Dude, I'm game."

Khaldon tramped deeper into the snow and over to a grove of huge pine trees with limbs that bowed out at least fifteen feet to the ground. We had to duck under the tree limbs to climb inside. Once we were safely ensconced behind the branches, I was surprised to learn how warm it was as the branches blocked the crisp night air and set the stage for our romantic dinner in the park.

Khaldon swished his hands in front of the couple, which looked like the Jedi mind-hand trick. Both the man and woman fell silent like they weren't even there anymore.

"What did you do to them? Are they asleep?" Sucking in a breath, I squealed similar to when I did the first time I killed a boss in a video game all by myself. Giddy with delight, I snapped my fingers and smacked their faces to see if they would respond. "Wow—it's like you used a freeze spell on them or something. Are they hypnotized?" I was way too easily amused at their submission. "Not even a blink."

"I want to explain to you about the *piquant*. This is how you commove them to the point of acquiescence."

"Huh—commove? Acquiescence? You mean something like ... they're so excited they can't move?"

"Precisely. That's a splendid way to explain it. I have them in a moment of repose, if you would."

"Then why couldn't you just say that? Where do you come up with these wild words?"

He ignored my question. "The trick to galvanizing your quarry is in your pheromones, which by the way, were spilling over capitally on the dance floor." Khaldon's grin revealed he was up to no good again. "It was all I could do to not eat you right there and then." He pulled me in sharp, so close I wanted to forget about the couple and dive straight into him.

Jealous words stammered out of my mouth, "I—I couldn't quite tell by the way you were dancing with Miss Chickadee if you wanted her—"

He cut off my words and kissed me with fierce abandon. We hadn't kissed like that since the night I found out he was Roxas Morgwain, my online boyfriend for over two years. Khaldon had been afraid to confess his true vampyric nature while I was human, but after the rogue vampire attack, and my transformation, he was able to finally divulge his actual self.

Since our plunge into the nightmare of kidnapped sisters, dhampir breeding dens, and illegal blood orchards, we hadn't had much time to rekindle our previous romance from our online avatars, Lady Cazenove and Roxas Morgwain. I had hoped now we might have a bit of quiet until we planned out the rescue for the remaining captives held on North Sentinel Island.

I was ready to take our relationship, in this physical world, to the next level.

Chapter 20

A shuffle beside Khaldon brought me back to the present moment while my mouth salivated with anticipation. Their scents cloyed on my taste buds like fresh baked bread in the oven.

He spoke to the couple in a melodic voice. "You are here to have a romantic romp under the trees and are open to our every suggestion."

My hand held Pony tail's chin and I moved her head from side to side studying her neck. "Okay—so this is going to sound dumb, but I've never in my life seen anyone walking around with two fang marks on their neck. If there're so many vampires in the world, why don't we see neck bites more often than with Halloween costume makeup?"

"Great question, Cheyenne, and that leads me back to the *L'Art de la Piquant*. In the movies, vampires are always portrayed as biting with both fangs, then sucking out the blood."

Not wanting to stop watching the couple, I eyed him with a questioning glance. "Are you telling me that isn't how you do it?"

"Have you ever tried to drink from two straws at the same time from opposite sides of your mouth?" He held the girl's neck for me to view.

I furrowed my brow and shook my head.

"Just for grins and giggles, try it sometime. Once the blood is flowing, it's difficult to suck from the two holes from opposite sides of your mouth." He pointed down mimicking the straws. "I'll bet you can't do it without spilling. If you think about it, a vampire doesn't need two punctures to eat."

I considered this new information, and it actually made sense.

"Now, answer me this: How many times have you seen people walking around with just one mark on their neck, their arm, or maybe on their leg? That doesn't seem out of place, now does it?"

"So you're saying that the *piquant* is only one puncture and you drink from one opening?"

His eyes brightened. "You see, with two punctures, it's difficult to control the flow. You end up wasting more than you consume. Any conservative vampire will want to keep from splattering their meal because: One, they don't want to waste the time hunting down another person, and two, blood stains can be a real bitch to remove from your clothes. Who do you think invented the original stain stick?"

"Khaldon, that makes total sense." I swallowed hard to gain enough nerve to ask my next question. "But do you ever get so hungry that you just want to rip out their throats and bathe in their blood?" I stood aghast at myself. I slapped my hands up to my mouth and shuddered. "Oh no! I'm becoming that monster who attacked me in the haunted house. How could I say such a horrific thing? What if I become like that hideous beast that attacked me and left me for dead?" I grabbed the collar of his shirt and pulled him tight to me. "I would rather die than do that to someone."

"Blimey, Cheyenne, not at all. Don't be so bent." He grabbed my hands and eased them down to my sides. "You'll need to come to grips with this. These emotions are perfectly normal."

I grimaced at the thought and tried to remember my promise to myself to make this work.

"I'm sure you've heard the old horror stories of Elizabeth Bathory bathing in virginal blood to keep her beauty? She was acting out on her vampyric hormones. They're natural instincts."

Heat flushed my face. "I must be sick. A blood bath sounds sensual and arousing to me."

"Bathing in vats of blood isn't something we do as much now, but there are niche spas where you can immerse yourself in human blood. I think Torchy has one of those spas at The Super Market in Orlando."

I reached for Khaldon's cheek and noticed the snow falling once again. Shrouded under the trees, the blanket of snow veiled us further, offering complete privacy.

"That's good to admit your instincts. It's okay—you haven't exactly had the opportunity to explore and get to know your new self. You've been surviving on the bloodwines, which is fine, but doesn't quite satisfy. There's nothing comparable to hunting your own prey and feeling their adrenaline surge, evoking your primal forces. Their emotions fuse the blood and the taste is simply intoxicating."

"Wait—what? You mean I can taste their emotions too?"

His eyes danced with electricity. "Oh yes, that's the best part. You'll begin to gain a specific taste after you hunt for awhile. Some vamps like the gamey, adrenaline rush a human will dump into their bloodstream after being chased and run down. Others prefer the heightened emotions of foreplay during sex. Whereas, others prefer their meals spiced with a heated argument or bellowing with laughter. Each emotion dumps a different brain chemical into the bloodstream and it changes the taste."

"Wow, I never thought of anything like that before. So it's not just the blood itself, it's the desired flavor. Man, if Briggs were a vampire, he would totally groove at making emotion flavored recipes for cocktails."

We both laughed at the possibility of seeing Briggs tending an emotion blood bar.

Fever spiraled up my legs and rollicked at my core. I flushed, feeling an awakening within me. Khaldon's strong hands guided mine to the girl's neck. I placed one hand on her cheek and one hand on her shoulder, stretching her throat on display.

"Now, embrace her and allow your fangs to slowly descend. Control the break through and relish in the sensations. Breathe her essence and then puncture her. Drink and ingurgitate her life force deep within your very core." His words were mere whispers. "There's nothing equivalent to fresh, sumptuous human blood coursing through you. Feel the electrifying animation absorbing into your cells and let it spark new life through your veins."

Khaldon stepped behind me, his body pressing tight up against mine as I inhaled her fragrance. Even though this girl had been enthralled, she must have been sexually stimulated because she gushed in the scent of sex. It drove me into a frenzy. Licking her neck, my tongue vibrated against the pulsating, rhythmic beat. *Thump thump, thump thump, thump thump.*

My fangs dripped with anticipation. I turned my head and punctured through to the breaking point. Her skin melted under my bite as though it were butter softened by the stove.

"Drink her in, m'lady—imbibe in her spirits. Intoxicate in her crimson liquors."

I removed my fang and her arterial fountain flowed. Her heartbeat grew louder, surging through my ears while I drank her deep into my soul. My eyes kaleidoscoped around and round as my thoughts filled with sex, pleasure, comfort, warmth, and peace. Her blood tasted of mother's milk, manna from heaven. I never wanted to stop bathing in this euphoric moment. No wonder rogues lived the way they did. How could I ever go back to bottled bloodwines after tasting this magnificent bounty?

More ... I want more!

Khaldon gently nudged my mouth away with his tongue. I moved over and allowed him a morsel of my delicious feast. But instead, he licked my puncture mark and lowered the girl to the ground.

Khaldon raised Ponytail's neck and pointed to where I bit her. "Now, Cheyenne, what do you see?"

I studied the mark and turned her chin back and forth to get a better view in the light. "It looks like any old red mark, or a mosquito bite. Maybe she scratched herself with a fingernail?" I mused.

"Righto! You were able to feed discreetly, and now she's left with a bite that looks like nothing. She'll either get drunk or high tonight, or sleep it off over the next couple of days. I usually offer a suggestion to take their vitamins and get a good night's sleep."

I stood up and gestured to the girl. "So by using the one prick method, vampires have flown under the radar for centuries?"

He gave me a sheepish grin.

Hmm ... I wonder if I had ever been bitten and not known it.

"Are you ready for dessert, my love?" Khaldon offered me Beer Guy's limp wrist. A wrist at odds with his upright posture and his full-on erection.

I pointed to Beer Guy's pants. "Is that normal?"

Khaldon's eyebrows shot up with an evil enticement. "Just as you can sense the arousal from her, he too has the same reaction. So yes, quite often, men will reward you with an erection. What you choose to do with it, of course, is your choice. Many vampires will take full advantage of a human's sexual arousal. Not that I want you to, my dear—just saying."

I winked at him.

Again, I performed the *piquant* controlling the blood flow and giving me time to suck down mouthfuls of deliciousness without causing a mess. Tonight, I was the apex predator. I could have easily ripped out this guy's throat, but for the first time, I was empowered to do what I wanted. Just knowing I could destroy this man's life sent heady, intoxicating passion shooting through my neural pathways leaving me panting for more.

I'm going to be all right. I can hunt and still be the same me.

Khaldon whispered in my ear as I continued to fill my belly with live human red blood cells. "Move to his neck just as you did with the woman." Khaldon pushed the man up against the tree, and I sank my controlled fang into his throbbing artery. Revitalizing fresh, carotid pulses gushed straight from his heart. The vital dynamics of the exchange ignited the kindling desires deep within me.

Khaldon consumed a small amount from the comatose woman and brought his attention back to me. His smile revealed a mouth stained with the beautiful elixir. "Had your fill, m'love?"

One seductive leer from Khaldon, and I knew what I wanted. I craved him. I hungered for all of him. Inside me, filling me to the brink of this eternal ecstasy.

"Are you ready to let our prey go on their way?"

I nodded several times in enthusiastic accession.

"Then release their enthrall and give them the mind messaging you desire, be it what may."

I gave him a devious, wicked grin. "Could I tell them to rob a bank or something insane crazy like that?"

"You could, but I always live under the laws of three. What you do will come back to you thrice. So unless you want someone to steal from you three times, I'd reconsider your temptation." He cocked an eyebrow at me seemingly to say, *it's your choice, but I wouldn't.*

I couldn't absorb enough of how Khaldon's verdant green eyes shone with the reflections of the soft snow light.

"Harm none, but take no shite—that's my motto. Or at least that's how I try to live my life now, anyway. There was another time when I wasn't as kind as I am now—but that was centuries ago."

I elbowed him in the ribs. "I'm sure Vhalencia and Chuck have a few sordid tales about you. It would be nice to get to know them one day."

"Indeed, not sure when, but as soon as we can, I'd love to have you visit my home in Dubai. Let's plan a vacation over there as soon we can. Would you like that?"

"Indeed, I would, Mr. Seters." I grinned ear to ear and I could feel my eyes sparkle with excitement for traveling abroad for a real vacation.I turned to Beer Guy and Pony Tail and considered what I would want a vampire to say to me if the situation were reversed. I didn't want to disappoint Khaldon and awaken these people to have them run screaming out from under the tree, so I did what seemed natural.

I pulled the couple close to me and wrapped my arms around them whispering, "Thank you for a lovely chat. Tonight, you will remember having a wild tryst under the pine tree together. You will walk away feeling satisfied, happy, alive, and very thirsty. You'll walk to the first drug store and purchase water and vitamins. You will have no detailed memory of us. You will always look upon this tree and smile to yourself. Now, go."

As though someone turned on a light, the couple awakened from their trance. They exchanged slightly embarrassed glances with us. The guy slapped Khaldon on the back and the lady kissed my cheek. Ponytail interlaced her hand with her boyfriend's and they scampered out from underneath the boughs of the trees. I heard Ponytail giggle while they headed toward the dime store across the street.

Khaldon put his arm around my shoulder as we watched the couple meander away. "Well done, m'lady. Well done!"

I kissed him on the cheek, allowing my lips to linger.

He turned his face to me and whispered into my mouth. "Did you enjoy the celebration of your vampyric virginity? The first step of your training is complete now. Now you'll need to do it on your own and alone to fully master the technique. Each hunt is different and challenging within it's own right."

Why do his eyes always seem so hauntingly familiar—like I've known him, loved him, all my life?

I listened to his words and realized I still had a lot of training before me. But tonight, Khaldon had taught me not only how to hunt humans, but he gave me style and panache with which to do it well. As we kissed for a few minutes longer under the tree, I realized the town had grown dark all around us. I broke our kiss and pointed toward the store. "Look, the lights. They've gone out. The music stopped too. I think we're in a blackout."

"Then this is a perfect time." He broke our embrace and reached into his jacket pocket.

"Time for what?"

Khaldon handed me a velvety crimson box about the size of my palm.

"What's this? A little something before the world ends tonight?" I shouldn't have laughed at the world's dire issues, but right at this perfect moment, under this romantic moon, it was my turn to finally find a slice of paradise.

For the first time in a long time, I didn't care what was going on anywhere else. My sights were laser-focused on Khaldon, and nothing would deter me from having the best sex of my life with the man I loved.

Khaldon gestured with his head toward the gift box. "I hope my gift isn't pretentious." He pulled me in closer and lifted my chin. His eyes bored deep into me. "But I wouldn't have this night commence any other way."

ುೆಯಾ

Puzzled at Khaldon's gift and not quite sure what to say, I decided to answer him with another kiss. I seductively slipped my arms around his shoulders and clasped them behind his neck.

My nervous laugh betrayed me again as I could sense the jittery anticipation of our coupling. Neither able to—nor wanting to—control my vampyric pheromones, I sensed our eager potency as our collected scents perfumed the hot, moist air between us. I stood on my tiptoes to kiss him and he lowered his mouth to meet my hunger.

Khaldon's lips were smooth and inviting. He was no slouch in the lip-works department. Most guys either choked you with their tongues, or painted-by-numbers with drool, but not Khaldon. He had the fine art of kissing down to a perfect science with a gentle nibble here, a tongue teaser there.

The best part was how tightly bound he held me. As though he didn't intend to allow the very air to escape from between us. His transfixed attention confirmed in my heart that I was the center of his universe and nothing else mattered to him at this moment. My heart knew I would never have to put up with another guy who kissed me with his eyes open watching a sports game.

Nothing would take his attention from me. Tonight it was us, and only us.

Our feverish pace picked up and instead of apprehension and embarrassment at my own clumsiness, I stepped up and pulled out all the stops determined to choreograph a night we would cherish forever. We threw ourselves into one another, and I reveled at the weight of his body next to mine.

"I hoped, perhaps, after tonight, you'd always stay with me. I can't tell you how long I've fantasized waking up with you in my arms." Khaldon nuzzled my neck, continuously kissing up my hairline with every breath.

Speechless, I swallowed down the emotion stuck in my throat.

Khaldon urged me to open the little box again.

I stole a glance up at his face and his features seemed to mimic my own emotions.

Is he biting his lip? Am I?

I took a deep breath and pulled the white satin ribbon. It was real satin fabric, not that cheapie stuff you get at the holidays. Taking the ribbon from me, he then tied it around a lock of my hair.

I paused and then looked in his eyes.

"It's all right, it won't bite." He urged me onward. "No spiders, I promise."

Opening the lid revealed an antique, ornate ring garnished in gems and hieroglyphs.

Khaldon's voice shook with emotion while he gently took my free hand and said, "Cheyenne, I have known you for two years, eight months, four days, twenty-two hours, sixteen minutes and..." He looked at his watch. "Eight seconds."

I swallowed hard to move that ever-growing lump at what might come next.

"During this time spent with you, I've been the happiest man, even as we have surmounted the challenges and tragedies we've faced. I want to get to know who you are in this reality, Cheyenne, as well as I knew who you were as Lady Cazenove in our virtual world. This recent time apart has convinced me of this. I never want to be away from you again. Ever."

The whisper touch of his hand sent electricity through me as the very breath in my chest escaped. Khaldon removed the ring from the box and knelt on one knee in front of me.

"Cheyenne Madeline O'Cuinn, I am asking you to share both my worlds and be mine for as long as we both shall live. Will you honor me and become my wife? Will you sleep beside me for the rest of our lives?"

In an instant, millions of memories flashed through my mind. Ones from when I was a little girl and dreamed about the man whom I would marry in a castle up in the clouds. Was I ready to make a marital commitment? Was Khaldon the man I knew to be the only man I would ever want in my life?

The heat in my face blossomed a red flush as my hands shook while I tried to cradle his face.

I wanted him. I wanted his soul. I wanted to know him more intimately than he knew himself.

"Yes—Khaldon—I would be honored to be your wife!"

Khaldon slid the gem-encrusted ring onto my left ring finger. His muscular strength picked me up and twirled me around as though I were a little girl running into her parent's arms after her first day of kindergarten. I squealed with excitement, at what our engagement meant between us, and the fact that my head hit an overhead branch. He lowered me onto his lips and kissed me most tenderly. He lovingly caressed the place on my head where the branch had made contact.

The kiss of a lifetime of coupling. Together we agreed to make our lives one until death do us part, and for Vampyre, our agreement truly meant forever.

"This was my mother's ring passed to her from our ancestor Sekhmet. This ring was the engagement gift from Ptah, Sekhmet's husband, and this ring has been passed down each generation since."

I gawked at him. "You mean *the* Sekhmet, the warrior goddess?"

He nodded. "Yes, Ptah had this ring commissioned for her in his everlasting love. She wore it until the day she died and told her son, Maahes, that one day he would find the love of his life and he should honor and laud her with this ring." Khaldon kissed my hand. "The ring has been bequeathed to me, and you will honor us all if you would wear it as my truest love."

I had so many words I wanted to say, to do, to express—but all I could muster without ruining the moment was, "I love you, Khaldon. Thank you for celebrating us."

I reached up and pulled him closer, kissing him again.

The energy between us solidified. Comfortable. Settled. Majestic.

Khaldon lowered us down onto the aromatic bed of soft pine needles. Our mouths and hands couldn't stop. Nothing was holding us back as the snow fell harder and our passion grew higher.

I wanted him.

I wanted to consume him on every level. It was as if another whole creature leeched out of my skin and I experienced a fever-pitch of need I'd never known before.

The heat of our bodies created a sort of steam vapor under the tree, and my world, my vision, was clouded over in complete submission and domination. Khaldon took me, and I took him. We rocked the rhythm of the silence until we could no longer breathe. Until we could no longer feel the difference between his skin and mine.

We were one.

At the height of our consummation, instinct plunged my fangs into his neck at the same moment his teeth punctured my own throat. The coupling—the bonding by me drinking of him and his consumption of me, became a symbiotic exchange of biblical proportions.

We shared our life-force energy. We were one in every sense of the word.

Completely lost within his empowering energy, my insides quaked, filling with every inch of him. Our bodies entangled in a web of arms and legs. I struggled to get closer to him. Simply to become him.

A dammed gateway burst open, and detailed memories of his childhood showcased in my mind. I watched his life's fondest memories through his eyes. A young Khaldon playing in the reeds near a pyramid, teenage Khaldon carving his a hieroglyph into a stone. Fast forwarding through the memory show revealed images of his computer monitor while he watched our avatars dancing on the bow of the Titanic, horseback-riding across Irish glades, spelunking in underground caves, and making love whenever we could.

I watched his mind movies as he meticulously oil painted the portrait of the two of us, which now hung above his fireplace mantel. Lovingly written in his own script with a feathered fountain pen, his letters scrolled out to me—ones he had never sent but which spilled forth in his prose of love. I drank him in on every pull of his blood's life force and shared my memories with him so he could also experience the undying love I held for him. Everything I knew, loved, and craved to know about him, was mine for the taking. Our union was complete.

We were bonded for eternity.

ॐ

Instead of relaxing into a climatic sleep into one another's arms, the realization of a branch sticking into my side and the hard, sharp bark of pine cones scraped my skin. My hands were sticky with resinous sap.

A pang of uneasiness slithered through me as images of my nightmare undulated behind my eyelids. I didn't want to share those dark moments from my rogue attack, but they kept coming stronger, rolling in with more detailed violence than I remembered.

Khaldon and I both tried to pull away from one another's embrace, but our mouths refused to release as though we were fused to one another's skin. The suction on our blood bondage would not unlock. Images of my vicious violation deluged my mind.

So many people dead.

The mermaid and her boyfriend ... consumed. I saw myself standing there in scraps of a bloodied mummy costume, bent over, crouched with a phone in my hand, surrounded by the thick, noxious fog. The severed hand holding on to the phone fell away and splattered against my foot and onto the floor. I slammed down the window panes to those horrific images in my mind, desperately struggling not to share my darkest moment with Khaldon.

The Red Man called out to me, "Please, help me!"

I tried to open my eyes, to break away from this nightmare before Khaldon learned too much, but inevitably we were bound to see it through. I watched his movie as I saw my pulse, hammering through my carotid and re-lived the same excruciating pain from when that monster savaged my throat.

Unholy hell! Am I reliving the attack ... through Khaldon's eyes?! How is this possible?

A muffled scream escaped my mouth as I struggled to pull away. My mind registered that I was consuming the very same blood, right now, at this very moment, from when I bit into the rogue vampire's hand flooding my mouth with his vampyric DNA.

I threw open my eyes and thrashed at Khaldon's chest. I pounded feverishly, breaking the hypnotic enthrall, and I pulled away as he pushed me at the same time, getting me as far away from himself as possible.

My fangs ripped through the muscle in his neck, leaving a double rake of torn flesh as the union between us was utterly shattered. An overwhelming, horrifying understanding came over me.

I relived the lust in his eyes.

His eyes—those haunting eyes. No, it can't be!

I shook my head. Rivers of blood ran down my neck and dripped off my breasts. Tears followed with the anguish of Khaldon's exposed knowledge.

My voice went raw with denial, "*No!* You? This—just—I can't believe—" I held my hands over my mouth and stared at him. "It was you?!"

His face seemed as aghast as mine and searched for what looked like an explanation. Khaldon stood wordless, shaking his head, one hand over his heart, and the other reaching out for me.

Khaldon, Roxas, my love, my best friend, my fiancé—the man I had pledged my life to—was my rogue vampyric attacker?

I whispered, "The demon, Red Man monster who left me to die last Halloween—that beast was you?"

He stood stone still, unable to speak, his face as tear-stained as mine. Life had given and taken away everything I ever wanted within a single blip of time.

In that moment, we were forever lost and I was truly dead.

Chapter 21

Flying F Ranch Guest House

Cheyenne O'Cuinn

The drive home was fast and silent. I jumped out of the car before it stopped moving.

"Cheyenne! Cheyenne, wait! Let's work through this," Khaldon implored me to speak with him while I tore my eyes away and raced through the doorway.

Beano trotted to my side and sniffed me up and down. "Good boy. Stay with Momma."

Sheridan met me at the bedroom door with Khai in her arms. Stormy ran out of the room behind her and nuzzled Beano's side.

"Hey, Chey?" Sheridan yawned. "Everything okay? Just gettin' a bottle for Khai."

Harris stopped practicing his new obsession, singing the cups game using a pistol as accompaniment. He pulled the bag of homemade venison jerky from a rear pants pocket. Torchy's Labradors, Ash and Soot, sat with rapt attention, their tails wagging, just waiting for their weird-looking pack mate to drop a piece of venison jerky onto the floor.

Harris spoke through a fresh mouthful of jerky. "Whazzup? You trying to wake the whole house? Want some?" Knowing it was one of my favorite snacks, he sing-songed, swinging the bag to tempt me with Uncle Charlie's smoked delights. "It's Teriyaki flavored."

Khaldon pounded through the door after me. "Cheyenne, please, wait. We can talk through this. Something's not right." He stood in the entry hall, his shirt half tucked and his belt unbuckled.

Torchy and Briggs stood up from the kitchen table, which they had covered in firearms in various stages of disassembly and cleaning. They held pistol magazines in their hands.

Harris raised an eyebrow and shot Torchy an *uh-oh, lover's quarrel* expression.

Torchy reached out to Sheridan and gave her and Khai quick pecks on the forehead. He redirected his attention toward us. "Everything al'right, you two?"

Flummoxed, I decided nothing good was going to come of standing still.

I needed to move.

"No—we're *not* all right. I need to disappear." I left Khaldon in the hall with the guys and rushed past Sheridan into the bedroom. "Sher, can you *please* come in here?"

She followed me, but then she stepped back into the hallway and whispered, "Torchy, can you warm a bottle for Khai?"

Beano and Stormaggedon scampered behind us and into the bedroom.

"Can you close the door?" I rushed her with flapping hand movements.

"Sure, what's going on? What in the world has you so upset?"

"I have to leave. I have to get out of here, and for your own safety we need to make Khaldon leave the ranch as soon as possible. It's not safe for anyone as long as he's here."

She scrunched up her face as though she'd encountered something rotten, but that could have been Khai's diaper. "Wait. Hold up. What's the deal here? Are you, okay? Are you hurt?"

"No, I'm not hurt."

Even though my heart will never be the same....

I rushed back to the bedroom and locked the door. "I just found out that he..." I heaved an unsteady breath and pointed toward the door. "Khaldon is my...."

"Cheyenne? Calm down. You're shaking like mad." Sheridan shuffled closer in her slippers while Beano sat on my foot.

"Khaldon is my rogue vampire attacker!" Turning away from the door, I snatched a couple of tissues out of the Kleenex box atop the dresser knocking over a vase of flowers. "He's the one who attacked and killed those people and left me for dead Halloween night!"

Sheridan's eyes widened. "What?! Are you feckin' kidding me?" She caught the vase and settled it with one hand while cradling Khai in the other. Her pulse quickened as she brought her hand to her mouth and rushed to my side.

Khai stirred in her arms.

Her voice quieted. "Khaldon?" She reached down and pulled Khai's sleepy head toward her shoulder while she gently rocked him on her hip. She lowered her voice to a whisper. "How's that possible? He loves you. Khaldon would never do anything to harm us." She grimaced, causing her eyebrows to tighten on her forehead. "Are you sure? What makes you think it was him?"

I squinted in defeat, rubbing my temples not wanting to tell my horrific tale. Frantically, I patted my pockets for my keys and looked around the room for my suitcases.

"Oh no, did he confess it to you?"

Loud exclamations erupted from the kitchen, but the words were too muffled to understand them. Khaldon must have been telling the guys his side of the story.

"No, I witnessed it through his blood memories. None of this makes any sense. He wants to talk about it, but I'm scared to death of him." I paced the room. "I'm afraid he'll try to hurt me again. I've been haunted by that feckin' Red Man all my life, and I can't face that hideous creature." I pointed to the kitchen through the wall. "He will kill me if given the chance. I just know it!"

Sheridan didn't say anything. She frowned and rapidly blinked in confusion.

"It's so horrific, I've never discussed it. I've never told anyone about what happened that night I was attacked. I didn't even tell the hospital shrinks about it because I was afraid they would lock me up for a long time with paranoid delusions. The nightmares have been haunting me, and now I know why."

"I remember how awful the Red Man dreams were when you were younger, but I'd no clue they continued to plague you as an adult." Sheridan rocked Khai back and forth and patted his behind. "I can't imagine the horror you must have felt to have those dreams come true." She raised her hand to her mouth. "Oh, sweetie." She hugged me as best she could with Khai in her arms.

"I've never been able to finish the dream. It's so terrifying and I have no idea what exactly is going to come next. It's just this steamy bathroom and it's hot and I can't see through the haze. Then the Red Man is suddenly there in the mirror behind me. Pouring blood all over me." I pulled on my hair in frustration and tousled the red, unruly curls out of my face. Pine needles and small pine cones fell to the floor. "To make everything worse, we just—we just—umm...."

Oh hell.

"He asked me to marry him, and I said yes. So we ... *ya know....*"

Sheridan grinned at me with a knowing curl to her lip. Her eyes twinkled. "Really? You're getting married? But what about ... oh, no!"

I watched as the realization of the situation fell over her in a shroud of understanding.

"Precisely!" I fumbled in the nightstand drawer for a ponytail holder and whipped my hair up on top of my head. Massive tears rolled down my cheeks, mourning the perfect relationship gone to shit as soon as it began. "That's just it. We exchanged blood during—"

She recoiled, hands-up, wrinkling her nose.

"Whatever. I don't think about you and Torchy and your little dragon sex quirks."

She pulled at her collar, covering more of her skin while clearing her throat. "This isn't about me. What are you going to do?"

"I'll hold you to that sister dragon sex conversation one day." I reached into the closet and grabbed my overnight bag.

She pretended not to hear and tugged on Khai's woobie as a distraction.

I threw the bag on the bed and opened drawers. Clothes started flying. Beano jumped onto the bed and hovered over the suitcase.

"I have to leave. I can't stay here. I'm not safe. None of us are. We exchanged blood and that's when I saw his memories through his eyes. It was like watching the worst horror movie—*ever!* I experienced him attacking all those other people, killing the mermaid, watching him tear hands and legs from people to bathe in their blood. Then he moved on to me, begging me for help, ravaging my throat, and draining me. Once the police sirens wailed, he dropped me to the cold floor and left me for dead. I watched him escape the park. Sheridan, he is the killer!"

"A mermaid?"

I stared at her. "I just said all that and you're stuck on the mermaid?" I waved her question away. "Never mind, it's complicated and gross."

She grimaced. "This is so not good. Are you going to the main house?"

"Of course not. I can't go to the main house. Aunt Maisie and Uncle Charlie don't know anything about Supernaturals. That's the last place I can go."

Exhausted from the emotional roller coaster, I wanted nothing more than to fall into bed, cry my head off, and drift off into a reality where vampires didn't exist. The survivor side of me, however, pushed onward. The safest act was to get the hell out of the house.

I frantically grabbed my ditty bag. "I just need to get away for a couple days and wrap my mind around this. Maybe drive down to Missoula."

"Is there a Lord Stovall type of person up here you can go to for protection?"

"I have no idea. I'll check it out, but bottom line, I can't stay here. There's no telling what Khaldon will do now that he knows I know. We have to make him leave for your own safety. What if he attacks you or the baby next?"

Her eyes widened in shock. "What the bloody hell, Cheyenne? Do you really think he's capable of doing that?"

My mind said yes, but my heart definitely said no.

⚜

Flying F Ranch Guest House Kitchen

Khaldon Seters

The guys stood staring at me in an uncomfortable silence. They each held a look of understanding of what it's like to be fighting with a woman.

"C'mon, let's grab a drink." Harris scratched behind his ears. "Lover's spat, I presume? She'll get over it."

I followed Harris, Briggs, and Torchy into the kitchen. "I wish it were that simple, but I've got a dangerously serious issue on my hands."

Soot's doggie nails clicked on the tile as he sauntered from the hallway and lay down on the kitchen floor, his eyes never leaving the bag of jerky.

Briggs placed his red Solo cups on the counter and tossed an empty beer bottle into the kitchen garbage with a *clang*. His french accent always deepened after a few beers. "We've been working on a trio gun cups 'and-jive action. I never knew Torch 'ad a wicked voice, and 'Arris is damn good at back up. We're gonna go on the road one day."

I smiled, but it faded quickly. The eight-hundred-pound gorilla in the room sat on it.

I stared at Briggs, my lips tight.

Briggs furrowed his brow. "Whaddya mean dangerously serious? Are dzere more cities without power?"

"No, this situation has nothing to do with the power outages and everything to do with the attack on Cheyenne at Halloween." I pointed to the red cups scattered around the room. "That's pretty bad ass by the way. Good thing you aren't practicing with live ammo."

Harris snatched four beers from the fridge and doled them out. Torchy placed the pistol and plastic bullets on the counter. He reached for a bottle of prepared whole blood in the side door. I leaned against the counter, inhaled a deep, laboring breath, and stood in utter denial at how I could possibly be Cheyenne's attacker. It was unconscionable to consider.

How could I have lost control like that? Was that really me?

"Chey Chey's attack?" Briggs popped off the top of his beer with his teeth. "Did dzey find dze sonofabitch?"

How am I going to possibly explain this without getting lynched?

I stared down at the ornate pattern in the mosaic tile, tracing the lines, stalling, searching for a way to explain this awful situation.

I pulled a long, slow swig of beer, and finally caved to the inevitable. "I asked Cheyenne to marry me tonight."

Torchy filled a tea kettle with water as the kitchen erupted with congratulations.

"That's fantastic! When's the unlucky date?" Harris jabbed.

Briggs punched me in the shoulder. "*Oui!* Rio de Janeiro bachelor party 'as our names all over it."

"What are ye daein, ya dobber? I cannae believe you're finally tying the knot." Torchy put down the tea kettle and jumped over to me. He picked me off the floor and hugged me tight to his chest. "I've got the perfect place for your honeymoon, mate. There's this place off the coast of—"

"Put me down, you pure wanker." I laughed and tried to hush the guys with my hands. The looks on their faces were confused. "Shhh." I held my finger up to my mouth. "Keep it down, fellas." I glanced toward Cheyenne's bedroom, praying she would come to her senses and talk to me. "Thanks, guys. But listen, something went deadly wrong."

"What are you getting at?" Torchy lit the stove and checked the temperature of the water. "She turned you down?"

"Nah, you numpty bogger, when she said yes, we—*ya know*...." I revealed a shy half-smile and ran a hand through my hair and picked out a few pine needles. They were sticky in my hand. I threw the sap sticks into the bin and pulled hard again on the bottle, emptying it.

"We had the blood exchange."

All eyebrows around the room went up in understanding and heads nodded.

Torchy poked his finger in the hot water to check the temperature. "How does this have anything to do wit' Cheyenne's attack? Did she dredge up some old memories or something?"

I stood straighter and squared my shoulders. "The blood exchange revealed hidden memories to both of us."

The guys looked perplexed. Harris' eyes squished up his face.

"I just relived attacking and killing all those innocents on Halloween through my *own* memories. Cheyenne was one of them."

The guys gawked at me. Dumbfounded shock graced their expressions. Not a word was said for a long minute.

"Somehow—and I have no feckin' way of knowing if it's true—but it seems as if I am the rogue vampire attacker."

The tea kettle screamed.

Ash barked at the high-pitched squeal.

"Get dze fuck outta here." Briggs snorted into his beer.

Harris stoically stood still with an *oh shit* expression on his face.

Torchy turned the heat off from under the kettle and chugged his beer. He cocked his head sideways. "Mate? What the bloody hell did you just say?"

"I know, right? I think I'm the rogue attacker who left Cheyenne to die in that wretched room. I don't understand how or why. I'm totally banjaxed to figure it out." I tried to swallow down the thick, hard lump stuck in my throat, but it was lodged sideways as if tentacles where holding on to it for dear life.

Harris asked, "Where were you that night then? Wasn't Cheyenne supposed to meet you at the waterfalls?"

"I've been wracking my brain about it and I honestly can't remember. I just don't know."

Briggs crossed his arms over his chest. "Whaddya mean you don't remember?" He leaned against the side of the fridge closer to me. "Dzat doesn't make any sense."

"I remember going to the park. Then, the next thing I knew Lord Stovall had called me to the yacht. He said there'd been an attack on the theme park. Shortly after that, I was on *The Resurrection*. Later that morning, Kiernan called and told me Cheyenne was in the hospital. It never occurred to me to think why I hadn't seen her."

"This is mad mental." Torchy poured the hot water from the kettle into a pan and placed Khai's bottle in it to warm. He grabbed the counter tight, and his knuckles turned white.

Harris opened his mouth to say something and then he closed it again before speaking.

"Something's rotten inside me, and I have to figure it out. Cheyenne is scared to death right now—and honestly, I don't blame her. She won't let me talk to her about it. You saw how she was."

Harris shook his head. "Dude, you remember what Cheyenne looked like in the hospital? She was almost dead. Of course, she's gonna be ridiculously scared of you. There's no way in hell I would talk to you either."

I blew out exasperated puffed cheeks, vibrating my lips. "Most likely, Sheridan is gonna come out of their room just as frightened of me, and I'm probably never gonna see Khai again."

Briggs put his beer down on the counter. "So wait ... you're saying dzat you dzink you're the attacker, but you don't remember doing it? 'Ow is dzat possible?"

"Bloody hell if I know. But the blood exchange opened locked memories inside both of us. We both watched as she saw me kill people and attack, leaving her for dead. There was this mermaid ... I heard the sirens and ran out the back door and swam across the lake." I rubbed my head as the flashes kept coming in waves. "The more I try to recall, the more I think Amicula was involved. That's where everything goes fuzzy. Like someone had written a script to blur out the faces."

Harris asked, "Wait—there was a mermaid?"

Torchy and Briggs looked at Harris and then asked the same question with their eyes as they looked again toward me.

"Never mind. It's kinda complicated," I explained.

Torchy asked, "How can you discover the truth? Do you honestly think you could kill like that, especially Cheyenne?"

"No, I don't believe I could do that now. Centuries ago, yeah, it was no big deal, but that was before the Human Preservation Act."

The guys nodded their heads, possibly recalling some of their own prior exploits. A sly smile escaped Briggs' lips as though he remembered something special or naughty. Or something especially naughty.

"I'm afraid the only way I'm going to learn the truth to these blood memories is to succumb to the blood trials."

Torchy took a defensive posture. "No way, mate. You're an idiot tube to believe this shite. I bloody well know you, and you wouldn't do this of your own accord. This is haverin' nonsense. That nutter Amicula bitch has to be behind this. I cannae believe it, and I won't let you do the exsanguination."

Briggs whistled. "Damn, man, dze blood trials? Dzat shit ain't cool. I've 'eard rumors—'ardly anyone ever survives dzem. If anyone does, dzey're never quite dze same."

I chewed on my lip and stared at him. At all of them. "What other choice do I have? How can I know the truth if I don't subject myself to this?"

"Wait, what's the exsanguination?" Harris asked. "What does our game have anything to do with this?"

"No, not *ExsanguiNation*. It's the draining of blood. The blood trials is a way I can test my blood memories and learn if there's anything I don't remember." I put down my empty beer bottle and stared at the ceiling. "It's like a blood lie detector test. The results reveal truths, even if you don't recall them."

"Is it possible someone or something could 'ave planted false memories into your blood?" Briggs asked.

"I've never heard of anything like that, Briggs. I guess anything is possible."

"What about hypnosis? Why do you have to drain your blood?" Harris opened the fridge and removed another beer. He handed it to me. "What'll happen if the tests prove you're the attacker? Do you have to go to some kind of silver encrusted vampire jail or something?"

I shook my head, almost disregarding his question, but thought better of it. "Hypnosis doesn't work on the Vampyric mind, only weaker human brains. Ultimately, it's up to the queen to decide my fate if I'm guilty. If I succumb to the blood trials, I can learn if my blood is clean. If it isn't, then I need to understand what happened to me, who did it, and figure out where to go from there. But to answer your question—there's no real vampire jail, but Queen Civetateo could have me put to death. And if I did kill those people, then don't I deserve it? Why should my life be spared when others have met the undeniable death for the same crime?"

"I appreciate your help guys. It means a ton. But I don't have any answers." I slumped against the counter and ran my hands down my face. "Guys, how is Cheyenne ever going to forgive me?"

The kitchen fell silent and we could hear Khai's cries through the walls.

I clenched my eyes shut and bound my fists together. My voice fell to barely a whisper. "I feel so out of control."

∞∞

Cheyenne O'Cuinn

"Hold up." Sheridan held up her hand. Her face stoic. She had morphed into CEO mode. "Look, there're three sides to everything. Yours, his, and the truth. Let's get to the bottom of this whacked out situation and figure things out. I say we talk it out in a safe environment and see what Khaldon can tell us. There's a lot more to this story than I think either of you realize."

I shook my head, smearing more bloody tears across my face. I kept on stuffing clothes and toiletries into my bag.

Beano sniffed at my clothes. "Get out of there." I gently pushed on his nose. "Don't worry, big fella, I'm not leaving without you."

Beano sat down next to the suitcase, and Stormy yapped to get on the bed. "Where's your suitcase? We need to pack you and Khai too."

"Cheyenne, I can see you're really scared. I would be too. But c'mon, let's go pour a tall glass of wine and work through this." She picked up Stormy and put her on the bed. "Hell, we're all scared with the shite hitting the fan the way it has tonight, but I'm sure Khaldon is just as upset over all this as you. He's done so much to help us. He's already a part of our family whether you like it or not. I can't imagine him doing anything to purposefully hurt any of us, especially you."

I listened to Sheridan's words, but I just couldn't make myself believe it. Her logic made total sense, and the little angel sitting on my right shoulder was rooting her on, but I stammered, "I ... I can't." My mind raced out of control. The little red demon on my left shoulder continued to stab me in the neck with the horrific images of Khaldon the Terrible destroying those people. The way he ripped Janie the mermaid in half and showered in her blood, the way he tore hands and legs from bodies all around me and laughed about it was more than my mind could bear.

I couldn't relive any more of it.

"Promise me you'll leave the ranch or you'll make him go. We have to get you to the main house tonight. Don't be alone at any time while he's here. Make sure Harris or Torchy stays with you and Khai tonight."

Sheridan put Khai back in his crib and he cried out for her. She opened up her arms and hugged me. "Oh, sweetie. I'm so sorry this has happened to you—to both of you. I love Khaldon like a brother, and I know how much you love him." She held me at arm's length and looked me straight in the face. "But I'm not going to move into the main house tonight. Torchy is here. I'm okay. We're fine. We're protected."

I vehemently shook my head.

She continued, "I know this is a real shock, for both of you. And now—you're engaged. How are you going to get through this?"

She reached in to hug me again, but I cut her off with a violent slice to my throat. "I can't ever trust that horrible creature. He's a real-life Jekyll and Hyde."

My sister's tone of voice changed as she firmly grabbed my shoulders. "Listen, it's obvious you're frightened, but dammit, you need to listen to me now. Get a hold of yourself. There's a worldwide crisis going on out there, and there's no telling what city is going to be hit next or what type of disaster you could be driving into. You need to stay here, on this ranch, where we know it's safe. I need you here to make sure *ExsanguiNation* is running and available for emergency help for people who are in real life-or-death situations."

I gaped at her insensitive words. Narrowing my eyes I could have spit poison at her but I knew she was trying to be. I certainly wasn't. "You don't think this is a life-or-death situation for me?" I seized my bags, jacket, keys, and cell phone and wrenched open the bedroom door, which led out into the main hallway. I stepped into the foyer and turned around with Beano hot on my heels.

The guys stared at me with forlorn expressions from the kitchen. They said nothing, but Khaldon reached out his hand to me. "Cheyenne?"

My heart urged me to converge, but I didn't move.

"I don't know what to do!" my voice broke from the hysteria and I tried to breathe and calm myself.

Obviously sensing I was terrified, Beano nudged my leg and whined.

Sheridan peeked out of the bedroom with the baby in her arms as I got to the front door. Torchy brought the warmed bottle out to Sheridan and put his arm around her, his face solemn. Ash and Soot sat by their feet.

Nobody said a word. They stood in shock, staring at me most likely thinking I was lying for accusing the wonderful Khaldon of such a heinous crime.

Khaldon took a tentative step toward me. "Please, m'lady?" He took another step and I dropped my bags onto the floor. Defeated, I had to try.

In less than an instant, he cradled me in his arms while I fell apart. We slid down the wall as I sobbed. "Who could have done this to us? Why?"

Khaldon stroked my hair and tugged out more pine needles. "I am reliving this just as you are. I don't have any conscious memory of that terrible night, Cheyenne. You have to believe me."

Sheridan spoke quietly, "We need to investigate, understand what's going on. Learn who's behind this and why."

I resigned and Beano licked my face. His doggy kisses were a welcome relief, a safe refuge from the terrors.

Torchy cleared his throat. "It's obvious. It's that crazy loon, Amicula. She *has* to be behind it. She is the common denominator."

Harris squatted down beside us. "We'll get to the bottom of this, Chey. You've got a lot to process. When we first change into Weres, the pack sends us off for a couple days to read and mentally work through things. Ya know, so we can wrap our heads around it. Then when we're ready, we come back for answers. You need to process this or it'll eat you up inside."

"He's right." Khaldon lifted my chin and looked deep into my eyes. Both of us, our eyes rimmed in bloody trails. "You need time to work through the myriad of emotions going through you. A good couple days would be good for you. I've got to get back to Florida. To find Stovall. He's the only one who can help me right now."

I reached out to cup his cheek and held tight onto his arm. "But the man I know and love, he—you would never have done this. My head and mind are telling me horrible things, but my heart knows you're innocent."

"It's the only way, Cheyenne. I have to learn what's inside my blood memories. Learn what else Amicula has been doing to me. She's raped me, and now this. It's out of control, and I can't allow it any longer. I've got to reclaim myself before I can be any semblance of a man for you."

Torchy asked, "Just what exactly will the exsanguination tell you?"

"The blood trials tell the truth, even if you don't remember it. If I've been wronged—"

I cut him off, my voice incredulous. "If? We've all been victims of her wrongs."

"Yes, once I can read and see the blood memories in their entirety, then I will have the proof I need to convict Amicula of her crimes and present the evidence to the queen. But I have to go to Stovall to do it. And I have to do this alone."

Khai slurped on his bottle and Stormy nudged her head into the palm of my hand. She licked my fingers. Briggs and Torchy helped us off the floor. I tried to smooth down my shirt and realized what a mess I was.

"I—I just don't know what to do. Everything is so confusing. And now this?" I lifted my left hand and indicated to the ring.

"I know, and I understand. Until I can figure out what I've done, and who I am, I want to put our engagement on hold." He kissed the ring on my left ring finger.

I wiped the tears from my eyes. "What? But I—"

"Cheyenne, look—bollocks, I know I said I never wanted to be apart again, but right now I don't deserve you. I'm not safe, and I can't trust myself to be around anyone until I can get control of this insanity." Khaldon beat his fist against the wall, puncturing the drywall. "If everything we saw tonight is true, the queen is going to—she won't let me live. I have the sword of Damocles hanging over my head. I don't want you to be engaged to a dead man walking. Until I learn what has happened, I have no right to keep you on reserve. I won't do that to you. Once I clear my name and prove Amicula has done this to me, then I can be the man who can truly honor you as a husband and a friend."

"But I don't care. We'll find a way, we'll get through it." The tone of my voice begged for his belief that I could be stronger, that maybe I could find a way to handle the Red Man. "Let me come with you. I can help—"

He cut me off and his eyes flashed with fire. "No, I refuse to give you a broken spirit, never really knowing what I might do. Always doubting, questioning, and, even worse, you'll be afraid of me. I won't have it, Cheyenne."

I heard the words, but my heart was rejecting every single one of them. My mind, however, believed in his logic. I *was* afraid of him—or afraid of what Amicula could do to him.

I breathed in a deep breath and stood taller. I stared at him and then everyone else in the hallway. Slowly, I nodded my head and stepped a little out of his embrace. "Yes—yes you're right. If I'm honest with you, myself, and everyone else, I would never fully trust you again after what you did to me. How can you expect me to?" My forehead knitted together. "There's no telling what you're capable of doing now. Why does Amicula always seem to have some kind of control over you? Can she turn you on with a remote?"

He pulled me in closer once again and held me tight to his chest. "Briggs said there's a flight in a few hours, and if the power keeps going out, this may be my last chance to get back to Stovall. And this can't wait. I have to find answers so we can be together again."

The decision had been made. Our eyes locked on one another possibly for the last time, and I so desperately wanted back what had been stolen away.

Without another breath, he whispered, "I'm not going to let this bat-shit crazy woman destroy us."

Trying to quell the nerves in my stomach, I looked at everyone mirroring the same expression as my own. I looked directly at Sheridan and asked, "Why is it that I have this overwhelming feeling everything we need to know is back on North Sentinel Island?"

She didn't answer but only shook her head. Her sympathy plumed out from around her filling the hallway with enough emotion for all of us.

Briggs downed the rest of his beer, and in his infinite wisdom he said, "Well, I guess dzere's only one way to find out."

"How the hell are we going to do this with terrorists blowing up electrical grids? How much longer can I allow this crazy queen to destroy our lives? Why this—why now?" I tried to calm my words, but something told me that this was just the beginning of the end. "Just when I thought our lives might start to heal and I could find some kind of normalcy again, this had to happen?"

Every single one of us spoke volumes of conversations with our eyes without saying a word. I nodded and it was silently agreed. At that moment, I had no idea when or how, but our return to that horrific island had been decided.

Khaldon had promised me I would never have to go back to North Sentinel again, and that we would never be apart. Both of those promises were broken now. His determination to work out his issues alone made me wonder just how many more promises would be broken before this was all over. Would we be irrevocably torn apart forever?

My heart grew colder by the beat as I watched what modicum of control I had over my life—fade to black.

Epilogue

~ Meanwhile, back in the Amazon ~

"I t's about time you've arrived. Where have you been?" Pouting, Queen Civetateo busily searched through her en suite for what to pack. "Dzis place has been insane without you."

Aisling O'Cuinn opened up her mouth to speak but was abruptly stopped with a wave of the queen's hand.

"I don't want to hear it. Have Antonia pack your bags immediately. We're heading out to North Sentinel on Dze Andamans Islands. I need you to prepare a portal for traveling."

Even if she couldn't talk to her family, Aisling stared at the stone floor already wishing she were back in Montana. Trapped in service to the throne, she was held at the whims of the queen to provide travel and consult in regards to the dhampir army.

"Kalina and Draconis La Rivière have promised me oodles of surprises at our latest blood orchard." The queen lifted up a pair of high heels against a gold brocade dress. Not satisfied with the contrast, she opted for the sequined heels instead. "It's become quite profitable now dzat it's at full capacity. Much better dzan we anticipated. We hit it big time with all the Malaysian *volunteers.*" She held up the other pair of shoes. "What do you dzink of dzese?"

Aisling gave her a big smile, nodded, and presented a thumbs up. They looked hideous with the dress.

"Will Amicula be traveling with us?" Aisling asked more out of planning protection for herself than caring for the queen's niece. "Do I need to make travel arrangements for anyone else? Any special requests?"

The queen stopped her search through the dressing chamber and slowly turned her head toward Aisling. A queer smile smeared across her face. Her eyes narrowed and her Brazilian accent thickened. "Oh jes, we definitely have a special guest who will be awaiting us on dze island, and I cannot *wait* until you meet her."

Glossary

In order of appearance

Kuthri - Noun *Hindi*
> Common curse word in Hindi. A spiteful or unpleasant woman. A bitch.

Kamina - Adjective *Hindi*
> Common curse word in Hindi. Rascal, a mean person.

Rakshasa - Noun
> In this mythos, the Rakshasa is the East Indian, Hindi version of a vampiric entity. A Rakshasa is a demonic being from Hindu mythology. Rakshasas are also called maneaters.

Cyberchondriac - Noun
> Cy·ber·chon·dri·ac sībərˈkändrēak/
> A person who compulsively searches the Internet for information on real or imagined symptoms of illness.

Trabuc - Noun
> A cylinder of tobacco rolled in tobacco leaves for smoking. Romanian version of the word cigar. https://ro.wikipedia.org/wiki/Trabuc

Feck - Verb
> An Irish word that has fallen into similar usage as fuck, made famous by Father Ted. Of Irish origin, feck is what a lady says when she really wants to say fuck.
> http://www.urbandictionary.com/define.php?term=feck

Shite - Noun
> The Irish/Scottish/ equivalent of the word shit. A very British and therefore great way of saying shit. Shite sounds much more effective than shit.

Iubirea vieții mele - Romanian words for "The love of my life"

Vrăjitoare - Romanian word for "witch"

Taarakian - Noun
> Warrior maiden summoned to defeat the Loc Nar. A fictitious character in the movie Heavy Metal in 1981. An adult animated science fiction anthology film.

Loc-Nar - Noun
> The Loc–Nar is the central villain of the 1981 adult animated film *Heavy Metal. A* green glowing sphere which self describes itself as "the sum of all evils" and melts people upon contact.

Ma chére - French word for "My Dear" an endearment said from a man to a woman pertaining to friendship.

Je t'aim - French words for "I Love You"

Je suis désolé - French words for "I am sorry"

Weres - Scientific Family Classification
> Weres is the familial name to all genus and species of Were creatures.

Witches - Noun
> Witches affirm the existence of supernatural power (as magic) and of both male and female deities who inhere in nature and that emphasizes ritual observance of seasonal and life cycles.

Vampyre - Scientific Family Classification
> The spelling with the "Y" refers to the familial name to all genus and species of Vampyre.

Vampire - Noun
> Being born or transformed into a living vampire. A human person who consumes human blood to support the vampyric DNA. Depending on their blood dynamics, they can easily ingest food, drink and walk in sunlight. They live among humans.

Draconian - Scientific Family Classification
> Draconian is the familial name to all genus and species of dragons.

Frog Hair - Noun
> Sounthernism for something that is very sparse or fine. A figure of speech.

Cinglé - French word for "crazy"

Gráim thú - I love you in Gaelic. One of many ways to say this phrase.

Woobie - A term of endearment for a child's blanket

Locations

North Sentinel Island - The Andaman Islands
https://en.wikipedia.org/wiki/North_Sentinel_Island

Walt Disney World
https://en.wikipedia.org/wiki/Walt_Disney_World

Music

"Another One Bites the Dust" by **Queen** (1980)
Album: The Game
Label: Elektra

"Happy" by **Pharrel Williams** (2013)
Soundtrack Album: Despicable Me 2
Label: Columbia - Back Lot Music

"1999" by **Prince**
Album: 1999
Label: Warner Bros.

"Three Little Birds" by **Bob Marley** (1977)
Also widely know as "Every Little Thing Is Gonna Be Alright"
Album: Single
Label: Tuff Gong

"Closer" by **Nine Inch Nails** (1994)
Album: The Downward Spiral
Label: Nothing/TVT/Interscope

"Shake Your Groove Thing" by **Peaches and Herb** (1978)
Album: 2 Hot
Label: Polydor

Videos

Montana Citizens Zombie Hack of the Emergency Broadcast System
https://www.youtube.com/watch?v=yld0o0nGHJg

Cups Game with Pitch Perfect with Guns!!!
https://www.youtube.com/watch?v=0QtM7X0xYN8

Taarakian Transformation from Heavy Metal
   https://www.youtube.com/watch?v=gmT79zMFh8s

People

Barry White (Born Barry Eugene Carter; September 12, 1944 – July 4, 2003)
   An American composer and singer-songwriter. A three-time
   Grammy Award–winner known for his distinctive bass-baritone
   voice and romantic image.

Julia Child (August 15,1912 – August 13, 2004)
   She is recognized for bringing French cuisine to the American
   public with her debut cookbook, Mastering the Art of French
   Cooking, and her subsequent television programs, the most notable
   of which was The French Chef, which premiered in 1963.

Annie Oakley (August 13, 1860 – November 3, 1926)
   American sharpshooter and exhibition shooter. Her
   marksmanship skills first came to light when, at the age of 15,
   Annie won a shooting match with traveling show marksman
   Frank E. Butler (whom she married). Oakley became a renowned
   international star, performing before royalty and heads of state.

Master Pai Mei
   Performed by veteran Chinese actor Gordon Liu
   As depicted in the film, Pai Mei was a powerful, very old
   practitioner of the Bak Mei style of kung fu. Pai Mei was the former
   teacher and master of The Bride, Bill, and Elle, although it is unclear
   whether he instructed the other members of the Deadly Viper
   Assassination Squad in the Kill Bill series.

Annie Wilkes
   Is a character in the 1987 novel Misery, by Stephen King. In the
   1990 film adaptation of the novel, Annie Wilkes was portrayed by
   Kathy Bates, who won the Academy Award for Best Actress for her
   portrayal. This characters ranks sixth most iconic villainess in film
   history. A nurse by training, she has become one of the stereotypes
   of the nurse as a torturer and angel of death.

Hannibal Lector
   Dr. Hannibal Lecter is a character in a series of suspense novels by
   Thomas Harris. Lecter was introduced in the 1981 thriller novel *Red
   Dragon* as a forensic psychiatrist and cannibalistic serial killer.

Companies

National Geographic
    https://en.wikipedia.org/wiki/National_Geographic_Channel

Coca-Cola
    https://en.wikipedia.org/wiki/The_Coca-Cola_Company

Utilikilt
    https://en.wikipedia.org/wiki/The_Utilikilts_Company

Rémy Martin
    https://en.wikipedia.org/wiki/R%C3%A9my_Martin

Cheetos
    https://en.wikipedia.org/wiki/Cheetos

Life Savers Candy
    https://en.wikipedia.org/wiki/Life_Savers

Movies

Must Love Dogs (2005)
    Warner Brothers
    https://en.wikipedia.org/wiki/Must_Love_Dogs

The Matrix (1999)
    Warner Brothers
    https://en.wikipedia.org/wiki/The_Matrix

Blade (1998)
    New Line Cinema
    https://en.wikipedia.org/wiki/Blade_(film)

Heavy Metal (1981)
    Columbia Pictures
    https://en.wikipedia.org/wiki/Heavy_Metal_(film)

Lord of the Rings (2001)
    New Line Cinema
    http://lotr.wikia.com/wiki/Lord_of_the_Rings_film_trilogy

Kill Bill (2003)
    Miramax Films
    https://en.wikipedia.org/wiki/Kill_Bill10 v

Alien (1979)
> 20th Century Fox
> https://en.wikipedia.org/wiki/Alien_(film)

Rosemary's Baby (1968)
> Paramount Pictures
> https://en.wikipedia.org/wiki/Rosemary%27s_Baby_(film)

Carrie (1976)
> United Artists
> https://en.wikipedia.org/wiki/Carrie_(1976_film)

National Lampoon's Vacation (1983)
> Warner Bros.
> https://en.wikipedia.org/wiki/National_Lampoon%27s_Vacation_(film_series)

Misery (1990)
> Castle Rock Entertainment
> https://en.wikipedia.org/wiki/Misery_(film)

Television

The Walking Dead (2010)
> Original Network: AMC
> https://en.wikipedia.org/wiki/The_Walking_Dead_(TV_series)

Cast of Characters

In Order of Appearance

Cheyenne O'Cuinn - Heroine of the story. Lead programmer developer for the mass-multi online role playing game (MMORPG) *ExsanguiNation*. Is afraid of haunted houses and has yet to embrace the vampiric lifestyle.

Khaldon Seters - Senior engineer for *ExsanguiNation* and online boyfriend to Cheyenne for over two years. Former lover to Amicula Darkrose and in ancient feud with Draconis La Rivière.

Tony Briggs - Dragon mafia hit man from New Orleans and senior programmer for *ExsanguiNation* who is in love with Dakota O'Cuinn. Family name Blaize La Rivière.

Ludovic Zyryanov - Vampire henchman who works for Amicula Darkrose and runs Breeding Den Facility #42. He is in love with Dakota O'Cuinn and regrets the things that have happened to her.

Torchy Gravenor - Welsh Dragon who is best mates to Khaldon Seters and is in love with Sheridan O'Cuinn. Torchy owns The Super Market locations all over the world.

Harris Archer - Game tester, hacker extraordinaire, and network programmer for *ExsanguiNation*. A werewolf who was Cheyenne's college roommate for three years. Has become like a brother to the O'Cuinn sisters.

Dakota O'Cuinn - Sound gaming engineer for *ExsanguiNation*. Cheyenne's youngest sister who loves makeup & high heels. She goes through men like Kleenex.

Kalina La Rivière - Halfling dragon demi-goddess and sister to Briggs. Daughter of Draconis and the Goddess Kali.

Draconis La Rivière - Father to Briggs and Kalina. Hates Khaldon Seters and holds confidential real estate properties for the vampire Queen Civetateo.

Kiernan O'Cuinn - Cheyenne's father who has been enthralled for years and is not aware of his wife's existence.

Vhalencia De La Fuente - Female progeny to Khaldon Seters. Is a master thief and locksmith. Proficient with the rapier sword and fashion.

Ichi Murasaki - Master healer of Eastern medicine and Kung Fu fighting bo staff. Owns the Chángshòu Apothcary inside The Super Market. Vampiric progeny to Vhalencia De La Fuente.

Devdan Sarat - Photographer and a clerical mage with a deadly prayer. Metalsmith extraordinaire. Master of the Eastern Indian Kalarippayattu form. Vampiric progeny to Vhalencia De La Fuente.

Chlodochar Lothar (Chuck) - German alchemist of the group, but very handy with a chainsaw. Heavy blacksmithing and sword maker. Vampiric progeny to Vhalencia De La Fuente.

Ruthie Anne - Grandmotherly type hospital nurse who takes care of Cheyenne and Sheridan in the Orlando Hospital.

Sheridan O'Cuinn - CEO of the MMORPG *ExsanguiNation* and Cheyenne's oldest sister who is falling in love with Torchy Gravenor.

Aisling O'Cuinn - Cheyenne's mother who was murdered nine years prior who is imprisoned to the vampiric queen in service to the throne. Her existence must be keep secret from her family.

Amicula Darkrose - Former lover to Khaldon Seters and is the niece of the vampire Queen Civetateo. Tasked to find breeders for her dhampir army and donors for the blood orchards.

Charlie MacCarthy - Uncle to Cheyenne who lives in Montana on the Flying F Ranch. Manages thousands of acres, cattle, and three nuclear missile silos for the US Air Force.

Maisie MacCarthy - Aunt to Cheyenne and runs the Flying F Ranch. A serious cook and generous heart but is a crack shot with any weapon.

Mason Jones - Flying F Ranch Foreman. Excels in hunting and tracking but always has to have the best story in the crowd.

Abbey MacCarthy - Charlie and Maisie's daughter who attends pre-veterinary college.

Queen Civetateo - Vampire Queen of the Vampyric race. Obsessed with eliminating rogue vampires and humans [especially politicians] trying to destroy the planet.

Thank You

Thank you for reading *Obfuscate*, book 2 in the World of Blood series. I hope sincerely enjoyed reading it as I much as I enjoyed writing it.

As with every Indie Author, your review on sites such as Amazon and Goodreads help boost my rankings to help others discover the book series too. If you loved Obfucate, please take a moment to let me know. I read every review and listen to your heartfelt words.

No—my books may not be for everyone. No author can be everything to everyone, and that's okay. But if you loved the book and want to see more, then please leave a nice review and help me continue sharing the world of our quirky characters. I am extremely grateful to your time and kindness.☺

What's Next?

Detonate - Book Three!

Obfuscate was originally over 135 thousand words. Yeah ... I know. There were story lines I wanted to expand upon and new characters to build out, so I chose to break the book in half. Detonate, the third book, won't be long a wait as most of it has already been written. My goal is get it published by winter of 2016.

The Super Market Anthology!

Yes, you've asked for it and you've got it! I am expanding the universe of The Super Market in the honor and style of the Thieves' World books by Robert Asprin & Lynn Abbey, and Disney Infinity gaming platform. I invited authors to collaborate and bring their paranormal and supernatural characters to come play in the World of Blood. Anticipated published date winter 2016.

Audible Version of Exsanguinate! YES! So many of you have asked for "When will it be on Audible?" Soon ... very soon. ☺ We anticipate having Exsanguinate available by summer 2016. That's just around the corner, folks. Looking for beta listeners if you want to provide feedback before it goes live.

Language Translations?

What language would you like to read the series in? I'm considering Spanish to start off with. What say you?

Talk to Me

Come visit with me any time on my website at https://www.killionslade.com I love hearing from you and your amazing ideas for the characters. I listen to all of them and am thankful for your time and kindness.☺ Connect with me on Facebook. Follow Me on Amazon, and if you loved the books, please leave a kind review on Goodreads and Amazon. Vote for Exsanguinate and Obfuscate to be on the Top Vampires, Witches, and Dragons Oh My! list and most of all – please purchase a gift copy and share it with another friend!

Kindest Regards,
~Killion

www.ingramcontent.com/pod-product-compliance
Lightning Source LLC
Chambersburg PA
CBHW020125180626
46810CB00004B/1412